Richard Kadrey has published twelve novels, including *Sandman Slim*, *Kill the Dead*, *Aloha From Hell*, *Devil Said Bang*, *Kill City Blues*, *The Getaway God*, *Killing Pretty*, *The Perdition Score*, and more than fifty stories. He has been immortalized as an action figure, and his short story 'Goodbye Houston Street, Goodbye' was nominated for a British Science Fiction Association Award. A freelance writer and photographer, he lives in San Francisco.

RichardKadrey.com

By Richard Kadrey

THE KILL SOCIETY

RICHARD KADREY

HARPER
Voyager

Harper*Voyager*
An imprint of HarperCollins*Publishers*
1 London Bridge Street
London SE1 9GF

www.harpervoyagerbooks.co.uk

A Paperback Original 2017

1

A catalogue record for this book
is available from the British Library

ISBN: 978-0-00-821906-2

This novel is entirely a work of fiction.
The names, characters and incidents portrayed in it are
the work of the author's imagination. Any resemblance to
actual persons, living or dead, events or localities is
entirely coincidental.

Printed and bound in Great Britain by
Clays Ltd, St Ives plc

MIX
Paper from
responsible sources

FSC
www.fsc.org

FSC™ C007454

For David Pomerico,
who keeps the trains running on time

ACKNOWLEDGEMENTS

Thanks to my agent, Ginger Clark, and my editor, David Pomerico. Thanks also to Pamela Spengler-Jaffe, Jennifer Brehl, Caroline Perny, Shawn Nicholls, Angela Craft, Priyanka Krishnan, Owen Corrigan, and the rest of the team at Harper Voyager. Thanks also to Jonathan Lyons, Sarah Perillo, Holly Frederick, Nicholas J.L. Beudert, and Tess Callero. Thanks also to Genie Casillas for Latin advice. As always, thanks to Nicola for everything else.

*It was written I should be loyal to the
nightmare of my choice.*

—Joseph Conrad, *Heart of Darkness*

*I got a paper cut writing my suicide note.
It's a start.*

—Steven Wright

So far, being dead is about as much fun as a barbed-wire G-string.

Yes, there is such a thing. They invented it in Hell, which is where I am. I already said I was dead. Where else would I be? Try to keep up.

Where was I? I was talking about fun. First off, there's the fact that I'm really, no shit, for sure, not coming back dead. I mean, I've been dead before, but now my body is stone-cold back in L.A., I'm in Hell, and I don't see any angles to play. So, that's a lot of laughs. As is the view. Up here on this spiky cliffside, Hell stretches out in all directions like the pockmarked belly of a gator with a bad case of just about everything. Acne. Psoriasis. Cancer. From the smell, gangrene and probably gingivitis, too.

Insult to injury: I'm stuck here with no weapons, no wheels, no fucking idea where exactly I am, and, oh yeah, there's a dust storm the size of Texas headed straight for me. It rolls and thunders across the hardpack in the valley below. This leaves me with exactly two choices: I can sit up here on this nameless mountain and get ripped to shreds, a speck of chickenshit on the rocky tip of nowhere. Or I can go down into the valley and look this dust devil in the eye.

Not a lot to think about there.

I kick a rock down the slope and follow it as it tumbles ahead of me into the valley. As it goes, I spot something on the trail ahead. Bend down to pick it up. Okay, I might not know where I am, but I know I'm being fucked with. What I'm holding is a dusty pack of Maledictions. But no lighter. Someone somewhere is having a good laugh. With luck, they'll choke on their good time while there's still a little piece of me left to feel it.

The dust cloud reaches up into the bruised Hellion sky. It looks miles away, but sand and grit already sting my face. I walk straight at it for a while, then start to run. If Hell is going to shred me, let's get it over with. I'm not even angry that Audsley Ishii murdered me right in front of Candy. Why would I be angry? I got to see Candy go Jade one last time as she ripped him to pieces. One last glimpse of her being exactly who she is. A gorgeous, perfect monster. My monster.

Good-bye, Candy. You made a stupid world hurt less and a place worth fighting for. And we broke a lot of furniture, the two of us. When this storm finishes me off and I fall into Tartarus—the only place lower than Hell—you'll be what keeps me from going crazy in the dark.

All right, maybe I am a *little* mad about being taken away from her. But it's too late now. The dust swallows me and Hell goes from a perpetual twilight to a rusty glow, the color of dried blood. My ghost nose closes with grit and my throat is rasped raw. I close my eyes and they instantly cement together. There's nothing to look at anyway. I've seen my skin peeled off plenty of times in the arena. I know what my bones look like.

After a few minutes of running, I stop and listen. There's a rumbling in the storm that's more machine than wind. I swear, I can smell diesel fumes. And as much as the dust boils and tears at me, it isn't nearly the storm I thought it was. It's not a cocktail party, and I've been to some bad parties. The storm isn't even what's sending the dust into the sky. It's something inside the storm.

I do a slow three-sixty. The rumble and smell of fumes get closer. When I'm facing it, I stop. Wipe as much grit from my eyes as I can. I can feel the sound in my chest, a deep shudder like someone running a drag strip through my ribs.

I'd do all kinds of depraved things right now for a smoke.

A second later, the rumbling stops. I don't mean the noise dies down. I mean that whatever is causing it stops dead in its tracks, but it's still growling and grinding as loud as ever. I stand where I am. Where am I going to go? Whatever it is, is a lot bigger than me, and if I'm about to get eaten, I'm going in facing the fucker. If I get lucky and it breathes fire, I might even get to smoke one last cigarette on the way down its gullet.

Choking dust billows around me, but I continue to remain uneaten. If whatever is out there wants to play games, it better be ready for a round of "Stark runs away and hides under a rock until the bad thing goes away" because without weapons, I'm not about to play Rock 'Em Sock 'Em Robots with a Hellbeast.

It's a good minute before the dust thins out and I can see well enough to look for a weapon. All I find nearby is a baseball-size rock. I pick it up and weigh it in my hand. Fuck. It's pumice. Light as a feather. I might as well throw marshmallows at the thing. I toss the rock back where I found it. I'm not sold on the concept of death with dignity, but I'd rather not be a story monsters tell each other around the watercooler.

The dust finally settles down and I get a look at what's coming.

Huh. I didn't think of that.

Turns out it isn't one giant thing. It's really a lot of big things growling and shuddering at the fucking sky. More than fifty of them.

The simple way to describe it is that I'm face-to-face with a smoke-belching desert rat parking lot of semitrucks and pickups, passenger cars, construction equipment, and motorcycles. There's even a few hellhounds with saddles and riders. Maybe I should have kept my rock. At least I wouldn't look quite so much like a deer caught in the headlights.

No. I'd look like a deer with a rock. Forget it.

We stare at each other just long enough for me to, one, notice that no one is offering me a ride, and two, get bored. So, I head over in their direction. I'm maybe twenty yards away when a Hellion in a jeep up front holds his fists over his head. The sound of the engines dies away. He's a big, spiky bastard, like a horned toad in a doorman's uniform.

"Stop," he says. "Where are you from and where's the rest of your group?"

"At the day spa at the Bellagio. Come on over. We'll have a shvitz and get to know each other."

4

The Hellion talks to a short, baby-faced damned soul in the jeep with him. The soul shrugs and points at me. The Hellion frowns. It doesn't improve his looks.

"What's a shvitz?" he yells.

"Really? You're driving up Hell's asshole with these *Grease* rejects and that's the first thing that falls out of your skull?"

The Hellion stands up a little straighter.

"What did you say?"

"I said, does Baby Face dress you? 'Cause from where I'm standing, I bet you don't know how pants work."

The Hellion gets out of the jeep. The damned soul starts to hand him a rifle, but Horned Toad shakes his head and starts in my direction.

Well, I got his attention. Everyone's attention. Now for the second part of my well-thought-out plan to get a vehicle and get out of this dusty shithole. If I stand still, I'll look scared, so I head straight for Horned Toad. Along the way, I look around for weapons, but all there is around me is dust and more of those light stones. Halfway there, I spot some animal bones sticking up out of the hard ground. Something the size of an elephant died out here and the wind scoured it clean. I need to think of something fast or my bones are going to be the next thing on display.

The real problem isn't that I don't have weapons, though; it's that I don't know anything about myself right now. Am I still strong? Am I fast? Can I still do hoodoo or manifest my Gladius and if I can, do I want a hundred or so Leatherface grease-monkey types knowing it?

I guess for now, part two of my plan is stay alive—so to

speak—see what I can get away with, and go from there. Yeah. That should work. No problem.

Another question that just occurred to me: In my present condition, am I still hard to kill? Will I heal if I'm injured or will I bleed out like any other sucker down here and wind up in Tartarus? Whatever the answer is, I think I'm going to have it in a few seconds.

Horned Toad stops about ten feet from me. I spot a gun on his hip and he catches me looking at it.

"Scares you, does it?" he says. "Don't worry. Got to conserve ammo these days, and anyway, I don't think you deserve a bullet."

"No. What I deserve is to be back in L.A. with my girlfriend, her girlfriend, and a bunch of other nice people who don't look like they eat bugs in a West Texas gulch."

Horned Toad pulls a knife the size of a labradoodle.

He says, "What I like to eat are eyes. I'm going to eat yours one at a time. Let you watch me swallow the first one before I cut out the other."

"It's good to pace yourself. You don't want to fill up before dessert."

"I know about your type. Talkers," he says. "Talkers are all cowards."

I check my sides, and while the ground is flat and even, there's nowhere to run to except the mountains. Besides, I'll never outpace all these trucks and bikes.

I point at Horned Toad.

"You look like an apple-pie guy. Me too. Except when they put cheese on it. Do you like that? Can toads even eat dairy? Is that why you eat eyes? Have you tried Lactaid?"

"Kill him," yells the baby-face guy from Horned Toad's jeep. Other voices join him, chanting for Horned Toad to gut me.

He lunges at me with the giant knife. I dance back and he misses me by a mile. He lunges again and I jump to the side this time. Okay. I can still move. That's the first piece of good news since I woke up here. I wonder what else I can do?

He lunges at me again, but it's a fake-out. Instead of going for my gut, he does a second lunge down low. I move out of the way, but he still gets a piece of my left leg. It burns like hell and the sight of my blood gets the peanut gallery going with whoops and catcalls.

When Horned Toad comes for me again, instead of moving back, I dive under his arm and drive a knee up into his lower ribs. I hear him suck in air when the pain hits, but the fucker swings his blade down and slashes me across the back.

"Watch the coat, asshole!" I yell at him. "They don't make these down here anymore."

"Maybe I'll leave your eyes and eat your arms and legs first. Would you like to watch me gnaw your bones?"

"I'd rather watch you do the backstroke in lava."

He smiles and I smile right back at him. I'm the one bleeding, but he's the one who just gave me an idea.

We go on like that for a couple more minutes. He lunges and I dodge the blade or the lucky prick gets a piece of me. I knock him back with some decent kicks and a few elbows to the head. The important thing is that I don't stand still and I keep him moving in the direction of the animal bones nearby.

By the time we make it there, Horned Toad is leaning a little to his left from all the shots I've given him to the ribs.

On the other hand, every time I move, my blood does a Jackson Pollock mural on the sand, so maybe we're even at this point.

We trade blows a little more until I'm near enough to the bones that I can make my move. I let him get close and swing at my head. When he does, I give him one more quick kick in the ribs that knocks him back and leaves him open. As he rocks back, I grab one of the half-buried ribs to smash him with.

And nothing happens. The rib is solid in the ground. It isn't going anywhere. Not with me yanking on it like a mouse trying to uproot a redwood.

I'd like to say that the laughs that go up as I pull on the rib don't hurt, but they do. Though not as much as all my knife wounds and the feeling that I'm running out of options.

Horned Toad is really feeling good now and runs at me like a lizard-skin freight train. On the ground next to the rib I can't budge is a big canine tooth from whatever died here. Just as he reaches me, I fall to my knees, grab it, and throw all of my weight behind a lunge at his legs. I drive the tooth deep into his thigh and twist it on the way out. Black Hellion blood splatters on my hands and coat. I roll away as Horned Toad drops to his knees. While he's down, I jump at him, swinging the tooth down at his neck.

I guess fucking up Horned Toad's leg in front of his friends really pissed him off because he does what every Hellion does when he's losing: he cheats. To be fair, I've cheated in plenty of fights, too, but he grabs his pistol when I thought this was a knife fight, and, well, it's a very upsetting moment.

I kick sand in his face, jump, and roll off to his right side.

Horned Toad fires blind and ends up popping off a couple of shots at his own people. They scramble out of the way like dusty roaches. I want to scramble, too, but I know that with a crowd like this watching, it's more important to stand my ground and risk being shot than to back down. With luck, I'll still heal fast. With all the slices Horned Toad has taken out of me, I'll know soon.

His Hellion Glock has an extended clip, and with the way he's shooting, he's bound to get lucky and hit me. It's time to take action. It's time to get strategic.

It's time to do something really stupid.

I work my way around behind Horned Toad, with just a few feet between him and the skeleton. From what I figure, I was able to get away from most of his attacks, so I have a little speed left. And I was able to hurt the fucker, so I'm still strong. I hope that's not all that's left of the old me. But I've got to be careful and not give too much away until I figure out all I can do and who this Wild Bunch really is.

While he's firing in the opposite direction, I run for the skeleton and grab one of the ribs. Like the first one, it doesn't budge. This time, though, I use the noise of the gunfire to cover me as I whisper some Hellion hoodoo.

For a second, nothing happens and I'm sure that I've reached a new level of fucked. Then the hardpack around the rib shatters and I haul it out of the ground like a deranged Fred Flintstone.

Horned Toad stops firing.

"Where are you, mortal? Come and fight me like a man."

From behind him, I say, "No."

And swing the rib over my head, crushing Horned Toad's

skull like an anvil landing on a soft-boiled egg. It's messy, and bloody, and I get toad juice all over my boots, but he's sure as shit not firing his gun at me anymore. I grab it and his knife as his body blips out of existence and starts the long, nasty fall into Tartarus.

I stand there, breathing hard, but with a dumb smile on my bloody face. I can still throw some hoodoo. That's the best news since I arrived here. Now I just have to keep all these creeps from finding out until I know how much I can do.

My little ego fest is cut short by bullets tearing up the ground around my feet.

Horned Toad's pal, the baby face in the jeep, is running at me, firing the rifle. I guess he's upset because he hasn't grasped the fact that it's really hard to hit anything when you're running and your gun is bouncing around like a rubber duck in a typhoon.

This time, I don't stand my ground. I run toward the fucker. The way he's shooting, he couldn't hit the sky from a weather balloon. When I'm close enough to see his pearly whites, I throw Horned Toad's knife, and nail Dobie Gillis right through the throat. He falls on his face, gurgling into the sand. It's an unpleasant sound, so I steal his rifle and drop to one knee.

More than Dobie, what I've had my eye on is another Hellion, this one a bit more human looking, in the flatbed of a small pickup truck, swinging a sixty-caliber machine gun in my direction. He has a good position and stable footing and I have a bad feeling that he knows what he's doing. I can't take a chance on missing him when I shoot. So I don't shoot him.

I shoot a jerrican of fuel strapped to the side of the truck.

It explodes with an extremely satisfying *whoomp*. Satisfying to me, at least. It would be nice to think that the screams from the burning Hellion are him cheering me on for making such a great shot, but that's probably too much to hope for.

I get a bead on the human torch while a group of Hellions and souls rushes to him with blankets and water to put out the flames. They're not going to make it in time. I squeeze the trigger.

"Excuse me," says a very human voice nearby. "Before you shoot."

I glance over and there's a small man in a white duster standing on the roof of what looks like an armored '69 Charger with tank treads instead of wheels. He's out in front of the pack, like maybe he's the one leading them through the desert.

"Excuse me," he says again through a megaphone.

I keep the rifle trained on Johnny Storm and yell, "What?"

"We would all appreciate it if you didn't kill Megs."

"Why should I?"

"Because I'm not aiming a gun at you. And I'm asking you politely."

I take quick stock of my situation. There are maybe a hundred idiots out there in those vehicles. My guess is that every one of them is heavily armed and eager to kill. There are more high-caliber guns mounted on other vehicles and other Hellion weapons that I don't recognize. If everybody opens up on me at once, hoodoo or not, I'm going to look like a flank steak shooting out of a wood chipper. Plus, I don't know where I am. I still don't know if I'm going to stop bleeding. I'm not sure that I can do hoodoo more complicated than yanking dead things out of dirt. I've swallowed enough sand that I'm going to shit cinder blocks. And I stubbed my toe on Horned Toad. It really hurts.

I lower the rifle and let the burning fucker's friends put him out.

"Thank you," says the man on the Charger.

I point at the pickup truck.

"I want that prick's water. And his ammo."

After a slight hesitation, he says, "That's fair."

"No, it's not," someone shouts. I look around and spot a leather-clad woman on a tricked-out Hellion Harley. I can't see her face, but she has her goggles pushed up to her hairline. "That's not how things work. He's not one of us. He obviously doesn't know anything. Just kill him."

Doesn't know anything? Doesn't know what?

She kicks her Harley to life and revs the engine. I raise the rifle again as she gets ready to charge me.

From behind her, a man riding a small hellhound cuts her off. She pulls her gun and sticks it right in his face. The man puts his hands up. Like her, he's wearing goggles, but he also has a rag around his nose and mouth.

"What the fuck are you doing?" says the woman.

"Don't kill him," shouts the man. "I recognize him. He can be useful."

I get to my feet and squint in the hellhound rider's direction. I can't make out a goddamn thing through his bandanna and goggles.

The man with the megaphone says, "You'll vouch for him as a reasonable man?"

"I will," says the rider.

I put the rifle back to my shoulder. "Reasonable? Call me that again and you'll do it without a head."

The rider turns to me, pushes up his goggles, and pulls down his bandanna.

I almost call out to him, but catch myself in time.

The man riding the hellhound is Father Traven.

I lower the rifle.

"Ah. So, you do know the father," says Charger Man. "What's your name, friend?"

I look at him.

"ZaSu Pitts."

That gets some laughs. Traven doesn't laugh, but he doesn't give me away either.

I look back at Charger Man.

"Who the fuck are you?"

"He's the Magistrate," says Traven. "He leads the havoc."

"Havoc? You assholes sound like more fun every minute."

"Are there others with you?" says the Magistrate. "Back on the mountain from where you came down?"

So they could see me. They knew I was here all along. That makes them more than a pack of Hellion one-percenters. And then there's Father Traven. He wouldn't throw in with a useless group no matter how bad things were.

I shake my head.

"No one I know about."

The Magistrate nods.

"Then that is where we will camp."

"You can't be serious," says the woman on the Harley. "He's killed two of us and burned another."

"Yet Father Traven says he's reasonable and I'm inclined to believe him." The Magistrate glances off in the directing of the mountain. "A lone traveler out here, confronted and attacked. What would you have done, Daja? Personally, I'd like to talk to Mr. Pitts."

Daja. Got to remember her. She backs down, but I can see it in her body language and hear it in her voice. No matter what the Magistrate says, she's not done with me.

"Just talk?" says Daja.

"Of course. And he will be judged just like anybody else," says the Magistrate.

"And if he's found guilty?"

"Then his fate will be that of all the ignobles."

Cheers. Fists pumps. It's a goddamn pep rally. All we need are cheerleaders.

The group around the burned Hellion steps back as he dies and his body pops out of existence. They all look in my direction. That's me. Making friends wherever I go.

The Magistrate points.

"We will camp at the base of the mountains. He said no one is there. That will be his first test."

I raise my hand like I'm in the third grade.

"Excuse me. What if I'm not in the mood to get tested?"

I prop the rifle on my hip, but Traven calls out, "Pitts. Calm down. It's going to be all right."

"Is it?" I say to the Magistrate.

He opens his hands.

"I cannot guarantee that. But consider this: Father Traven has vouched for you. That means he, too, will be judged. If you are not a reasonable man, if you are a stupid man, he will die with you."

Slowly, I let the barrel of the rifle drop so it's pointing at the ground.

The fucker called my bluff. He points to the half-burned pickup truck.

"Can you drive that vehicle?" says the Magistrate.

"I usually steal better, but yeah."

"Then ride with us when we make camp tonight. If you try to leave the havoc or attack anyone else, I will personally kill the good father. Understand?"

"Yes."

Daja looks around at where her dead friends used to be. "And what about the two, now three, dead?"

"We will have a memorial service tonight," the Magistrate says.

He calls to a patched-together ambulance.

"Mimir, come and ride with me. I will need an oracle tonight."

A woman in a ratty fur coat, with some kind of plastic mask over the lower part of her face to filter out the dust, steps from the ambulance and goes to the Magistrate's Charger. Without another word, he points to the mountains and the vehicles rumble to life.

I walk to the charred pickup truck as Traven rides his hellhound up beside me. Dressed in boots and a ragged leather duster, he gives me that sad smile of his and I shake my head at him.

"It's good to see you, ZaSu," he says.

15

"You've got some explaining to do," I tell him.

"So do you."

I start the truck.

"Do those bastards have anything to drink?"

"Of course."

"And food?"

He nods.

"Good. At least I'll get a last meal."

He takes off the rag that was covering his face and wipes the blood from some of my worst wounds.

"Don't talk like that," he says. "It's going to be fine."

"Yeah? If Ahab up there has a real oracle, he's going to find out I'm lying about who I am."

"We'll deal with that when the time comes. Have a little faith."

I look at him.

"When you died, faith got you sent to a frozen gulag at the ass end of Hell, remember?"

He nods.

"And it got me rescued. By you. You're who I have faith in."

Some riders nearby signal us forward.

"These days, Father, I'm not worried about dying. I'm just worried about doing it hungry."

Traven and I pull out, joining the havoc convoy heading for the mountains. The only thing I'm wondering about besides what time they're going to kill me is the thing at the back of the havoc. It's under a giant tarp and being hauled by the construction equipment on a double-length sixteen-wheeler bed. People like this, they don't take anything with them that they don't need. So, what do a bunch of Hellions and damned souls need with something the size of a Saturn V rocket? Maybe I'll live long enough to find out. The way the day is going, though, I'll be lucky to make it through the appetizer course.

WE DRIVE TO the base of the mountains, a herd of lumbering, smog-belching dinosaurs. Maybe ten yards away, Daja is riding parallel with me on the Harley. I'd rather be on the bike than this trashed pickup, but I don't think she'd trade me.

When we reach the mountains, the vehicles fan out in a semicircle, forming a defensive perimeter. That means they know what they're doing and they're worried that someone out there might be gunning for them. Whoever thinks they're hard enough to take on this crusty bunch, I don't want to meet. I stay put in the jeep while the others set up camp. It's a cruel joke. This thing was on fire a few minutes ago, but now I can't find a damned thing I can use to light a Malediction.

Father Traven leaves me and disappears into a small teardrop-shaped camper being hauled by a rusty tow truck. I wonder if I hopped on his hellhound and headed straight up the mountains, how many of these assholes could follow me? Hellhounds can climb like goddamn apes and go places no ordinary vehicle would dare. On the other hand, I spotted plenty of Hellion Legionnaires on the drive over. All it would take is one good sniper and off I'd go to a time-share in Tartarus. No thanks. Mason is still down there and I couldn't stand his gloating if we ended up roommates. I'll stay put, play dumb, and see what happens next. Besides, being murdered made me hungry. If these clowns are going to stone me in the public square, I'm going out with a full stomach.

While they set up camp, most of the mob goes out of their way to ignore me. I wave my unlit cigarette to a couple of the ones that dare look at me, but I get the finger, not a light. I settle back looking bored, but watch them while they work. They're fast and efficient setting things up. Everybody knows their job. That means they've been doing this for a while. Daja doesn't do any heavy lifting, but moves from group to group answering questions and moving people around when there's a group that needs help. We lock eyes for a second and I give her a little wave. She turns away and gets back to work. Okay, she's smarter than I was hoping. Not so easy to provoke. That means I'll have to go for someone else.

Everyone in the camp is armed. While that sounds bad, it works in my favor. It means all I have to do is find someone weak enough, hurt enough, or stupid enough that I can kill them and grab their gear. While I'm scoping out the rabble for easy pickings, Traven comes over. He smiles like he can read my mind.

"Relax," he says. "You have business with the Magistrate. No one is going to bother you."

"Meaning, I won't be stuffed like a turkey and cooked until afterward. That's a comfort."

"No one's resorted to cannibalism, yet."

"Unless that's why they're in Hell."

Traven smiles.

"True. But as long as they're part of the group, there are rules of conduct that everybody follows."

"Even the Magistrate?"

"Even him."

I nod and look back at his trailer.

"I never took you for a ramblin' man. When did you decide you didn't like Blue Heaven?"

Traven glances at the ground. The last time I had seen him, I was hiding him in a funny little burg called Blue Heaven. It isn't Heaven or Hell, but exists in a funny limbo zone between each. It's a kind of sanctuary for people with nowhere else to go.

"It's gone," he says.

"Blue Heaven? What do you mean it's gone?"

Traven looks around the mob like he's nervous about someone listening.

"The Magistrate and the havoc appeared there a few weeks ago. They told the ruling council they were looking for something he called the Lux Occisor."

"I learned a little Latin when I was in Lucifer's library. I know *lux* is 'light.' What's the other word?"

"'Slayer.' 'Killer.' Take your pick."

"Fun. Do you know what it is?"

Traven runs a hand through his hair. I swear he has a few gray ones he didn't have before.

"If we did, maybe we could have given him . . . something. The Magistrate doesn't talk about it in specifics."

"And when Blue Heaven couldn't come up with the light killer?"

"The havoc killed anyone who ran. Then they burned Blue Heaven to the ground."

So much for my former life as a savior. A lot of the people I try to save have a bad habit of not staying that way.

I look over my shoulder and across the camp.

"This all has to do with whatever is under the tarp, doesn't it?"

"That would be my guess," Traven says.

"Do you know what it is?"

"'Salvation.'"

I give him a look.

"What the hell does that mean?"

"I don't know. It's all the Magistrate will say about it."

"You're hauling around a ten-ton leap of faith."

"Isn't a leap of faith what salvation is?"

"I wouldn't know."

I feel stupid holding an unlit cigarette, so I put it back in the pack.

"Let me see if I have this straight," I say. "The Magistrate and his party boys show up in Blue Heaven and have a barbecue. So, how is it you ended up joining them?"

He looks back at the tarp, too.

"When the Magistrate found out I was the librarian and Blue Heaven's historian, he *strongly* encouraged me."

"And who's going to say no to King Kong?"

He draws a breath.

"I wish I could say that I was brave enough to refuse. I took some of the most important books, my pens and ink, and I've been with the havoc ever since. The Magistrate wants a record of the crusade. He thinks it will be important. So do I, but not for the reasons he thinks."

I'm still bleeding and my left leg hurts. Horned Toad got my quadriceps and the meat isn't healing fast enough for my taste. I shake blood off my boot onto the sand.

"They don't have Nuremberg trials in Hell, Father."

"No. But perhaps they do in Heaven."

"Always the optimist," I say, and he shrugs. "As for the other thing, I would have joined him, too."

He turns his head toward me.

"That's nice of you to say, but I know you wouldn't."

"That's where you're wrong. When a tidal wave washes out the luau, you surf it and look for land."

"Thank you," he says. "I'm sorry. I know this is a strange moment for you, but I have to ask . . ."

I put a hand on his shoulder.

"Brigitte is fine. She's working. Doing auditions. She got a part on some cable-TV series."

He puts his hand over mine for a minute.

"Thank you."

"She misses you."

He takes his hand away.

"It's mutual."

Brigitte Bardo and Father Traven were an item back in the world. A defrocked priest and an ex-porn-star zombie hunter. A Hollywood love story if there ever was one.

"And how are the others? How's Candy?" he says.

Now it's my turn to get awkward.

"Everyone is fine. Candy's doing good. But she goes by a different name now. I'll tell you about it later."

"Of course," he says.

We stand there in awkward silence, and I think about all the life leaking out of me. There's only one thing that's going to take my mind off all this blood.

"I don't suppose you have a light, do you?"

Traven goes to his camper and comes back with a match. I take out a Malediction and he lights it for me. Breathe in a big lungful of the beautiful poison.

"Bless me, Father, for I have sinned."

"Then you'll fit in just fine around here," he says.

He nods to the camper.

"I have some work to do. I'll come back when the Magistrate calls for you."

"Don't worry about me. I bet I'm the only one here with cigarettes. The rest of these assholes are smoking locoweed and pocket lint."

Traven gives me a small smile and then heads back to his camper.

"Enjoy the smoke," he says.

I sure as hell will. It might be my last.

I COOL MY heels in the burned-out pickup for an hour. Smoke one Malediction and light a second off it. But I stop there. Got to ration myself, which isn't in my nature, but these are weird times.

The good news is that while I was bleeding when I started the first cigarette, I've pretty much stopped by the time I flip the butt of the second away. That's means I still heal quickly. Good news there.

The cigarette arcs through the air in the direction of the mountains and almost hits Daja, who's headed my way. She doesn't even flinch. Just tracks the flying smoke's flight with her eyes and watches it miss her by a couple of inches. Nice.

She crooks a finger at me.

"Let's go," she says.

"Where to?"

"The Magistrate wants to see you."

"That's okay. I like the view right here."

She rests her hand on the grip of her pistol, cop-style. She's packing a Colt 1911. Not a new gun, but it still blows nice holes in things.

"The Magistrate wants you with a clear head, so I'm not going to shoot you anywhere that'll kill you. Just where it hurts."

"Fine. I'll go to prom with you, but you're paying for the limo."

I swing my legs down out of the truck and yell, "Father! We're up."

Traven comes out of his camper, putting on the ragged duster.

We follow Daja to a Hellion motor home. It looks less like something your grandparents would drive to the Grand Canyon and more like a Gothic mansion on wheels—one designed by insects and decorated by something with more tentacles than taste. Hellion chic. Daja opens the door and we go in.

The light inside comes from glowing glass globes that seem to float above the furniture. A cramped sofa along one wall and a small table with chairs in the center of the claustrophobic room finish off the nightmare.

The Magistrate sets down a book he was reading when we come in. He points to chairs at the table for me and Traven, then sits down across from us. Daja doesn't sit. She stays behind me doing her best to loom. At another time and place I'd say it didn't work and I'd mean it. But right here and right now, I'm a little off my game and I don't like her and her gun behind me.

The Magistrate says, "Thank you for coming without causing any more trouble. I somehow think it's not in your nature to so graciously respond to a summons."

I shrug. "It beats bleeding in a truck. Do you have anything to drink around here?"

The Magistrate turns around, takes a glass off a small table, and sets it in front of me.

"I had a feeling you might be thirsty."

I sniff it. No smell.

"Water?" I say.

He nods.

I squint at him.

"You wouldn't try to roofie a guest, would you?"

"Do I strike you as that sort of man?" says the Magistrate.

"No. But I've been wrong before. And we *are* in Hell."

Back in the world, I can usually tell when someone is lying. I can hear their heart, watch the pupils of their eyes and micro-expressions on their face. But most of that doesn't work on the dead. No heartbeat. Micro-expressions dulled by death. And it's too dark in here to see the Magistrate's eyes.

I down whatever's in the glass, though, because at this point I'd drink paint thinner out of a hobo's galoshes.

What I swallow seems like water. There's no weird aftertaste and my eyes don't start spinning. So far so good.

"Feeling better?" he says.

"Okay. But I'd feel great if you had something stronger."

The Magistrate moves his head from side to side. "We shall

see," he says. "Now that you're feeling better, are you still Mr. Pitts in here or can we start off on a friendlier footing?"

"Are you still the Magistrate in here?"

"Of course."

"Then I'm still Mr. Pitts."

Traven gives me a look, but I give him one right back.

"As you wish," says the Magistrate. "What were you doing on the mountain?"

His speech is clipped, like English isn't his first language. But I can't identify his accent.

I say, "I have no idea."

He cocks his head.

"You weren't spying on us?"

"Until you stopped I thought you were a dust devil come to pick my bones clean."

"Who else is on the mountain?"

"No one that I know of. I told you that when I fried your friend."

I hear Daja move behind me, but she stops when the Magistrate holds up his hand.

"How did you get onto the mountain? Where did you come from?" he says.

"I was busy getting murdered on Earth."

"You're *dead*?" blurts Traven.

I hold up my left arm to show him that it's my old human arm again and not a biomechanical Kissi prosthetic.

The Magistrate looks to him, then me, then back to Traven and his big goddamn mouth.

"Why would Mr. Pitts being dead surprise you, Father?" he says. "Hell is a place of the dead."

Traven mumbles, "It's just that . . ."

"This isn't my first time in Hell," I say.

The Magistrate leans back.

"I see. Another mortal foolish enough to make a deal with the Devil. Did he send you back with promises of immortality? How did it feel when you realized you'd been tricked?"

"It wasn't like that," I say. "In fact, Lucifer and me are pretty simpatico these days. The old Lucifer. The retired one. He's the one who thought it would be funny to leave me on the fucking mountain."

The Magistrate continues to lean back, but he doesn't look so smug anymore.

"You mean the Lucifer who has become Death?" he says.

I upend the glass and get a few more drops of water.

"Do you know a bunch of other Lucifers?"

He leans forward and rests his arms on the table.

"You are friends with Death. My, how special you must be."

"We don't go to karaoke or anything, but we've had a cocktail or two."

"I find it hard to believe you, Mr. Pitts."

I push the glass back to his side of the table.

"I don't give a single fuck what you believe. Unless it means I don't get a drink later. Then I care a lot."

The Magistrate takes the glass and puts it back on the small table.

"Why would your 'friend' Death leave you here in the middle of nowhere?" he says.

"Isn't it obvious?" says Traven.

"No. It is not. Why do you think he was there?"

Traven opens a hand to the Magistrate and then to me.

"For *this*. This moment. This meeting. This is why Mr. Pitts was on the mountain. Death wanted us all to meet."

"To what end?" says the Magistrate.

"To help with the work, of course."

"You're so sure?"

Traven leans forward, speaking quietly, but intensely.

"Death could have left him in Pandemonium or at the gates of Heaven with the other refugees. He could have left him in the wilderness where no one would ever find him. But no. He left him right here in the Tenebrae, directly in our path."

"Perhaps Death left him so that we could dispatch him to Tartarus," says the Magistrate.

"Perhaps he has something we need."

"Or perhaps Death was having a joke on all of us."

"I vote for that," I say. "Death loves a joke. Pull my finger he says and *poof,* you're gone."

Traven lays his hand on the table.

"I'm telling you. Death has sent us a gift. This man is useful to the cause. I don't know exactly how, but it will reveal itself."

"How do you know that he isn't lying about everything?" the Magistrate says. "From where he came from to his alleged friendship with Death?"

"Because I knew him."

"When you were alive."

"Yes."

"How do you know he is the same man you knew then? Perhaps he's gone mad. Perhaps he's a spy."

"Excuse me," I say. "What time does the buffet start? The service here it terrible."

"Stop it, Pitts," snaps Traven.

The Magistrate shakes his head.

"Yes. Stop it, Mr. Pitts. We will know everything when Mimir gets here," he says.

Fuck. The oracle. I'd forgotten about her.

"But for my own curiosity," the Magistrate says, "what is the new Death like?"

"Is this part of the interrogation or are we just dishing?"

"It is simply a question."

I look at him for a minute. He didn't poison me and he could have. He also hasn't let Daja shoot me and I know she'd love to.

I say, "Death is pretty much like he was when he was Lucifer. He didn't much like that job either, but he was good at it. Truth is, I haven't seen him much since he's become Death. It's like being a cabby. Long hours."

"You were friends, then?" says the Magistrate. "Confidants?"

"Why not? I'm a people person."

The Magistrate aims a finger at me.

"The Devil had many secrets. What was his greatest?"

"Now it's twenty questions? Fuck you," I say. "That's his secret and mine."

Daja moves again. I'm getting really tired of this.

"Please answer the question," says the Magistrate.

"Please answer," says Traven. There's something in the bastard's eyes. It takes me a while, but then I recognize it: now that he's seen a familiar face, he doesn't want to be alone again. I can't blame him.

"There are a couple of things it could be," I say. "But what I think you mean is the wound. The one Dad gave him during the war in Heaven. The one that never healed. Until recently, at least."

"You are saying the wound is healing?" says the Magistrate.

"*Healed.* It started getting better when he went home."

The Magistrate stays silent for a minute. Then he whispers, "Interesting," and looks at Daja.

When no one else says anything, I say, "Now I have some questions for you."

"I am sure you do. Father, would you bring in Mimir?" the Magistrate says.

"Of course."

He gets up and goes outside. I lean my head back and look up at Daja. She doesn't look any better upside down. Her dark, dusty hair is long and she wears it tied back. Her leathers are light and worn. She's strong. She could wear heavier leathers, but she likes the light ones because they let her move faster, so she's down for a gunfight, a knife fight, or fists. I smile up at her wondering which one she'd like to start with on me. She scowls back.

Traven comes back in with Mimir in tow. She's still in her ratty fur coat, but she's taken the bandanna off her face. Turns out it was hiding a respirator attached to a small oxygen tank under her coat. She sits across the table, next to the Magistrate. I can hear her labored breathing all the way over on my side.

The Magistrate gently takes her hand.

"Thank you for coming, Mimir."

"Of course," she says, her voice muffled by the oxygen mask. "How can I help?"

The Magistrate looks at me.

"Mimir, I am concerned that Mr. Pitts here might be a spy or intend to harm us in some other way. He says that he found himself on the mountain and that he was placed there by Death himself. Is he telling the truth?"

"Do you mean, did Death leave him or that he believes Death left him?"

"How did he get onto the mountain, Mimir?"

She opens a canvas Safeway shopping bag (Have I mentioned recently that they bootleg a lot of our stuff in Hell? They steal cable, too. Don't tell anyone.) and lays a whole spook show on the table. At the center is a bowl made from the skull of a Hellion with three horns that make three perfect little legs for it. She pours in powders, a few drops of a potion, a seed pod, and a lot of other crap I can't identify. As she grinds it all together, I wish Vidocq was here. I bet Vidocq wishes he was here. The alchemist in him would be going nuts right now. He'd know what kind of moonshine Popcorn Sutton here is brewing. All I know is that I don't want to drink it when she's done. Things might get tense soon.

When she's finished, I put my hands on the table, ready to push back and try to knock Daja off balance before she can shoot me.

But Mimir doesn't come up with the glass. She pulls a match from her bag and lights the mess in the bowl. Just as it starts to stink, she unhooks her respirator from the oxygen tank and puts the tube over the Dumpster fire she's started.

I start to say something stupid, but Traven's hand closes on my arm in a goddamn death grip.

Mimir sucks in the smoke and suddenly I want another Malediction. Her eyes roll back in her head. She begins to shake. She mumbles something unintelligible, like she's chanting or speaking in tongues. It's your basic oracle carny act. I've seen a million of them. They always look like they're about to have an aneurysm. If they didn't, the rubes wouldn't think they were getting their money's worth.

After a long moment, Mimir pulls out the tube and puts a lid on the skull bowl. She blows a long trail of smoke from out of the tube, clearing her wheezing lungs, and hooks her respirator back to the oxygen tank. She takes several long, deep breaths.

"What did you see?" says the Magistrate. He looks at me. "Is he telling the truth, Mimir?"

I get ready again to bash Daja.

Mimir takes one more long breath and nods her head.

"He is not a spy?"

"He is not," she rasps.

I hear a rustle of leather behind me and the quiet *click* of a small hammer being lowered onto a small gun. Daja was playing me all along. She knew what I'd do if things went bad. I was ready for her to pull her pistol, but she had a little pocket gun—a Derringer or something—on me the whole time. Suddenly I hate and like her even more all at the same time.

"How did he make his way up the mountain?" says the Magistrate.

"Death placed him there," says Mimir.

"Why?"

"Death's reasons are his own. To look too closely is to risk having his gaze fall upon you."

"I understand," the Magistrate says.

He pats Mimir's shoulder as her breathing returns to its normal wheeze.

"I have one more question for you," he says, and looks at me. "The gentleman that Death so graciously brought us calls himself Mr. ZaSu Pitts. Is that, in fact, who he is? And if not, who is he really?"

I tense again. This time Daja pulls her big pistol. The barrel brushes my ear. It tickles, which pisses me off. I don't want to go to Tartarus giggling.

Traven looks at me and I look back at him. I'm stuck between a witch, a dime-store desert prophet, and a gunslinger who wants me extremely dead. And I can't even reach my cigarettes.

Mimir takes the bowl and tosses the burning herbs outside. She comes back to the table and, lucky me, begins mixing a whole new brew that this time is going to reveal that not only am I a big fat liar, but so is Traven. I wonder if I should tell the Magistrate who I am. But that would make us liars. We're fucked either way. Better keep quiet and play this out.

When she gets her hoodoo herbs piled up nice and high, Mimir sets them on fire. A dull yellow smoke drifts from the bowl, filling the camper with a smell like boiling cabbage in scorched motor oil. I start to say something when the contents of the bowl flare up, sucking the smoke back inside. An orange flame rises from the bowl, kicking up sparks. When it's about a foot high, the flame begins to turn until it's a miniature tornado, twisting and writhing above the upturned skull.

I say, "If you're trying to make fondue, you're doing it wrong."

Mimir waves a hand in my direction. I stare at her.

"What do you want? Applause?"

"She wants you to put your hand in the fire, asshole," says Daja.

"Yeah. That's not happening."

"I am afraid you must," says the Magistrate.

I look at Traven.

"What do you say, Father?"

"You were brought here for a reason," he says. "Do as they say."

I shake my head. "You people have a shitty way of treating guests. I'm never staying at this hotel again." But I put out my left hand. The heat hits me at the edge of the bowl. I hesitate.

"Daja. If he does not put his hand into the flame, please shoot the father."

I hear her pull back the hammer on the pistol.

I push my hand forward.

"Mr. Pitts," says the Magistrate. "I believe that you are right-handed. Please use that hand."

I look at him.

"Is Magistrate *your* real name? Why don't we both put our hands in the fire?"

Daja grabs my shoulder.

I put out my right hand.

"At least I'm not going to die in Fresno."

And in I shove my mitt into the tornado.

I've been burned before. I've been shot, stabbed, poisoned, beaten, chewed on, and called rude names. I want to say that because of my vast experience in getting my ass handed to me that the fire is no big deal. But that would be a lie. This fire is a big deal. A huge deal. A giant, flaming, goddamn, piece-of-shit, agonizing, I-want-to-rip-my-own-head-off deal.

I lower my head. Close my eyes and grit my teeth. I'm sweating like a hog tap-dancing in a sauna. I want to scream the paint off the fucking walls. But I don't make a sound. If I'm going to end up Captain Hook at the end of this, at least they won't get that little piece of satisfaction.

I open my eyes. The flames are more intense than before and have changed color from a deep orange to a pale blue.

I lock eyes with Mimir. She nods and waves her hand again. I start to pull my hand back, going slow because I'm not looking forward to the sight of my charred stump. The moment I move, the Magistrate leans across the table, grabs my wrist, and shoves my hand back into the flames.

I'm close enough that I could lunge across the table and shove his smug face into the tornado until his eyes burn out. But Daja has the gun on Traven. I really want to do something, but I don't know what. The pain is really getting to me and I think about Candy and everything I've lost and left behind, and it's all so goddamn sad it's like a Roy Orbison song, so I do the only logical thing.

I start singing "In Dreams."

The Magistrate's face shifts to somewhere between pissed and puzzled. But I keep singing, staring into the fire. Mimir sees an opening and snatches the bowl off the table. She douses the fire and slams the bowl down hard. The Magistrate lets go of my wrist and sits down, staring at Mimir. Fuck 'em both. I pull back my hand and look it over. Not a scorch mark or even a blister. The Magistrate's oracle has some good hoodoo.

Mimir slaps the table. "If you wish to keep my services, do not interfere with my work again," she shouts at the Magistrate.

He holds up his hands.

"My apologies, Mimir. It will not happen again," he says. "But what did the flame tell you?"

The oracle gets up and dumps everything outside again. When she sits down she looks at me.

"He is who he says he is."

I feel Daja shift her weight. I don't have to look to know her pistol is now pointed at me.

"He is Mr. Pitts?"

"Yes."

That was unexpected. Leave it to lunatics like this guy to hitch himself to a third-rate seer. Still, it's nice for me. I don't have to start killing people right away.

"Thank you, Mimir. Again, my sincere apologies."

I take a big breath and let it out, happy me and Traven are still in one piece.

The oracle gathers her gear, wheezing in the respirator. As she gets up, she gives me a look. I have no goddamn idea what it means or why she lied or why Traven and I are still alive. When she leaves I look from Daja to the Magistrate.

"I think your pet monkey is getting tired. Why don't you throw it a banana and send it home?"

Daja smacks me on the side of the head with the gun barrel.

"Daja. It is over," says the Magistrate. "Put your gun down. Mr. Pitts has passed his first test. He will be staying with us for the time being."

I rub the side of my aching head and raise my eyebrows.

"*First test?* I am going to crucify you people on Yelp."

Traven gets up.

"Pitts passed the test. May we go?"

The Magistrate shakes his head.

"No. Mr. Pitts I would like to leave. You I would like to stay," he says. He looks up at Daja and frowns. "And I would like a word with you as well."

Traven pulls me to my feet. I'm a little light-headed from the pain and it's hard to stop rubbing my hand. The father gives me a little shove to the door. I look back at the Magistrate.

"What's under the tarp, Roy Bean?"

"The future," he says. "Ours and now possibly yours."

"I've got my own future. I don't need yours."

The Magistrate gives me a tiny smile.

"Thank you, Mr. Pitts. We will talk again soon."

On the way out I bump my shoulder into Daja's like an annoyed sixth grader. She's already in trouble with Dad, though, so she doesn't say a word.

Outside, I have to lean against the side of the motor home for a minute. The fire test took more out of me than I was ever going to let those assholes see.

The camp is weirdly quiet. A handful of Hellions attend to cook fires. A few others move trucks and construction equipment around. But the vast majority of the havoc is gathered by a hill of burning crosses erected on the other side of whatever is under the tarp. Their heads are down as a group of robed creeps perform some kind of ceremony.

So, this really is a crusade after all. And now I'm part of it. Hallelujah.

I listen at the motor-home door, trying to hear if Traven is all right. But if the Magistrate got the answer he wanted from the oracle, he has no reason to hurt the father. Anyway, I can't hear a damned thing.

I walk back to Traven's camper thinking that maybe I'd've been better off if there had been a storm and it snuffed me back on the plains. It would be simpler than dealing with this sideshow.

THE SERMON BREAKS up a few minutes later. Hellions and damned souls straggle back to camp. They're pretty buddy-buddy for a bunch of torturers and torture victims. I guess there have been weirder alliances Downtown.

Grating Hellion music blasts from a tricked-out Impala lowrider. When you get down to it—mysterious religious services aside—the havoc is like any camp. The cooks start filling dinner plates. Damned souls and Hellions argue, while others laugh or barter. Shooters load up on ammo from a Hellion APC. It has massive bullhorns on top and iron shark teeth welded on the front. Someone strapped broken mannequin parts in between the jaws. Cute gag, but where did they get dressing dummies way out in the Tenebrae? They must make runs into Hell itself, maybe even Pandemonium. That's good news for me. If I have to make a run for it, I can disappear in ten seconds flat there. All I have to do is survive until then. When I get back to Hell I can start figuring out a way to get back home.

I wonder who Daja has spying on me? No way this bunch is letting an outsider stroll around without surveillance.

There's probably a rifle sighted on me right now. Or am I just being paranoid? Being dead has thrown me off my game. I need some privacy to figure out how much of me is left. I have some hoodoo and I didn't bleed out. Good news there. But how strong am I? How fast? Is the angel part of me powerful enough to manifest a Gladius? And yet, for all those questions, the one that's truly bugging me is this: Why the hell did it have to be Audsley Ishii who killed me?

I've fought Hellions, slimy monsters, armed-to-the-teeth mortals, scary little girls, and forgotten, pissed-off gods. And it was a third-rate shitbird I got fired from his lousy job who finally did me in. Maybe it was poetic justice. Maybe it was me getting soft. Every time I decide to take things easy or deal with my PTSD, something rotten happens. There won't be any of that down here. Hell is a Zero Slack zone. No one gets a second chance from me down here. Which means I need weapons. But first I need something to eat and a little sleep. Dying is like the worst jet lag you've ever had.

Rubberneckers from the havoc wander by, but none of them will meet my eye. They just want to sniff the new meat. That's okay. I'd do the same thing. I keep still and look as oblivious as I can. Today's lesson, kids, is to not look for trouble until I have a better handle on the situation. I'm perfectly prepared to look a little dumb if that's what it takes.

Just as I'm getting bored and cranky, Traven comes out of the Magistrate's motor home.

He gestures and we head to his camper.

"You were in there for a while," I say.

"These things take time."

"Complaining that no one responded to his birthday Evite, was he?"

Traven nods to someone.

"I was taking his confession."

"You're back in the priest game?"

"I don't think excommunication counts for a lot down here," he says.

That actually makes me smile.

"Did you do the other thing?"

A bug-headed Hellion in a sombrero and dirty serape glowers at me. I smile like a dummy and keep walking.

"You want to know if I ate his sins," Traven says.

"Did you?"

"Of course. It's always been part of what I do."

I look at him.

"Even in Hell? What does anyone care about sins down here?"

"It's an individual thing. The Magistrate's job is difficult."

"Believe me, I know."

Traven looks surprised.

"You know the Magistrate?"

I shake my head.

"I know a killer when I see one and he's one cold Charlie Starkweather motherfucker."

"It's not that simple," says Traven.

"That isn't criticism. I'm just trying to figure out how things work down here."

"I told you. It's a crusade."

"Because the Crusades worked out so well back home."

"I've pointed that out, but he isn't interested in mortal history."

What a shock.

I look at him.

"But you sound like you believe in this guy's half-assed jihad."

Traven puts his hands in his pockets.

"I've believed what I've had to in order to survive. And even then, I've questioned his methods."

"I'm guessing a guy travels with his own personal havoc isn't the candy-and-flowers type."

"I'm afraid not."

"So, you're raiders. How bad is it?"

"Bad. When it happens . . . just don't try to stop it."

We reach the camper and Traven opens the door.

"There it is," I say. "I came all the way to here just to be the biker trash my mom always warned me about."

"Death does have its fun with us," he says. "Would you like some food?"

I lean against the side of the camper with the open desert at my back so I can keep an eye on the camp.

"Does that mean I'm not being executed?"

"Not tonight."

"Food sounds good, but what I really want is another light."

I take out the Maledictions.

Traven points to the pack.

"Could I have one of those, too?"

"Sure."

I tap one out and hand it to him. He lights mine, then his.

I say, "I found them on the mountain."

"A good omen."

"Or bad housekeeping."

"Let's go inside," he says. "You're not a popular man around here."

"I'm getting that impression."

He hesitates in the doorway.

"You know, I can do it for you, too."

"Eat my sins?"

"Yes."

I shake my head.

"Thanks, but sometimes I think my sins are the only thing holding me together."

"That's not true. You have a higher calling, Mr. Pitts."

"I'm God's special little snowflake. You don't have to tell me."

I take a pull on the cigarette. Watch Daja moving smoothly through the havoc, a wolf watching over her flock.

"What's Daja's story?"

"Her name is Dajaskinos," says Traven. "She's the Magistrate's second in command. She's very devoted."

"They lovers?"

"No. More like father and daughter."

"Was the guy I fried her lover?"

"I don't know."

"She really hates me."

"She's suspicious. You didn't come to us in the usual way. Usually, we pick up new members from volunteers among groups we encounter."

"The ones that survive the havoc."

"That's usually the way it works."

I watch Daja until she steps into a city bus blaring smoke and music. The smoke from whatever they're cooking doesn't smell bad.

Traven.

g to have to kill Daja?"

"Please don't," he says, his eyes going a little wide. "And don't talk that way around here. She is powerful and respected."

"I was afraid of that. The worst kind of boss: a good one. Don't worry. I'm not killing anybody. I'm just making conversation. It would put you on the Magistrate's shit list and me back where I started."

"Which is?"

"Dead, lost, and with only half a pack of smokes. The dictionary definition of Hell."

"Amen to that," Traven says. He goes into the camper and I follow him.

IN A FEW minutes, he goes out and comes back with a couple of plates heaped with Hellion meat and something that's sort of like gluey mashed potatoes. The meat is a little gamy, but I dive in headfirst and don't come up until I've finished every scrap on the plate. Traven offers me some of his dinner, but I wave a hand at him.

"I don't want you eating my sins and I'm sure not eating yours."

He laughs and goes back to his food.

When he's through, we smoke and talk. I tell him more about Brigitte. Everything I can think of. Later I explain how we had to fake Candy's death and how she's Chihiro now. When Traven asks about my murder I tell him what little I know. Ishii. Me letting down my guard. The funny hoodoo knife he used.

"If Ishii is the lowlife you describe, where would he get a knife like that?" says Traven.

Why the hell didn't I think of that?

I sit there like a dummy trying to come up with an answer. Did he buy it off some witch with a grudge? Maybe from the White Light Legion? There was also one of the Augur, Thomas Abbot's bodyguards, who didn't like me. What was his name? Maybe he could come up with a weapon like that. Then something else occurs to me.

Wormwood.

I lay it out for Traven as simply as I can.

Wormwood is like a mob-run bank if the mob was a Hellion horde and the bank was the world. They make money when the stock market goes up and when currencies collapse and a few million poor slobs starve to death. They make money on terrorist bombs, and where and when the next Ebola outbreak kills the most people. They make money on who is or isn't damned.

And they make money on me.

Who I kill. Who I don't. Whether I'm a good boy or bad, they make a profit. And it pisses me off. I can't say for sure that they're behind my murder, but I know this: someone just made a fortune off my currently decaying ass.

MY EYES HAVEN'T completely focused yet, but I can make out a silhouette in the door of Traven's camper. It's a man and he has a knife in his hand. I kick him with my good leg and he bounces off the camper's roof and comes down onto me.

The guy stinks. Like a T-bone steak that's been left out in the sun and gone maggoty. He wheezes while he tries to shove the knife through my throat. He doesn't feel that strong, but he's on top of me with all of his weight centered on the blade.

My eyes finally focus, but it's too dark in the van to see who it is. This seems like as good a time as any to see how strong I am and toss the killer's ass outside. Of course, if my aim is off, he's just going to land on me again, and maybe get lucky with the knife and my throat.

I shouldn't have had that Hellion wine with Traven. Between it and my murder jet lag, my reflexes are all off. There's nothing subtle I can do from this position, so I just work on pushing the fucker off me.

I'm able to move Mac the Knife's body without too much effort. Good news. I'm still strong. Bad news. There's something wrong with the guy's skin. A big piece of his left arm slides off like a snake shedding its skin and the bastard comes down hard, knocking the wind out of me. While I'm trying to catch my breath, he rears back with the knife, ready to pig-stick me.

Instead, he stays up there and just twitches. A couple of big shudders. Then he sighs and does a backward swan dive out of the camper. By now, Traven is awake.

"What's happening? Are you all right?" he says.

Mac the Knife is gone. There's someone else silhouetted in the door, and she's holding a knife. I'm sure it's Daja, but instead of attacking me, the silhouette pulls off a respirator mask and says, "Jimmy, you are such an asshole."

I squint at her through the dark. Something about the voice . . .

"Cherry Moon?"

She glances around and steps into the camper. Still wrapped in the ragged fur coat, she drops onto her knees and slithers over me like a shaggy snake.

"Seeing as how we're both dead, can we finally fuck?" she says. "Right here. In front of the preacher."

I push her off me.

"Thanks, but I'm busy bleeding right now."

She glances back at the stab wound in my leg.

"I've seen you with worse. Now get that ass in the air and call me Mommy. And don't pretend you're not a bottom. I knew it the first time I met you."

She climbs back on top of me, jamming her stupid knee into my knife wound. I reach up to push her off and she slides my hands over her breasts. She's laughing when I notice Traven's head looming over us in the dark. He looks confused.

"Wait," he says. "You know the oracle?"

"She's no oracle," I say. "She's Cherry Moon. A lunatic from my dim, dark past."

Cherry was part of the magic circle I was in when Mason Faim sent me Downtown. She used the hoodoo he gave her to turn herself into an underage Lolita manga fuck doll. And alive or dead, she's been screwing with me ever since.

Traven stares at Cherry grinding away on my crotch. He looks like the most puzzled holy man since Jesus saw Judas order fajitas at the Last Supper.

"No. She is the oracle," he says.

"Oh, all right," says Cherry. "Everybody get their pants off. You too, choirboy."

She pinches Traven's cheek.

"Me love you long time."

I finally shove her off me. Cherry slams into the wall, shaking the camper. She's still laughing.

"If the house is rocking, don't bother knocking!"

I sit up and check my leg wound. It's deep, but not too wide, like the knife went straight in. It'll heal in no time.

"Stark, what is going on here?" says Traven, then corrects himself. "Pitts."

"Don't bother, Father," I say. "Cherry knows me. She's known it was me this whole time. What I don't get is why she didn't give me away."

Cherry sits up, takes her time adjusting her miniskirt and coat. I pull the camper door closed.

"ZaSu Pitts. That's the best you could come up with?" she says. "And why the funny name at all? Every asshole in Hell is afraid of Sandman Slim. Don't you want that? Fuck, you could probably kick the Magistrate out and take over. We could ride the havoc all over Hell. One big party till the end of time."

Traven looks at Cherry.

"You're not a real oracle?" he says.

Cherry rolls her eyes and shoves one of her high heels into my leg. Like all my dealings with her, it hurts.

"You have any smokes left?"

I find my coat and give her a Malediction. She sparks it with a gold lighter in the shape of a Crucifix. Cherry looks at me, then turns her eyes to Traven.

"Did prickless here tell you that he killed me?"

Traven starts to say something and I cut him off.

"I didn't kill her. I just didn't get to her in time to save her. Mason's attack dog—a guy named Parker—killed her."

"Details, details," says Cherry. "I'm still dead and it's still your fault."

"I'm sorry. If you were any less annoying, I'd be even more sorry."

She looks at Traven.

"See? He admits it's his fault. And I just saved his worthless ass. Doesn't he owe me one quick fuck for that, Father?"

Traven takes a breath. This madness is way above his pay grade.

"So, you're not a real oracle? Does the Magistrate know?"

She swats away the question.

"No. I'm a real oracle. I learned the whole seeing thing from a Hellion street swami. He did it for cash back in Pandemonium, but after everything went to shit because of this one."

She digs her heel into me again.

"The swami took off and left me high and dry. Of course, I'd already learned the tricks by then . . . and helped myself to enough of his toys to set myself up when some bleeding hearts gave me a ride out of the city."

"Where did you meet the havoc?" says Traven.

"We left Hell altogether and lit out for the Tenebrae. I'd spent some time here, so I knew my way around."

"But you didn't count on the Magistrate showing up," I say.

She sighs and puffs the Malediction.

"Everyone who didn't join up . . . well, the pope there can tell you all about it."

I nod to the oxygen tank.

"What's with the wheezing gaff?"

Cherry puts the respirator over her mouth and makes a silly face at me. She lowers it and says, "I've been a few places and done a few things since the last time we saw each other, Jimbo. I couldn't take a chance on anyone recognizing me."

"That doesn't explain why you didn't rat me out to the Magistrate today."

She frowns.

"I'd never do that, ZaSu. The world—even this one—is a lot more fun with you in it." She taps her ash onto Traven's floor. "Besides, if things go belly up here, maybe Sandman fucking Slim can step up and actually save me this time."

She blows smoke at me. I wave it away.

"As much of a pain in the ass as you are, you know I would."

She points at me, but looks at Traven.

"Is he all right? What's with the Boy Scout act?"

"We've been talking," says Traven. "He's trying to be a better person and deal with some of his mental issues."

Cherry stares at me, a little horrified.

"He's *nothing but* mental issues. You can't fix him. You do and you'll fuck us all. But especially me. I killed for this piece of shit today. He owes me."

I limp to the camper door.

"That reminds me. If it wasn't Daja who tried to kill me, let's see who it was."

"It's Megs," says Cherry. "Didn't you smell him? You burned him up good, Jimmy. He looks like a s'more that fell in the fire."

I get out of the camper and look at him. Cherry and Traven follow me.

We're at the far edge of the camp, away from anything important. A nice place for an ambush. I look at the pile of meat on the ground.

"It's Megs all right."

He moans quietly, leaking blood.

The ground leading back to the main camp is a flat surface, and the desert floor is too hard to leave footprints. Nothing useful there. I kneel down and look Megs over.

"You two have been around. Does Lobster Boy look like he could get here under his own power?"

"I doubt it," says Traven.

"Definitely not," says Cherry. "I saw him at center camp. He was a goddamn basket case."

I reach back in the camper and pull out the piece of Megs's arm that came off in my hand. Toss it down next to him.

"That means someone helped him here. Carried or wheeled him over. We would have heard a vehicle."

Cherry gives Megs a light kick.

"Making friends wherever you go, eh, Jimmy?"

"It's Mr. Pitts," I say. "If you want rescuing when the time comes, that is."

Cherry drops the Malediction and crushes it under her shoe.

"Speaking of the time," she says, and pulls the respirator up over her chin. "Time for me to get back to the peanut gallery. There'll be rumors about you by now."

She winks and pulls the respirator up over her face.

"Don't worry. I won't tell anyone what a shy flower you were in the face, so to speak, of free pussy. A rare commodity in Hell, Jimmy, but you'd remember that if you hadn't gone soft living the good life back home."

"I'm bleeding and I just got murdered, Cherry. Give me a fucking break."

"Keep an eye on him for me, Father," she wheezes in her mask. "If anyone's going to kill him down here, it won't be Daja."

"It will be you?" says Traven.

Cherry gives us a fingertip wave and heads back to camp.

Traven looks at me.

"Well. That was unexpected."

"That's one word for it."

He looks down at Megs. "What are we going to do with him?"

I reach down and snap his neck. He blips out of existence a moment later.

Traven turns away.

"Please warn me the next time you're going to do something like that."

"Sorry."

He looks back at where the body was a second before.

"There's a lot of blood."

"We're going to need to cover it up."

I look around.

"We're close to the base of the mountain. I remember loose soil down there," I say. "I'll bring some over and cover the blood when things settle down."

"You'll need help."

I look around for something else to cover the blood with, but there's nothing.

"You're in good with the Magistrate," I say. "I won't fuck that up. If things go wrong, it should be me they come after."

"That's not fair."

"We're in Hell. I just got knifed by a charcoal briquette and molested by a witch. Talk to me some more about fair."

"At least let me be your lookout," says Traven.

"Fine. But not now. When most of them are asleep."

We go back into the camper. Traven settles back down on his cot and I lie on my coat on the floor with a couple of pillows. It's not exactly comfortable, but it beats sleeping anywhere else at this crummy summer camp.

He says, "This has been an unusual day."

"And we're just getting started."

"I know."

"Good night, Father."

"Whatever happens, it really is good to see you."

"You too. Now shut up and let me rest awhile."

A minute later Traven sits up.

"I'm sorry I snapped at you earlier."

"When I broke Megs's neck? Don't sweat it. Think of it like someone putting a dog out of its misery. Only he really, really hated the dog."

"Maybe I was wrong earlier," he says. "Maybe I *can* get excommunicated in Hell."

"Pull that off and I sure as shit will let you eat my sins."

AT LEAST ONE thing goes right. We get enough dirt to cover the blood without anybody seeing us. The rest of the night, though, Traven tosses and turns.

A few hours later, I wake to the ground shaking and a roar like Mechagodzilla. I run outside, but it isn't an earthquake or a metal Kaiju invasion. It's just the camp waking up and getting ready to move out. Vehicles gun their engines. Trucks maneuver out of the camp to clear a path for the cars. The semis and construction equipment get chained to the double-length flatbed carrying the tarp. It looks like complete chaos at first, but the moves are smooth and practiced. The havoc is one big, well-oiled machine.

Traven comes out of the camper and stands next to me.

I say, "Is it like this every day?"

"Not every day. We've camped for as long as three days while scouts have gone out surveilling the territory."

"Hell's own alarm clock."

"We're not in Hell, remember?"

"Right . . . I've been wondering about that. Why search the Tenebrae?"

He sits in the camper doorway with an old book in his lap.

"We go where the Magistrate leads us and whatever it is he's looking for led us out here."

He's holding a book.

"Doing a little light reading?"

"I wish. This is an old Hellion treatise on ley lines, holy sites, and places of power down here."

"If it points out any Dairy Queens let me know. I could sure go for a sundae."

He gets up and heads to where Daja, Cherry Moon, and the Magistrate are studying a map spread out on the hood of his Charger.

I shout after him.

"The Magistrate seems like the Holy Roller type. Could the tarp be some kind of church on wheels?"

Traven stops.

"I doubt it. From what he says, it has to do with the war in Heaven."

"Which side is he on?"

Traven pauses.

"Sometimes I'm not sure. He's so full of righteous anger. Still, I like to think that, despite some of his methods, he's one of the good guys."

"Define 'good guys.'"

"I'll have to get back to you on that."

"That's not a comfort, Father. You could at least give your flock comfort."

He makes the sign of the cross and ends it by giving me the finger. It actually makes me smile.

"That's more like it," I say.

"I'll see you in a little while."

"A little while" is relative—the four of them go over the map for a long time. Cherry throws stones. Traven consults his books. The Magistrate plots a course using a pile of shiny Hellion tools that make it look more like he's dissecting something than reading a map. After a half hour of good old-fashioned geomancy, the Magistrate hops onto the hood and then the roof of the car like a goddamn gazelle. As he scans the horizon with a telescope, the others gather up the map and tools he scattered all over the ground. A minute later he jumps down just as gracefully as he got up. I didn't expect that. I'd pegged him for a desk warrior. Serves me right for assuming too much too fast. I wonder what other tricks he can do?

By now, all the vehicles are ready to go. Traven heads back in my direction while Cherry goes back to her ambulance and

Daja fires up her Harley. The Magistrate guns the Charger. As it belches black smoke a small cheer goes up. He pops the clutch, turns a donut, and blasts out into the desert at the head of the havoc. When Samael was Lucifer he could have learned some tricks from this guy. The prick knows how to put on a show for his people.

As the rest of the vehicles pull out, a Mohawked Hellion woman heads straight at me. I shift my weight, ready for a fight. Instead, she walks right past me and unlocks the cab of the pickup truck. When Traven makes it back, she comes around and locks his old book in the camper. She tosses me a set of keys, then she peels out after the others.

I look at him.

"I might be in charge of the library and records, but it doesn't mean I'm trusted with them," he says.

"He thinks you wouldn't run off without your books."

"Exactly."

"Would you? Run off? I need to know if you're with me when I see an opening to get clear."

"Do you think that's possible?"

"I don't know, but I want to be ready. You with me?"

"Yes," he says, but he's not exactly excited about the prospect. I'm worried, but this isn't the time for a heart-to-heart. Most of the havoc has already moved out and the half-dozen members left as our watchdogs are looking antsy. Traven wraps his bandanna around his face and steps onto his hellhound. I go back to the burned-out pickup and try the key.

Damn. It starts.

We head out after the others with our babysitters hot on our heels.

WE TRAVEL FOR hours across the Tenebrae's monotonous plains. Imagine an optical illusion where you're on a flat, endless road. There are mountains in the distance on both sides and low peaks in the far distance. And nothing ever changes. Nothing moves. Nothing gets any closer or farther away. You know you're moving because you can feel the motion, but nothing ever fucking changes.

I've heard of souls who refused to enter Hell getting lost in the Tenebrae and wandering for years before going flat-out crazy. That's a whole new level of fucked. Dying, escaping Hell, then finding yourself someplace worse. If the Church had afterlife travel agents, they could make a fortune. Pay now, then later see the most colorful views of damnation from a double-decker, air-conditioned tour bus. Stop for lunch at the damned soul deli, where you can try Phil, your racist neighbor, on whole wheat. Or roast hot dogs over the lava pits where crooked politicians and show-business accountants do synchronized-shrieking shows every . . . well . . . forever. Don't forget to tip your driver on the way out or you'll end up with the other stingy bastards, growing gold teeth and pulling them out with pliers for eternity while other stingy dumb-asses pound them into coins with their faces. Where do you think Hellion money comes from?

The other part of this Bataan death march across nowhere: I'm still in this goddamn fried truck. There's no material left on the seats, so I'm riding bare springs all day. My bruised ass feels like it's welded to a demon pogo stick.

I'm a little worried about Father Traven. Has he gone a little too native? There's things you have to do to survive, but that doesn't mean you have to believe whatever mad shit your torturer is feeding you. I don't think he'd rat me out, but I'm worried that maybe he's got a bad case of Knights Templar and has actually bought into the idea of a holy crusade. I'll have to keep an eye on him. When I make a break for it, I'll drag him by his heels if I have to.

But Cherry is the one I'm really worried about. She's too crazy to predict what she'll do. I mean, she wasn't exactly stable when she was alive, but after she died she did a deep dive into unstable. She refused to leave her dead body for a long time and lived as a jabber—an animated corpse—clawing her way through the dirt and filth under L.A. When I finally got her to leave her body, she lived in the bombed-out version of L.A. in the Tenebrae. She played a sexpot ghost for a while and I don't know what else since I've last seen her. And now she's here with a whole new act. I don't think she'd deliberately let on who I am, but who knows what twisted stuff she might blurt that could make things a lot more difficult for me.

When my mind drifts back to Candy and home, I push the thoughts away as hard as I can. I'm dead. There's no going back now. None that I can figure, at least. But fuck everyone down here if they think I'm staying. All that matters is getting through this mess and figuring out what to do after that.

I lose track of the time on the plains. Bits of paint flake off the truck's crisped body and stick to my face and hair. That's fun. Traven rides beside me. He seems like a real natural. Maybe I'm selling him short. Maybe he likes being out of the library. He used to help us track bad guys back home before he died. Maybe this is like that and I should ease up on the guy.

About the time I'm wondering which of the babysitters I'm going to run off the road so I can steal their vehicle and save my aching ass, there's something new on the horizon. The ruins of a town. Of course, everything is ruins in the Tenebrae, but this looks more ruined than most. I wish I could get a look at the Magistrate's map. If I could place the town, maybe I could navigate my way back to Hell. That's something else to think about. The map.

Up front someone, probably the Magistrate, sends up a red flare. The havoc spreads out across the plain, zeroing in on the town. Me and Traven are at the rear of the joyride, between the main havoc and the trucks pulling the tarp. When the flare goes up, our babysitters peel off to join the main group. I look at Traven and point out into the open desert. He shakes his head. He's right. I'm getting ahead of myself. There's nowhere to run to yet. Sit tight and learn how the havoc works. Then disappear at the moment of maximum confusion. For now, though, I hit the gas. At least if we stop somewhere, maybe I can get out of this damned truck for a while.

By the time us stragglers reach the others, they have the town surrounded. But no one is going Hell's Angels on the place yet. They're just sitting in their cars, gunning the engines and looking like hard desert bandidos. It isn't exactly a stretch for them.

At a signal from up front, all the engines cut off at once. I pull to a stop and shut mine down. While the dust settles, I crawl out of the driver's seat. My ass and back ache like someone gave me a baseball-bat massage. I stretch, trying to work the kinks out, when Traven comes over.

"What now?" I say.

"It depends. It isn't always the same."

"But this is where the havoc gets to havocking."

"Maybe today will be different."

"Sure. Maybe today."

We're pretty far back in the pack, so I climb on the hood of the truck trying to see something. I can't make out much besides a crowd gathered at the edge of the town. Nothing happens for a while. I think the Magistrate is having a nice chat with whoever runs the burg. After all the driving and the last day of abject terror and confusion, frankly, it gets kind of boring. Traven climbs up on the truck with me.

"See anything?" he says.

"The Wizard gave the Scarecrow a heart. I hope he has something for Dorothy."

Traven points into the distance.

"What's that?"

There's a plume of dust winding its way through the havoc in our direction. A few seconds later I hear the roar of a bike engine. A sweaty soul on a dirty Hellion Ducati stops next to the truck.

He pushes up his goggles.

"You Pitts?"

"Last time I checked."

He moves up on the seat.

"Get on. You're riding bitch."

"What makes you think that?"

He looks up at me.

"The Magistrate wants to see you right fucking now. So get on, bitch, before you get us both in trouble."

"When you say it nice like that how can I resist?"

I climb down and head over to the bike. The rider is a big bare-chested sweat pig. To be clear, I mean he's literally a sweaty, upright pig—busted snout-like nose and everything. I stand there for a minute looking over his wheels.

"You checking out my ass? Get on, faggot."

"Sure."

I move like I'm getting onto the seat, but instead I swing my leg around and kick him in the back of the head. He falls forward and dumps the bike. I drag his sweaty ass off and haul the Ducati upright. I didn't hit him hard enough to knock loose anything essential, but he's going to have a long, embarrassing walk when he comes to. Traven comes over but doesn't say anything. He just raises his arms and drops them again like he's exhausted. I give him a little salute, gun the bike, and head for the front of the pack.

No one tries to stop me as I weave through the havoc. When I spot the Charger, I open up the throttle and hit the brakes just right to land in a nice stoppie up front.

Daja looks at me blankly while the Magistrate frowns.

"Where is Billy?"

"Taking a nap."

The Magistrate comes around the car.

"Then he is alive?"

"I'm not that dumb."

"I'll go check," says Daja, but the Magistrate lightly touches her arm before she can get on her Harley.

"No. I want you here with Mr. Pitts and myself."

He waves to a couple of riders in an El Camino covered in Nordic runes.

"Bring back Billy and the father," the Magistrate says, and they peel out.

I know the Magistrate added Traven to his delivery list just to fuck with me, so I brush it off. Don't give him the satisfaction or the ammunition.

When the car is gone, the Magistrate gestures for me to follow him over where the residents of the town are gathered. Daja comes, too, hooks her arm around mine, and—smiling like a blushing bride—drags me with her.

The Magistrate waits by a small group of the least pathetic souls in town. That said, they look like they spent the night in the drum of a cement mixer. Tattered clothes hanging off their bodies in gray rags. Dust in every crease on their desiccated faces. They sag in front of the havoc like kids who know they're about to get a spanking. Another twenty or thirty souls are bunched behind them. They look even worse.

The Magistrate says, "I am a student of human nature, did you know that, Mr. Pitts?"

"It beats beekeeping, I guess."

He smiles infinitesimally.

"I sent Billy to you knowing exactly what you would do."

"You sent one of your own people to get his ass kicked? That's not the way to build brand loyalty."

"Everyone in the group has their role," he says. "Some are more demanding than others."

"You mean, me turning out Billy's lights was some kind of prize?"

"I told you he wouldn't understand," says Daja. "He'll never understand."

"She's right," I say. "I never got fractions either."

"Come now, Mr. Pitts. Everyone is a good student with the right teacher and the proper motivation," the Magistrate says.

He pulls me away from Daja and the three of us go to the group of pathetics. The town council, local Shriners, or something.

"Hold up your hands," says the Magistrate.

When I do, he puts a corner of the map into each of my hands and lets the rest fall open, facing the pathetics. Great. I have the damned map, but I'm on the wrong side of it.

The Magistrate pulls one of the town council over and gestures to the map. The ragged bastard raises a hand and says something in a language I don't understand. The Magistrate answers him back in the same language. When he gets fed up with contestant one, he pulls contestant two forward. She's dressed in a filthy evening gown like she's heading for drinks at the Copa with the Rat Pack. Again, the Magistrate points to the map and the woman answers. Again it's in a language I don't understand—but different from contestant one's—and again he answers her. How many languages does the bastard speak?

He takes a piece of parchment from a pocket of his duster and shows it to the group. A couple touch it, then point into the distance. The Magistrate speaks to each of them, switching languages when he has to without missing a beat.

Daja stands with me behind the map.

"Having fun, sweetheart?" she says.

"Always with you, dear. Did you book the cruise next year?"

She looks behind us, searching for the El Camino.

"You won't last that long."

I turn to her.

"Bet I outlast you, Nancy Drew."

The Magistrate reaches over and pulls me back into place.

"You might not even make it past today," she says.

I give her a look.

"This isn't the first time I've heard that line."

She leans over and whispers, "I didn't say you were going to *die*. Just not make it."

Before I can ask her what the hell she's talking about, the Magistrate hands the map to Daja and she folds it up.

"Mr. Pitts, would you join us?" he says.

I go over as he pulls the town bigwigs he's been talking to aside.

"I have tried reasoning with these people," he says. "I have tried cajoling them and even promising rewards, but none has taken it upon themselves to be cooperative. What do you think of that?"

I look over the sad sacks. Shrug.

"Maybe they don't know anything. Look at them. I'm surprised they can even talk. Where the hell are we?"

"On an important ley line that passes right by this town."

"What makes you think they know that?"

The Magistrate brightens and sweeps his hand across the crowd.

"Because we are in a town of holy people. Priests. Nuns. Rabbis. Mullahs."

I point at the woman in the evening gown.

"Then why is she dressed like Joey Heatherton?"

"She has been here so long that her vestments rotted away, the poor dear. She had no choice."

"And you think these losers know something about your crusade?"

"I told you I was a student of psychology. I know they know something."

"You're a goddamn mind reader, too?"

"The Magistrate knows something about everything. He's a genius," says Daja, a proud kid who knows that her daddy can beat up your daddy.

"Fine. Say you're right," I say. "Maybe you should give these poor slobs some food or water. Then maybe they could think straight."

"They have gone without for too long. The shock to their system might send them to Tartarus without us lifting a finger. What a waste of scant resources," he says.

"Why are you telling me all this? Why am I even here?"

"This is my domain. What exists here without knowledge exists here in defiance."

"That doesn't even make sense."

"He's calling them liars," says Daja.

I look at her.

"Again I ask: What does any of this have to do with me?"

The El Camino pulls up behind us. Billy staggers out. Daja brings Traven over. An old military truck, its rear covered by a canvas awning, pulls up next to the El Camino.

"Like these people, the Father is a holy man," the Magistrate says. "But unlike them, he is not a liar. Is that not right, Father?"

Traven nods.

"Of course, Magistrate."

He doesn't know what's going on. He's scared.

"What does the Bible have to say about liars? I believe the Revelation to Saint John mentions them," says the Magistrate.

Traven looks blank.

"I'm not sure which passage you mean."

The Magistrate smiles.

"Do not be shy, Father. Now is a time to shine. Come. Say it with me: 'But the fearful, and unbelieving, and the abominable, and murderers, and whoremongers, and sorcerers, and idolaters . . .'"

Traven joins in.

"'And all liars, shall have their part in the lake which burneth with fire and brimstone . . .'"

The Magistrate stops and lets Traven finish on his own.

"'Which is the second death,'" he says.

"The second death," says the Magistrate.

He turns to me.

"Do you see?"

I look at him, wishing for a cigarette I could grind into his face.

"I used to go to a club called Second Death," I say. "Skull Valley Sheep Kill played there. Are we going to a show?"

"Yes," he says. "Yes, we are. And you shall be the ringmaster."

"It's been a tough day for Billy. Let *him* have a little fun."

"Billy is a good boy. His reward will come soon enough. As will yours. Come."

I follow him to the town's pitiful leaders. He pulls five forward. I look around and find Cherry in the crowd. I wonder if this freak show is because she said anything about me. I need to get her alone later.

The Magistrate clears his throat and speaks to the five.

"Mr. Pitts here is a man of great violence. He proved that yesterday. He proved it a few moments ago. And soon he will prove it again."

He repeats his little speech in several languages for the town leaders. They shuffle their feet and look at each other.

"I don't know what you have planned, but you can leave me out of it," I say.

"No, I cannot, Mr. Pitts. This is for your benefit as well as theirs."

"What is?"

At the Magistrate's signal, the canvas covering the old truck is pulled back. There are upright posts at either end of the flatbed, with a longer post connecting them. Every few feet along the horizontal post are knotted ropes. I've seen some shit, but this makes me blink.

It's a traveling gallows.

"Which one?" says the Magistrate, pointing to the five losers.

I look at the gallows.

"For that?"

"Of course."

I point to Daja.

"How about her?"

I point to the Magistrate.

"How about you? Think I can't make it happen?"

He laughs and turns to the townspeople.

"See? As I said, man of great violence."

He walks over to me.

"Do not pretend that you have never done something similar

in the past. Decided who in the crowd, even among innocents, should die."

For a fraction of a second, I flash back to fighting in the arena in Pandemonium. I killed everything they threw at me back then. I never asked who they were or why they were there. But this feels different.

I shake my head to clear it. The Magistrate is spookier and spookier. I don't want to take a chance he can read something in my face that will give me away.

I say, "What if I don't want to play?"

"Come come. We both know the answer to that."

Daja doesn't go for her gun. She pulls out a *tanto* and holds it across Traven's throat.

"It's all right," he says. Traven even smiles. "Let them have me. I'm ready."

"What a brave man. What a great soul," the Magistrate says. "Such a shame it would be to sacrifice him because of your inaction."

I stare at the five quaking assholes in front of me. I hate the whole town for being here. For choosing the Tenebrae over Hell. They thought their punishment would be too much and that they could run for it. But punishment doesn't give up, and it has all eternity to find you down here.

"Mr. Pitts?" says the Magistrate.

"Give me a fucking minute."

He checks his watch.

"Exactly one minute."

I glance at Traven. He nods to say it's all right. The prick is way too eager to go to Tartarus, for my taste. I bet Cherry's heart is doing backflips watching the Magistrate make me do his monkey dance.

"Thirty seconds, Mr. Pitts," the Magistrate says.

I look over the townies' faces. Spot someone trying to pretend none of this is happening. His hands are in his pockets. I can see their outline as he moves them around.

I walk over.

"What's in your pockets?"

"Nothing," he croaks.

I grab him by the collar and rip off a pocket. A collection of doll heads, large and small, falls onto the ground. He begins to shake. There's something else. A small pocketknife. I squat down, pretending to examine the doll heads as I slip the knife into my boot. Then I drag the guy back to the Magistrate.

"Him," I say.

"I've already picked the volunteers," he says.

"You told me to choose. I chose."

The Magistrate looks at his watch, then at me.

Traven shouts, "What are you doing? Let them take me."

The Magistrate turns to him.

"You never volunteered before, Father. Are you embarrassed now that you have a friend here? Does it make you afraid that God can see you, too?" He turns to the city council. In several languages he says, "Do you understand what is happening? Will one of you take his place?"

None of them makes a peep.

The Magistrate comes closer to me and says quietly, "Why him?"

"He kicked my dog."

The Magistrate grins.

"Then by all means let us rectify this atrocity. Bring him," he tells to the crew on the gallows truck. They climb down and drag the doll man over.

"What are you doing?" says Traven. "Why him over me?"

I show him a couple of doll heads I picked up.

He says, "You think he hurts children."

"He did something to get damned."

"But you don't know. They could belong to his own children."

"They don't."

"Are you sure?"

"Completely."

I get close enough to whisper to him. Daja pushes the knife into his throat hard enough to draw a bead of blood, and it takes a lot to ignore that.

I say, "You're the one who told me that when things happen not to try and stop them."

"Not like this," he says.

I step back.

"Then you should have been more specific."

What happens next doesn't take long at all.

The doll man is dragged onto the gallows, his hands are tied behind his back, and one of the crew puts the noose around his neck. The Magistrate says something to him and stands at the edge of the flatbed, a preacher addressing his flock. Charlie Manson laying out the plans for Helter Skelter.

He says, "As Father Traven reminded me, Revelation 21:8 tells us that liars 'shall have their part in the lake which burneth with fire and brimstone: which is the second death.'"

As he finishes, someone pulls the lever. The trapdoor opens. And the doll man falls through. The havoc howls and cheers, which covers up the sound of his neck snapping. Doll Man swings at the end of the rope for a few seconds before disappearing, his soul sucked into the Hell below Hell. A few last doll heads fall, bouncing out of the truck and onto the ground. Damned souls and Hellions scramble to get souvenirs.

I watch it all thinking one thing: *Survive.* Revenge and pity and whatever else there is comes later.

I guess my chances of getting over my PTSD just went out the window.

Daja puts her knife back in its sheath.

"Welcome to the team," she says to me.

"I'm not on your team ever, sister."

"You are and you don't even know it. That's how it was with the father. Isn't that right, Padre?"

She smacks Traven on the ass and walks away.

I go over to him.

"Did you have to choose?"

He nods.

"In Blue Heaven. I did what you did. I picked the worst person I could find."

"You did the right thing."

He shakes his head. Draws in a breath and lets it out.

"I was a man of God. Now I'm just a murderer."

"Why don't we ask God what he thinks? Oh, that's right. He isn't around anymore. We're on our own."

"I don't believe that and neither do you."

"It's done. We do what we have to do to survive and we get away the first chance we get. Right?"

"I'm not sure I can do that."

"You can. Trust me."

He gives me a look.

"You're sure about the man you chose?"

"One hundred percent."

"I want to believe you."

"We're in Hell. No one is innocent."

"Especially us. Because we know better."

"I'm getting out of here and I'm taking you with me. What you do after that is your business."

Traven walks away as a stream of havoc members come by to pat me on the back, punch my arm, and shake my hand. I smile and nod like it's the Oscars and I just won Best Supporting Asshole.

The Magistrate is off talking to the rest of the town. In ones and twos, they drift over to the havoc looking miserable. Reluctant new recruits to the cause.

I walk to the truck and drop back into the driver's seat. I don't want to let Traven see me feeling the way I feel. Did I just cross a line I can't uncross? I know the doll man was a bad guy. I *know* it. This isn't the first time I've executed someone. I murdered a whole houseful of Wormwood bastards just a few weeks ago. Still. This feels different.

The next time the Magistrate tries to rope me into a dog and pony show like this, I'll kill him, no matter what.

Daja rides up on her Harley. She pulls a couple of Hellion beers out of her saddlebags and hands me one. Clinks hers against mine and takes a long drink.

"We'll be moving out soon," she says. "When we get settled I'll see about getting you better wheels."

"Don't bother."

"It's no bother. *Brother*."

She drives away.

I sit there for a while looking out at the desert, not thinking. Letting my mind go blank for a few minutes.

Then I drink the beer.

THAT NIGHT IN Traven's camper, neither of us has much to say. I hear a motorcycle stop outside and go to see who it is.

It's Daja with another woman as big and bad as she is. Her hair is buzzed almost skinhead short, her face is fine-boned and graceful. Her skin is dark and heavy with Downtown warrior sigils. She almost looks like someone I could have met in the arena. She and Daja are on spidery Hellion Harleys.

I close the camper door and say, "It's late and we need our beauty sleep. What do you want?"

They get off the bikes.

"Nothing," says Daja. She throws me a set of keys. The other woman gets on the back of her Harley.

"Leave that piece of shit," she says, pointing to my burned-out dream car. "This is yours from now on."

I look the bike over. It's a beautiful, horrifying machine, screaming power.

"And it's not even my birthday."

I look at both women.

"What if I don't want it?"

Daja shrugs.

"No sweat off my ass, but the Magistrate would take it hard. You don't want to upset him now that you're best friends, do you?"

I weigh the keys in my hand. Put them in my pocket. When the time comes, it will be a lot easier getting away on the bike than the burned-out shit box I've been driving.

"Anything else?" I say.

"A thank-you wouldn't hurt."

"Yes, it would. I'd have bad dreams all night."

Daja kicks her Harley awake and revs it a couple of times. Before she pushes up the kickstand, she takes something small from a jacket pocket and holds it out.

"Here," she says. "The bike is from the Magistrate, but these are from the havoc."

I go to her and take what she's holding. It's two packs of Maledictions.

"For these, I'll definitely say thanks."

Daja leans back to the woman behind her.

"What did I tell you? Ugly, but at least a cheap date."

The other woman laughs as they start away. She blows me a kiss and spits at my boots, but misses by a mile. No sharp-shooter there. As they peel out, I go back inside the camper.

Traven looks up from a book. He's been reading it all night. It looks holy. Probably trying to figure out a loophole in salvation.

"What was that about?" he says.

"Blood money."

He makes a face and I put the Maledictions on a table well away from me. He goes back to reading and I curl up on the floor. For about five minutes. Then, without getting up, I grab one of the packs and rip it open.

Fuck it. I was headed for Hell the day I was born. A nephilim Abomination and natural-born killer. Where else was I going?

I take one of Traven's matches and light a cigarette. Hold it out to him. He hesitates, doing calculations in his head. Sins versus cigarettes. How many wheezing angels can smoke on the head of a pin?

Finally he takes it and I light one for myself.

"We shouldn't be doing this," he says.

"Yep."

"It's a sin."

"Smoking is part of God's great plan, Father."

"Did he tell you that?"

"I inferred it."

"I'm not sure that's how it works," he says.

"He forgave Cain for cracking open Abel's head."

"No. He didn't."

"No? I thought he did."

"No."

"Funny. He said he did."

Traven coughs.

"You knew Cain?"

"Yeah. He was the doorman at Second Death. Nice guy."

Traven taps some ash into an overturned jar lid.

He says, "Lying is a sin, my son."

"I'm an angel. Sin washes right off."

"Half angel. Part of you is still human."

"Not the fun part."

"I wish I could say the same about myself."

"We'll get through this and you'll have a billion years to repent."

"I'm not sure that's enough time."

I tap some ash into the lid.

"If Brigitte was here, what would she say?"

"I don't know."

"She'd say shut up and smoke."

He thinks about it.

"Yes. I suppose she would."

So he does and we do. I lie down on the floor when I finish the Malediction. He blows out the lamp.

In the dark he says, "Do you think we could burn that gallows truck before we leave?"

"I was just thinking the same thing."

WE STAY ON the ley line the Magistrate plotted. It's nice to be on a bike again.

Travel is like Traven said. What happened in the little town isn't an everyday thing. Sometimes we travel for days without seeing anything, and even if we find a town, chances are it's deserted. The Magistrate, Cherry, and Traven check the map each morning, but I think it's all for show. We're just going to follow this line until the Magistrate changes his mind or we fall off the edge of Hell into a deep, dark void. Some days, that doesn't sound half bad.

Then we hit a string of populated ghost towns along a range of mountains so dark they could be piles of black powder ready to explode everything in sight. Not a bad idea.

In some of the towns we even find a few Hellions, fallen angels who've run away from the chaos of Pandemonium to the monotony of the desert. But it doesn't matter who's there. Each town is the same horror show we had the other day. The Magistrate interrogates a few bigwigs, pulling more languages than I thought possible out of his ass. Then the gallows come up, and someone—sometimes more than one—gets the rope. The only difference is that I don't have to choose again.

When we camp, the Magistrate has a regular swami session with Cherry. I get the feeling that whatever he's after, he's been looking for it for a long time. What the hell could pull someone like him all the way through Hell, Blue Heaven, the Tenebrae, and who knows where else? I need to see what's under the tarp.

Now that I can walk around more I can get my own food at center camp. Even though I'm theoretically part of the group now, no one seems to want to buddy up to me, which gives me a lot of time alone. Fine with me. It gives me a chance to watch the guards around the tarp truck.

Daja acts friendly enough, but she or the other woman—Wanuri is her name—always seems to be around. I don't know if they're spying on me, or now that I can sit at the cool-kids table, Daja wants to draw me deeper into the havoc. I'll go along with whatever happens for now and see where it gets me.

THE PROBLEM WITH the Tenebrae isn't just the monotony of the landscape, but how your sense of time evaporates. A few days in, it occurs to me that it might be more than a few days. A week. Two? Hell, months, for all I know. I wonder how long some of these bastards have been riding with the Magistrate. Maybe years and they don't even know it. Maybe that's what's going on with all the funny languages. Some of the townies—and even a few in the havoc—could be goddamn antediluvian.

We pull into a town a lot bigger than the others. Not quite a city, but it's more than the usual scattering of buildings. Around us are dead neon signs and dusty hotels sporting roulette wheels and slot machines. A post-apocalyptic Reno.

These days, I ride up front with Daja, Wanuri, and some of their dog pack. They don't talk to me much, but I don't let it hurt my feelings. I get to see a lot more up here. Some days more than I want to. Like today.

The routine is the same. Round up everyone—not an easy job considering the size of the place—find the leaders or the least brain-dead, then settle in for an afternoon of twenty questions. The Magistrate does a bang-up job today, playing for a larger crowd than usual. His gestures are bigger, his voice louder. He laughs like a hyena and snarls like a Bengal tiger when anybody gets out of line. He practically dances up and down the line of mopey skeletons he's decided to interrogate.

A dozen members of the havoc run crowd control on the losers crowded along the road. I try counting them, but give up after ninety and leave it at an even shit ton of walking ghosts.

The Magistrate pulls two people from the silent mob and has them hold up the map. One by one, he walks the leaders over and questions them. Sometimes he puts an arm around their shoulders. Sometimes he whispers or laughs with them. Sometimes he slaps the shit out of the ones who can't stop crying. In the end, everyone answers his questions. When they're done, he politely escorts each one back to the line. The problem—and the one way today is like the others—is that no one knows a goddamn thing.

For the first time on the trip, he looks genuinely annoyed. Plunging into the crowd, he shouts orders, questions, threats, promises, and, for all I know, Bundt cake recipes. Daja pulls her gun and plunges in after him. She and the others on crowd control clear a circle around him as he preaches to the dead-eyed townies.

Nothing. They shuffle and stare at their shoes, stoned emo kids playing in the dirt.

Suddenly he gets quiet. Throws out his arms and starts talking again, faster this time. I can't hear what he's saying, but it doesn't matter. I can see him just fine. He pulls things from his sleeves. Gold coins. Doves. Playing cards. Each disappears as quickly as it appeared.

The lunatic is doing a magic show for these mummies.

When the havoc catches on, they begin to laugh. I have to admit, I do, too. It's all so mad, pathetic, and weirdly beautiful at the same time.

He links and unlinks rings. Breathes fire. Pulls a rabbit from his hat. He actually gets the mob to pay attention. A few even clap.

He puts a finger to his lips, clearly getting everyone ready for the climax of the show. Slowly, he opens his duster and takes something from inside. With one hand he points at the map. Shouting nonsense in a dozen languages, he uses his other hand to hold up what he took from his coat.

A bottle of water.

The crowd surges forward, but Daja pops a couple of shots in the air and they back off.

The Magistrate does a theatrical half bow with a hand to one ear. Waits.

From the middle of the crowd, an old woman shouts something. He points at her, and without a word the crowd parts, letting her up front. Her wild hair hangs down like dead weeds and she's wearing a dress that looks like she took it off a Disney princess, tossed it in a grain thresher, and got an ape to sew it back together.

Gently taking her hand, the Magistrate leads her to the map. They talk for a couple of minutes. He points out landmarks and she points out others. He listens, cocks his head, and studies the woman as she chatters away. When she's done, she looks at him shyly, like a dog hoping it fetched the master's right slippers. Guess she did. The Magistrate opens his arms wide and pulls her into an embrace. He hands her the old water bottle as he releases her. Daja leads her to the havoc. The woman drinks greedily, dribbling all over herself, not caring where she's going or who's moving her away from the others. When the Magistrate turns back to us, he's smiling in a way I haven't seen before. I don't like it.

Walking to his Charger, he gracefully hops over the hood and onto the roof.

"My friends, this is an auspicious day. Our new friend, the lovely Empress Consort Hristova, a wise woman who wants only to do God's will and advance his just cause during these troubled times, has given me information that I believe will propel our crusade into its next stage. Soon, perhaps just a few days from here, lies the treasure we have sought for so long. With God's blessing and this good woman's help, we are one step closer to paradise," he says. A dramatic pause. "And war!" he shouts.

The havoc loses its fucking mind. It's like every Motörhead

fan in the known universe stomping and screaming for an encore.

Me, I clap politely.

The Magistrate holds up his hands and the cheers die down.

"But there is still work to do. We will camp here tonight." That gets a round of cheers.

"Empress Consort Hristova will be my guest," he says. "As for the others . . ."

He looks over the rest of the poor slobs he's gathered together.

"Kill them all. Take everything useful from the town and then burn what is left."

I thought the first round of cheers was loud, but this one makes my head hurt. All around me, the havoc surges forward. Humans and Hellions pull guns, knives, and swords. They rush the townies before they know what's going on. The only good part is that their shouting covers up any screams. And when the slaughter is over and the townies have blipped out of existence on their way to Tartarus, there aren't even any bodies.

When that's done, there's a second surge of motion as the havoc rushes in to loot the town. I let them go around and some slam into me. I stand my ground. As the Magistrate climbs down, I circle around to him.

Someone grabs my arm.

I whirl around, my hand closing on a throat. It's Traven. He grabs my hand and I let go of him, but he holds on to me. It takes him a moment to get his breath and speak.

"Not now," he says. "I know how you feel. But not *now*. He'll see you coming. He probably expects it."

I look over at the Magistrate. He has the map spread on the hood of his car. Cherry and the Empress stand on either side of him, moving their hands along roads and lines I can't see.

I turn to Traven.

"Who the fuck is this guy? How does he do all those things?"

"I don't know."

There's a distant *whoomp* as a couple of small buildings catch fire.

"And why kill everyone? Why burn the town?" I say.

"He found something crucial today. My guess is that he doesn't want to take a chance on someone else finding it."

I look around at the chaos, and something hits me. "I'm getting a look at what's under that tarp."

"This might not be a good night. It will be well guarded this close to an unknown town."

A soul with no ears and no nose runs by with a Molotov cocktail in his hand.

"That might be a good reason to do it. It's the last thing they'd expect."

"I had a feeling you'd say that. Please be careful."

"I'm always careful. It's the whiskey that isn't careful."

I get on the Harley.

"Where are you going?" Traven says.

"I'm going back for my stuff." I had left my coat, cigarettes, and the little knife I took off Doll Man in Traven's camper. "In case things go wrong, I'm leaving you a pack of Maledictions. You should stay away from me for a while."

Traven looks at the fire.

"If that's the way it has to be."

"It is," I say. "Don't worry. We have unfinished business."

"What's that mean?"

"I'll tell you when I see you."

I gun the bike and grab my stuff out of the camper. When I get back to the road, I leave the Harley by a giant earthmover covered in spikes like a prehistoric porcupine. I walk into the town as members of the havoc carry out furniture and craps tables. The smart ones grab armfuls of chips and cases of whiskey. I wave and give a thumbs-up to some of them as they go by. I look like an idiot, but that's okay. I want to be seen. I want to be part of the group. The more they're used to me, the more invisible I can be later.

Outside a burning bank someone dropped a torch. I pick it up and light a Malediction. Then I stroll downtown to join in the animal fun.

Survive. That's all that counts. Survive and find a way home.

THE HAVOC HAS been looting clothing stores. They're dressed in golf shoes, wedding dresses, and tuxedoes. I help a group in marching-band uniforms set fire to a library.

Walking along the main road through town with my torch, I hum an old Circle Jerks song, "Wild in the Streets." I think of Candy. What would she think of me now? I like to think she'd understand, but who knows? Anyway, this is no time to contemplate that. Tonight, smile like a shark and mean it.

I help some Hellions push a fire truck through a casino lobby. They don't steal anything. It's just good fun.

On a side street is a gun shop. I push my way through the crowd and grab a Colt Peacemaker. Stick it down the back of my waistband. Of course, by the time I get to the ammo case, it's been picked clean.

Fuck my luck.

Pretty soon the whole town is burning.

On the way back to camp, a Christmas elf hands me a bottle of good whiskey and runs off hand in hand with a Playboy bunny.

I drink enough of the bottle that there's liquor on my breath. Throw the rest through the window of a drive-through chapel.

Fuck you, Elvis.

"Wild, wild, wild, wild
Wild in the Streets"

THE MAGISTRATE AND the Empress are holed up in his motor home while the kids play kid games. Everyone is drinking. I pick up an empty bottle and weave a little as I walk, hoping to look a lot more drunk than I feel.

It looks like half of the havoc is gambling at the casino tables while the other half is fucking on every conceivable piece of looted furniture. Some are fucking *on* the tables while the games go on around them. Everything else that isn't useful or fun gets tossed into a giant bonfire at the center of camp. The cooks burn big haunches of meat in the flames. I'm sure I don't want to know where they got it.

I head back to the earthmover, where I left the Harley. Settling down on the edge of the bucket where I can be seen, I nurse the bottle against my chest. Havoc members weave by drunkenly, dance or run by. I give a tipsy wave to anyone who looks at me.

When the first wave of elation settles down into the kind of steady low-level craziness that can go on all night, I slip out of the earthmover's bucket and stagger closer to the flatbed.

Traven was right. Six souls are on guard. However, people have been running booze to them all night. Five of them look pretty wasted and the sixth is trying to catch up. But even this fucked up, they're too awake to sneak past. I can't spike their drinks because Vidocq isn't here with one of his sneaky potions. All I can think of is to try some hoodoo. I consider putting them to sleep, but I'm not good at subtle stuff. More than likely I'd pop their heads like a shotgun in a jack-o'-lantern. And that gives me an idea.

When you can't go subtle, go loud.

I hold up the bottle like I'm taking a swig and whisper some Hellion hoodoo. Across the camp, a Lamborghini explodes. I never did like those cars. Show ponies for day traders with more money than taste. Whatever part of the havoc that isn't fucking or rolling dice rushes over. The ones that stay put . . . well, they're fucking and gambling. The flatbed's guards come to the front to whoop it up at the flames.

I slip into the shadows around the back of the truck and crawl under the tarp.

The material is something like canvas and all the fire outside lights things up pretty nicely inside. I walk the length of the dual flatbeds, running my hand along the Magistrate's secret. It's a long iron tube mounted on a metal turntable. Along the sides are bas-relief scenes of angelic warfare. There are heavy wheels and at the back is something that looks distinctly like a breech.

Shit.

It's a gun, and a fucking huge one. What the hell did the Empress point out to the Magistrate? An ammo dump? That doesn't make sense. He could find it or make it back in Hell.

This is one huge goddamn disappointment. I don't know what I was expecting, but it wasn't this popgun. The thing doesn't even look Hellion made. More like the too-pretty stuff I've seen angels carrying from Heaven.

Wait. How did the Magistrate get a gun from Heaven? Okay. That's a lot more interesting. But I can't fuck around forever under here.

I crawl back to where I got in and drop down to the ground. Right in front of me is the sixth guard, pissing on one of flatbed tires. He squints at me like he's trying to figure out if I'm real or a whiskey phantom. He must decide I'm real because he springs into truly inept action, fumbling for his rifle with one hand while finishing his piss with the other. It's not a pretty sight, nor is it sound decision making because before he can complete either task, I grab him and slam his head into the side of the flatbed. Now I hope my decision making is better than his.

I could kill him and he'd disappear without revealing that he'd seen anyone skulking around the tarp. Or I can leave him and hope, one, that he can't identify me, and two, that he's wasted enough that no one believes anything he says. Of course, there might be a third option—I could always try some of the subtle hoodoo I was afraid to use earlier. The more I think about it, the more it's the only thing that makes sense. Killing him would raise too many questions and leaving him means he could rat me out. That's it, then.

I don't have to do much to him really. He's drunk, his cock

is out, and there's piss everywhere—plus I already gave him a concussion—so everyone will think he stumbled and cracked his head on the flatbed. Okay. Just wipe out, say, the last hour or so of his memory.

This will be interesting. I've never tried it before. Still, I'm good at improvising hoodoo. I bark a few Hellion words at him.

The first thing I note is that my hex doesn't make him explode. So far, so good. I grab the booze bottle he set on the ground and pour some over him so that he really reeks of the stuff. There's nothing else I can do if I'm not going to kill him. I need to get moving or risk more guards coming back.

I make a wide circle from the flatbed to the trucks and construction equipment, staying in the shadows as much as possible. Eventually, I come out at the earthmover and slip back into the bucket from the far side, hoping that no one came by to check on me and found me gone. At this point, though, there's nothing to do about it but curl up with the empty whiskey bottle and pretend to sleep it off while worrying about the fifty things I probably forgot while trying to cover my tracks.

The sounds of the camp have settled down again. Either they put the Lamborghini out or they're using it to roast marshmallows. Now that I think about it, I probably should have killed that guy. But ever since I got Doll Man hanged, I feel like I want to ease back on the homicide for a little while. Just a little.

That said, I probably should have picked up a bottle with a little whiskey left in it. Or gone looking for the greatest Hellion libation of all—Aqua Regia. But what are the chances of finding that out here in the boonies?

I lie in the earthmover's bucket, staring up at the bruised eternally twilight sky wishing I hadn't thought about Aqua Regia. My big decision now is whether I lie here until we break camp or give in to one of my mother's favorite expressions: beggars can't be choosers.

In the end, I decide to go and beg for a drink. Anything is better than lying here hoping I got the hex on the guard right. If I fucked up and gave that idiot superpowers, I'm going to be really pissed.

The ground at center camp is littered with empties. I walk around like a true wino, checking each one to see if there's enough to get one good belt. After striking out a good dozen times, I drop-kick a couple of empties into the bonfire in frustration.

"Here," someone says. "Before you hurt yourself."

When I turn around, Daja is there holding out a mostly full bottle of . . . hell, I couldn't care less. It's liquor. I accept the bottle and take a couple of long pulls. When I hand it back, it's considerably emptier than it was a minute ago.

"Sorry," I say. "I've been looking for a while."

"No problem. We got every bottle in town. We're set for a month."

"A month? How do you tell time out here? I don't even know how long we've been in this town."

She upends the bottle, drinking a good potion of what's left.

"It's just an expression. I count the days by when we reach a new town or the Magistrate says to camp."

"He's Father Time, too? The guy knows a lot of tricks."

"That he does."

She hands me back the bottle. The stuff we're drinking is vile. Greasy and fishy, but even flounder-flavored turpentine will taste good when it's the only drink in town.

I say, "How long have you been with him?"

Daja shakes her head. "I don't know. There weren't a lot of us back then. Hardly any vehicles." She holds out her arms and turns in a half circle. "But now look at us."

I hand her back the bottle.

"You're a whole army."

"Damn right," she says.

"Onward Christian soldiers."

Her eyes narrow.

"What does that mean?"

"It's an old hymn back where I grew up . . . not that I actually spent a lot of time in church."

"Must be a Protestant thing. What were you? Methodist? Baptist?"

"I have no idea."

"I figured. My family practically worshiped the pope. It felt like I was in church all the time," she says. "Four times a week at least. Not that I minded. Except I couldn't be an altar boy, but I'd sneak in after services and put on their gear anyway."

"You ever get caught?"

"Never. But it was still a sin, so here I am."

I hand her back the bottle.

"You think you were damned because you played dress-up?"

"Why else?"

"You never killed anybody or robbed a bank or short-sheeted the pope?"

Daja smiles.

"Nope. I was a very good girl."

"And here I was thinking you were Ma Barker back upstairs."

"Nah. I didn't learn to ride till I got here. I never even threw a punch back home."

She looks me over.

"I bet you were exactly the way you are now."

"Only prettier."

She drinks most of what's left, but offers me the last swig. I shake my head so she finishes the bottle and tosses it into the fire.

"What happened to your face?" she says. She pulls down my shirt a few inches. Spots more scars. "And the rest of you."

"Never follow a foul ball into a wood chipper," I say. "We didn't even win the game."

She ignores my stupid joke and says, "Were you a soldier? A boxer?"

"You got me. I fought a bit," I say, wondering if she ever saw the gladiator pit in Pandemonium.

"You must not have been very good at it."

"On the contrary. I beat pretty much everyone. Just some were harder to knock down than others."

I flash on Hellbeasts, the ones that spit fire, the ones with pincers as big as a man, the ones with teeth like buzz saws.

Daja says, "I didn't have my first fight until after I was damned. Isn't that funny? I was scared as hell."

"Did you win?"

"Nope. But I got better."

"And now look at you. No one here would lift a finger."

She looks at me.

"Even you?"

"I'm not looking for trouble."

"Uh-huh," she says, not sounding entirely convinced. "Did you hear the explosion before?"

"What explosion?" I say, as innocent as a newborn bunny.

"One of the cars. The gas tank went up. It's been burning all night."

She points and I follow her finger.

"Oh, that. Yeah. I saw that."

"And you weren't interested enough to crawl out of that bucket?"

I pick up another bottle. It's empty, so I drop it.

"I'm from California. Pretty much everything is on fire these days."

She gives me a look.

"There's a drought."

"Mmm."

"And we kind of had an apocalypse thing not that long ago."

"Mmm."

We stand there for an awkward minute, staring into the fire.

I say, "Why are you over here talking to me like we're friends? You wanted me dead a couple of days ago."

"Who says I wanted you dead?"

"I burned your friend."

"Megs?" she says, and laughs. "He wasn't my friend. He was useful, but he wasn't anyone's friend."

"Still, you would have killed me when I first got here."

"Of course. You came out of nowhere with that story about walking down the mountain."

"It was all true."

"The Magistrate believes you, so now so do I."

"But," I say.

"But what?"

"No—you were going to say 'but.'"

A leg collapses on a nearby roulette table and a mob of naked people tumbles onto the ground.

"You have secrets," she says. "I watched you in that fight with Asodexus . . ."

"The guy who looked like a horned toad?"

"Yes. That wasn't an ordinary fight. You *did* something."

I wonder for a second if she spotted the hoodoo, but I'd be dead by now if she had.

"And you want to know what I did."

"Yeah."

"Maybe you saw wrong and it was just a fight."

"I've seen fights. I've seen souls and Hellions kill plenty. What you did wasn't like that."

"I can't tell you."

"Why?"

I give her my best shit-eating smile.

"If I tell you now, what will we talk about on our next date?"

Wanuri and the earless, noseless guy call to Daja from over by the fire.

She looks at me.

"You're with the havoc now. Don't forget it."

"I won't."

Daja walks backward away from me, pointing at me with both hands.

"And I know your name isn't Pitts, no matter what Mimir says."

I wave to her as she leaves and head back to my bucket, suddenly wanting to be alone.

I take off my coat, roll it up, and put it under my head. Settle down for a nap. The last thing I think before drifting off to a slightly dizzy whiskey sleep is, Daja's a lot more interesting than I thought. But I really am going to have to kill her.

A FEW HOURS later in whatever counts for morning around here, someone knocks on the side of the bucket. I sit up, a little cramped from my steel crib. The Magistrate leans on the edge of the earthmover's bucket, a bottle of water in his hand. He tosses it to me. I catch it, unscrew the top, and take a drink. It feels good. Whatever was in that flounder whiskey last night left me with a headache, but the water eases it. I finish the whole bottle.

"Good?" says the Magistrate in his clipped diction.

"Very. Thanks."

"I'm glad. Come. Take a walk with me."

I crawl out of the bucket and follow him. The camp looks like a tornado passed through during the night. I don't see a stick of furniture that isn't broken, cracked, or burned. Gambling tables are overturned or were propped up and used for target practice. The havoc is scattered on the ground, in the backs of vehicles, or on the remnants of the furniture. It's like a company picnic that turned into Altamont and everybody loved it.

Me and the Magistrate walk out of camp and into the desert. A nice open space to kill someone. But which one of us is it going to be?

We're about fifty yards out when he stops. He stares out into the distance not looking at me. He seems completely relaxed. But he doesn't say a word. Finally, I can't stand the silence anymore.

"Nice magic show yesterday."

"What?" he says distractedly. "Oh, that. Yes. Another interest of mine. You see those mountains in the distance?"

"There's nothing else out there."

"What do you think they are made of?"

I look hard and say, "Rocks?"

He takes out his telescope and scans the horizon. When he finds what he's looking for, he hands me the glass and points to a spot in the distance. I don't see anything but more of the monotonous land that we've passed through.

"I don't see a damned thing."

He points again.

"Your answer was more correct than you think. You said rocks rather than the more logical 'stone.' In fact, what surrounds us are not mountains, but rocks. Brilliantly huge rocks that giants might have used to mark the edges of their domain."

"Are you saying there are giants out there?"

He shakes his head.

"No. Those rocks weren't thrown by giants, but by angels.

During the first war in Heaven, they were hurled at the fallen angels as they plummeted to their new existence below."

"I thought the angels fell into Hell."

"Falling bodies tend to drift as they spin through space."

"Nine days is a long time to drift. I guess they could fall all over."

"Exactly."

"I never heard of ecclesiastic geology before. Daja said you knew something about everything."

"*Ecclesiastic geology.* I will have to remember that," he says. "Yes. Daja told me that you two had a talk last night."

"She was doing most of the talking."

"I doubt that. In any case, when she gets an idea in her head, it is hard to dissuade her."

"What idea does she think about me?"

"That you are an assassin sent by my enemies to kill me."

I snort back a laugh.

"I don't know your enemies. Hell, I don't know you at all."

"Of course you know my enemies," he says, and turns to me. "The God of Gods burns in my blood. His enemies will be annihilated."

I give him a look.

"Right. After all the massacres, I knew you were all about the God of Love."

"Don't forget, he is also Lucifer these days. God's nature has always been multifold, and never more than now. He dances with a dove in one hand and an ax in the other."

"So, you're fighting for the nice God and executing helpless slobs for the other. That's a pretty convenient philosophy."

"In time, you will see the wisdom."

"If you say so."

"Don't forget. You have the blood of innocents on your hands, too, Mr. Pitts."

"You sure talk about blood a lot."

The Magistrate leans back his head and laughs. He looks like a maniac, but I'm sure now that he's not. He's something more complicated, but I don't know what.

I say, "Did we come all the way out here so you could tell me that Daja is gunning for me?"

"Quite the contrary," says the Magistrate. "She wants you to come deeper into the fold and learn more about our work."

"Is that what *you* want?"

"We shall see."

"What's under the tarp?"

For the first time, he faces me.

"Do you not know? I thought you got a good look at it last night."

I shake my head. All innocence.

"I don't know what you're talking about."

"An unexplainable explosion. A guard injured, but with no memory of how. And you sleeping in such an uncomfortable, yet highly visible spot. It is all a very good scenario for a lost soul to get up to mischief."

"I played minigolf once, but the windmill scared me. I try to avoid excitement these days."

"Naturally," he says. "Mimir speaks highly of you. She seems to think that you are more than a mere ruffian."

Dammit, Cherry.

"Mimir might be more than a mere swami," I say.

"What do you mean?"

I put my hands in my pockets.

"She just seems like an interesting person. Maybe she started the fire."

"Why would she do that?"

I feel the pistol against my back and wish to hell I had some ammo.

"You know how oracles are. Huffing locoweed all day. Makes them unstable. Maybe she has a kind of vision she hasn't told you about. Maybe she's on her own side."

The Magistrate stops for a minute and seems to consider the idea. Eventually he says, "You haven't seen Megs around, have you? He seems to have gone missing."

"He unfriended me when I set him on fire."

"How sad for us all," he says, then sighs. "The universe has drifted off its axis. It teeters from side to side. There is a chance it will tumble into oblivion."

"Like a man once said: 'I'm not afraid of death. I just don't want to be there when it happens.'"

The Magistrate takes a step closer to me and says, "We live in a time of so much secrecy. Let us play a game. Tell me one of your secrets and I'll tell you one of mine."

Daja again. I bet she's been telling him my name isn't Pitts.

"You first," I say.

"All right. I know you have a gun. There. Now tell me one of your secrets."

"It doesn't have any bullets."

He laughs another one of those uncomfortable big laughs.

"That's no secret, my boy," he says. "Do you think I would have brought you here otherwise?"

"You knew I had a gun but no bullets? How?"

He leans in even closer.

"Souls are so easy to read if you know the trick."

"That's a secret I wouldn't mind knowing."

"Perhaps I'll teach you someday."

We head back to camp.

"When are we pulling out?" I say. "It sounded like the Empress lit a fire under you."

"We'll go soon. Perhaps tomorrow."

"It'll be quiet tonight. I think everyone is partied out."

"Still, we must be on our guard."

"Your enemies. Right."

"The closer we come to our goal, the more dangerous things will become."

"I'm sure I'll be very useful throwing rocks at them."

"No need for that," he says.

He takes something from his pocket and presses it into my hand. It's a box of bullets. They're even the right caliber. He couldn't have read that on my face.

Right?

When we reach camp, the Magistrate shakes my hand.

"It was lovely chatting, Mr. Pitts. I hope we can do it again."

I weigh the bullets in my hand. Someone must have told him about the Colt. That's the only explanation. Or did I say something that gave me away? Am I that much of a rube?

When he lets go of my hand, I say, "Seeing as how we're friends now, why don't you go ahead and call me ZaSu?"

"I think I will stick to Mr. Pitts. It suits you more."

I take a few bullets and start loading the Colt. The

Magistrate heads back to his motor home. When I look up, I swear that every single person awake is looking at me. I guess not everyone gets face time with the messiah. I spin the cylinder on the pistol and snap it closed.

I didn't want this high a profile, but at least now everyone knows I'm armed.

IN THE MORNING, we burn all the furniture and anything in town left standing. Burning ruins seems a little gratuitous even to me, but everyone seems to have a good time and the smoke gives us a good perspective when we hit the road. Unlike those days when it feels like we're making no progress at all, watching the smoke recede behind us is nice. Proof we're actually moving.

As always, the Magistrate is out front in his Charger. Daja darts in around traffic, staying up front with him, but sometimes veering off and exchanging hand signals with other vehicles, relaying orders from the big man.

I'm a few car lengths behind her dog pack. That is, until she falls back and cocks her head at me to follow her. I hit the gas and move up with the other bikes and muscle cars in a line behind the Magistrate. From what I can make out, there are eleven of them. Six women and five men. Am I supposed to be the new guy to bring the numbers even? There's a good chance. A messiah needs twelve disciples.

Wanuri is up here. So is the earless, noseless, mutilated guy. I like that. If I'm part of the pack now, I won't be the ugliest one.

I ride next to a young black kid whose dreads stand out straight behind him in the wind. His leathers are as roadrashed and worn as anyone's, but he's noticeable for one reason: he's smiling. I guess damnation is working out for him. He's handsome, like prom-king handsome. It's unnerving in the middle of the havoc, where most of us look like we've been dragged behind a truck.

A few hours into the ride, Daja drops to the back of the havoc, then speeds up and exchanges signals with the Magistrate. A blue flare flies up from the Charger and the havoc begins to slow. When we've stopped, Daja does a one-eighty and peels out for the rear of the havoc. For everyone else, it's a pit stop. We get off our bikes and stretch. Souls and Hellions climb from their cars and exchange beer and water, nursing their hangovers.

I go to Wanuri.

"What's wrong?"

"It looks like something is up with one of the trucks. Probably snapped a chain."

"One of the ones pulling the flatbed?"

"Yeah. It happens. Too often for my taste."

"Old gear?"

"Maybe."

I look at her.

"The Magistrate mentioned he has enemies. You think someone might be fucking with the equipment?"

"It's one theory."

"Any suspects?"

"A couple."

I don't need hoodoo to read her. She wasn't trying to be subtle. Great. I'm already on the saboteur list. That's probably why Daja wants to keep me close.

"You said it's happened before."

"It has," says Wanuri.

"Then there's no reason to blame, for instance, someone new. The fox is already in the henhouse."

"Just because there's one with us doesn't mean they don't have a partner."

Okay. Logic isn't working. Let's try something else.

"Do you have extras or do we need to burn another town looking for one?"

She gives me a look. "Don't worry your precious little head. We have plenty."

"The Magistrate thinks of everything."

"*Everything,*" she says. "Don't forget it."

The dog pack smokes and drinks around us. Wanuri looks to the rear of the havoc, then at me.

"We might as well get this over with. Daja usually plays social secretary, but she's gone, so I guess it's up to me," she says. "Come along, buttercup. Time to meet the others."

One by one, she introduces me to the other members of the dog pack. The mutilated guy calls himself Johnny Basher. He has an Aussie accent and Hellion runes branded all over his face, the mark of an escape artist, but not a very good one. Runaways in Hell get marked so the guards will know to keep an eye on them. Johnny's got at least a dozen brands. Maybe he's not smart, but you have to give him an A for effort.

Most of the others in the pack are the same forgettable assholes you meet in any gang. Loyal idiots with a chip on their shoulder, but a talent for following orders if you keep them simple like "Kick that guy to death." There's a toothless weather-beaten one-percenter with HEIL tattooed on one hand and "1488" on the other. An older woman with a Louise Brooks haircut who looks like she'd be more at home baking cookies for the PTA, except for the small *panabas* and butcher knives hanging from her belt. A square-jawed guy named Frederickson who looks like an ad executive if it wasn't for the fact that the whole top of his head is crudely stitched together and looks like it might blow away in a strong breeze. Somewhere, sometime, someone scalped the fucker. I hope he did something to deserve it. The Mohawked Hellion woman who drove Traven's truck one day is there. The sweat pig whose bike I stole after kicking him in the head. Billy. He's looks utterly delighted to have me in the fold. Two of the women are twins with mismatched eyes. One has brown and blue. The other has green and gray. Everyone calls the handsome black kid Gisco.

"He sings like an angel, but don't try talking to him," Wanuri says. "He only speaks some gibberish. Old Greek or something."

"Carthaginian," says Johnny.

"That's it. Something old as dirt. The Magistrate is the only one who can talk to him. With us, it's mostly grunts and charades, ain't that right, Gisco?"

He raises his eyebrows and makes a series of quick hand gestures. Everybody laughs.

"Same to you, sweetheart," says Wanuri in a teasing way.

I say, "Gisco. You understand what these animals are saying?"

He nods.

"But they don't understand you?"

He nods again.

I look at Wanuri.

"Interesting. At least I know who the smart one around here is."

"Fuck off," says Frederickson.

"Watch your mouth, mate," says Johnny.

The sweat pig says, "Anyone can sucker-punch, faggot. Fight me face-to-face sometime."

I say, "I don't think I could stand looking at you that long."

"That's enough," says Wanuri. "Yes. The kid is smart. That's why we like having him around."

"Was Megs smart?"

Everyone laughs at that.

"Is a dog smart?" Wanuri says.

"I don't know, but one time at a carnival a chicken beat me at tic-tac-toe."

"Megs couldn't beat a rock at tic-tac-toe."

"That why I'm his replacement?"

"You're in because Daja says you're in. Anyway, you're not in yet."

"Now you're going to make me cry."

"Soon, Sonny Jim, but soon," says Johnny.

Apparently that was hilarious. Laughs. High fives. Fist bumps. Great.

I'm joining a community-college frat.

The little celebration is still going on when Daja rides up. She looks tired and annoyed.

"Truck's fixed," she says. "But since we're stopped, they want to check the other chains and do some other repairs."

I don't want to hang around with the dog pack long enough to get into a brawl, but I don't want to disappear and make people more suspicious.

I say, "When will we start moving?"

"When the Magistrate says," she snaps.

Wanuri hands her a bottle of water. Daja finishes it. She points at me.

"You introduce the asshole to the pricks?"

Wanuri smiles.

"He's been charming. We're all looking forward to tea with him."

"I'll serve," says Daja.

Daja puts her arm around my shoulder.

"You look like the milk-and-sugar type."

"I don't drink tea," I say.

"Everyone drinks tea here. But you only have to do it once."

Quick as a bunny, she swivels and plants an armored fist into my gut. I'll admit it. She catches me off guard. It knocks the wind out of me, but before I can return the favor, the twins smash clubs into the back of my knees, knocking me onto the ground. Right. I get it. Teatime. Dog-pack initiation. It's like getting knighted. The king or queen touches you with a sword and it's the last time anyone can touch you with a weapon without having every other knight gunning for them. Sadly, the dog-pack version isn't as classy. Basically, everyone in the pack gets to punch and kick the shit out of you until the boss calls time. It's all good alpha-wolf fun. No one is trying to kill you, but I get the feeling a few of these boots are coming in a tad harder than is technically within the rules. I just curl up and take it. I've taken worse beatings than these creeps can dish out, but that doesn't stop it from hurting.

"Enough," shouts Daja.

Everyone backs off. I open my eyes and start to sit up when Sweat Pig gives me one more good kick in the ribs. Without missing a beat, Frederickson swings a fist and bloodies Sweat Pig's nose.

"What the fuck?" he yells.

"She called time," says Johnny. "Open your ears, you lardy bastard."

Sweat Pig wants to pop Frederickson, but he knows the rules. If he made a move, the rest of the pack would be on top of him and give him worse than they gave me. At least these idiots *have* rules. Points to them for that. First chance I get, I'll use them against them.

Gisco helps me to my feet. I hurt all over, but I still have all my teeth. I wobble a little more than is strictly necessary, making a show of what rough customers they are.

Daja comes over with a bottle of the fishy whiskey.

"How was that?" she says, and hands me the bottle.

"My crippled grandma hit me harder from her deathbed."

I take a mouthful of the flounder juice and hand her back the bottle. She drinks and passes it to the next person in line. It goes all the way around the pack.

"Welcome to the family," says Daja.

I nod to everyone. They're better about it than I expected. Hard, but friendly punches on the arms and chest. The twins get on either side of me and peck each cheek.

The PTA mom says, "Do you have a knife?"

I take out the little pocketknife I took off Doll Man.

She laughs and hands me one of the butcher knives from her belt. Wags a finger at me.

"Don't go cutting yourself."

"Yes, ma'am. Thank you."

I slip it into my jacket, where I used to keep the black blade. Thing could cut through anything. Thinking about it makes me think about the world, though. This isn't the time to start feeling sorry for myself. The rest of the pack moves off to smoke and argue about who got in the hardest shots at me.

I spit some blood on the ground, and when I look up, I spot Traven watching me from the back of his hellhound. He looks me over as I limp up to him.

"What was that about?" he says.

"I get to sit at the lunch table with the cool kids."

"Is that what you want?"

"For now. And I wasn't exactly in a position to say no."

"I know the feeling," he says, and I imagine him in Blue Heaven going through his library, deciding which books to save before the Magistrate ordered the havoc to burn the place to the ground.

"Listen," I say. "I'm going to come see you tonight."

He sits back on the hellhound.

"Is that wise? I'm not sure your friends would approve of you spending time with a librarian."

"Fuck them. Have your bread and salt ready."

"You're going to let me eat your sins?"

"No. We're going to bake brownies. Just have the stuff ready."

"I will."

He looks past me.

"I think your friends want you over with them."

"I should go. Have you heard anything interesting from the Magistrate?"

"He's very excited about finding what we've been looking for soon."

"I bet he is. By the way, what's under the tarp is a gun."

"A gun?" he says. "That's strange."

"No shit. Also, rumor is there's a rat around here sabotaging equipment."

"It's only a theory."

"Well, some people think it's me, so I'm going to try being a good boy for a while."

"Good luck with that."

"I'll see you tonight."

"I'll have things ready," he says, and rides his hound away. I go back to the dog pack.

"Giving the old man a kiss good-bye?" says Wanuri.

"He's a friend. I'll talk to him when I want. Unless a bookworm makes you nervous."

"Hey, the Magistrate likes him, so he's all right with us. Just remember who your real friends are now."

"How could I forget?" I say, rubbing the back of my neck. I take out my Maledictions, but the pack got crushed during my initiation. Fucking barbarians. I pull out a broken smoke and offer her one. She takes it and throws it on the ground. Takes out two of hers, hands me one, and lights both.

"Thanks."

"Daja gave you those smokes, but remember: cigarettes aren't a gift anymore. They're part of your place with us."

"Can I give someone outside the group a cigarette?"

"All you want. Anyone you want. Just be careful."

"Why?"

She looks over her shoulder at the rest of the havoc.

"You might find you bought yourself a boyfriend or girl-friend you didn't want."

"That's not the kind of trouble I want out here."

"I heard that. Still, it's nice to blow off steam every now and then."

"I suppose. But what if steam's all you've got?"

She pokes me in the chest.

"Then you need to find something more."

"You're right. What I need now is another drink."

"Right this way. Drinks are part of who you are now, too. Whiskey, water. Whatever you want."

"Hell, if I'd known that, you could have kicked me a lot longer."

"Everybody says that."

"But I mean it."

"Trust me. We all did."

TURNS OUT THAT the truck repairs take longer than expected, so we dig in for the night. I sit in a circle with the dog pack. They pull camp chairs and even a beanbag chair from the trunks of the cars. If I'm not in Traven's relatively cushy camper, this will do. It beats the earthmover.

Everyone shoots the shit at dinner. They ask me about my life back home, so I tell them the truth. I ran a video store. That gets some laughs. Then we move on to the inevitable *What did you do to get here?*

"I'm like all of you," I say. "It was all a big mistake. I'm supposed to be playing Candy Land in Heaven with the baby Jesus."

The dog pack finds that funny enough. All except Sweat Pig.

He says, "Fuck the baby Jesus. Fuck him like I fucked the preacher before I burned him and his church."

I spit out a piece of gristle.

"Wow. You beat up a preacher. That's like beating up, what, a math teacher?"

People look from me back to him.

"You never killed anybody, I bet."

"Look at his face, you drongo," says Johnny. "You don't get a face like that just running a shop."

I rub my chin.

"My mom says I'm the handsomest boy in the world."

"Your mother needs glasses," says the twin with brown and blue eyes.

"It's true. She used to chase my dad around with a rolled-up newspaper thinking he was the dog. 'Course it was his fault for shitting on the carpet."

The Mohawked Hellion hands me a beer for that one. Sweat Pig is the only one not smiling.

He throws down his plate.

"No more bullshit. We all told our stories, but this fuck gets to sit there cracking jokes. And you let him get away with it. I say he tells his story or he gets out. Or he fights me right now."

"Calm down, Billy," says Daja. "No one wants to hear that shit now."

I push my food around with a fork, singing quietly.

"'Jesus loves me this I know, for the Bible tells me so . . .'"

Billy jumps to his feet. I let him take one step toward me before I snap my wrist with the fork in it. It slices across the circle of seats and buries itself in the bastard's right cheek. He howls like a brontosaurus and comes at me with the fork still stuck in him. At the last minute, I get up and toss my chair at his feet. Billy stumbles over it and falls, driving the fork deeper into his stupid face. As he hauls himself up, I pull the knife PTA Mom gave me, but I don't make a move in his direction. I need to gauge the room. If everyone is going to jump me, I want to know.

"Billy!" shouts Daja.

She points at me.

"And you. Get your chair and sit the fuck down."

I pick up my chair from where Billy kicked it, and sit.

"And put the damned knife away," Daja says.

I slip it back into my coat.

Billy is on his knees pulling on the fork and moaning.

The toothless old man with HEIL on his fingers brings Billy a bottle of whiskey.

"Drink this. All of it," he says.

Billy upends the bottle and hands it back to the old man, who takes it and cracks Billy across the side of the head. Billy rocks back. While he's still dizzy, the old man plants a boot on his chest and yanks out the fork. Billy howls again and falls forward onto his arms, cursing at the dirt. When he's done, he looks at Daja. She's on her feet.

"Get up," she says.

He scrambles to his feet, knowing he's fucked up.

Daja turns to me and says, "You too, slick."

"You just told me to sit down."

"Get up!"

I get up.

"The two of you are going to shake hands in a minute," she says. "But, Billy, since you started the fight, you owe Pitts something. What are you going to put up?"

"I don't have anything," he says like a whiny kid.

"You know the rules. You better find something."

He goes to the saddlebags on his bike and comes back with something cupped in his hand. When he hands it to me he says, "Don't tell the others."

It's a Saint Christopher medal. Protector of travelers and children. I doubt that he knows that. He just saw the little kid and the old man and liked it. Probably thinks it's Santa Claus. I wink and put the medal in my pocket before anyone can see it.

Daja says, "Now, Pitts. You give him something."

I pat my pockets. There isn't much there. I don't want to give him the butcher knife because it might piss off PTA Mom and I have policy against pissing off women with that many knives. And I'm sure not going to give him my Colt. I reach into a pants pocket and find a thousand-dollar poker chip. I put it on my thumb and flip it to him. He catches it and looks it over.

"Don't spend it all in one place," I say.

He holds it up and looks at me, apparently satisfied with the trade and that I didn't rat him and Saint Christopher out.

"Now shake," says Daja.

I put out my hand and he wraps his big mitt around it. It's a fast, limp shake. He's not fucking with me. Now that I know his secret, he just wants to get things over with.

We both look at Daja.

"Now both of you sit down and no more of this shit to-night. You make us look bad in front of the havoc. People look up to us. They're afraid of us, and that's how it should be if we're going to take care of the Magistrate."

She looks at me.

"And that's job number one for us. Everyone is expend-able. Except him. Understand?"

"I got it."

"Good. Now everyone eat your fucking dinner."

Billy picks up his spilled plate and goes to get more food. Everyone else eats in silence for a while. In a few minutes Johnny says, "A video-store clerk, eh?"

"Owner," I say. "Completely different thing."

"Well, that explains it, then."

Gisco signs something.

"He wants to know your favorite movie," says the twin with the green and gray eyes.

I look over at him.

"They have a lot of movies in Carthage?"

"No, stupid," she says. "We find them here sometimes. Some of the truckers have players."

Hellions bootleg movies. They steal cable, so why not?

"What's your favorite?" I say.

Together, the twins say, "*The Red Shoes.*"

"What's his?"

Gisco signs something.

"*Spartacus,*" says one of the twins.

"I agree. Those are my two favorites, too."

"Oh God, a diplomat," says Wanuri.

"Or he's trying to get into someone's trousers," says Frederickson. He looks from the twins to Gisco to me. "The question is whose."

"How do you know it's not yours?" says PTA Mom.

Frederickson shifts in his seat so his ass is aimed in my direction, and lets rip with a tremendous fart.

"That's what I think of that idea."

I point at him.

"He's your fucking diplomat."

He laughs.

I look at Daja.

"I don't suppose there's a special, secret toilet reserved for us, is there?"

She waves an arm at the horizon.

"It's the Tenebrae. Nothing but toilet for as far as the eye can see."

I get up.

"In that case, I'm going to take a walk and defile this little slice of Heaven."

Wanuri says, "Careful. There's sandworms out there. They'll swim right up your ass."

"Don't worry. I had a buzz saw installed. My ass can chop wood."

"I'll remember not to let you sit on my lap."

"But you said you'd tell me a bedtime story."

"That's *your* Heaven, but my Hell. Next lifetime, Suzie Q."

"I'll take you up on that."

I head out well past the edge of the camp and piss in the direction of hills spiked like upturned knives.

Or are they more Heaven rocks? Or was the Magistrate

just screwing with me? He climbs like a cat, can read maps, do magic, and speak Carthaginian. And has a flock of psychos hauling a gun to who knows where. Oh, and maybe the bastard can read minds. Nothing scary about that. I'm going to stay as far away from him as possible from now on.

I'M CIRCLING THE camp, heading to Traven's camper as discreetly as possible, when, out of goddamn nowhere, Gisco runs up and grabs my sleeve.

"Hey, Gisco. How's it going?"

He says a few unintelligible words and signs with his hands.

"Sorry, kid. It's going to take me a while to understand the hand stuff."

He waves and makes a face. I think telling me it doesn't matter.

He points to me, then points to himself.

"Pandemonium," he says in a thick accent I've never heard before.

"Pandemonium? You were in Pandemonium . . . and you know I was, too?"

He nods and signs.

"Yeah, I was in Pandemonium," I say. "We were all in Pandemonium at some point. No big deal, right?"

He shakes his head like he's frustrated and points a finger at me.

It takes me a minute to understand through his accent, but I finally get it.

"Sandman Slim," he says.

Great. Now I'm going to have to kill him, too.

I put a hand on his shoulder and lead him away from camp out to where it's darker.

"Did you see me fight in the arena?"

He nods.

"How? Did you fight there? Work there?"

He nods and signs at the second question.

"Have you told anyone else about me?"

He shakes his head no.

"You sure? 'Cause if I have to kill a bunch of people, I'm going to want a list."

His eyes go wide and he tries to take a step back, but this time I grab *his* sleeve.

He gestures wildly. I don't break his neck right away because I think he's trying to tell me that no one else knows. But I don't let go of him.

"Let's say I believe you. Why are you telling me? What do you want from me?"

He holds up his hands and slowly raises a bag. Gestures that he wants to take something out. I pull the Colt and press it to the side of his head.

"Go ahead. But real slowly."

He does what he's told. Reaches into the bag and pulls out a black cylinder. He holds it out to me.

It's a na'at. My favorite Hellion weapon. I used it all the time in the arena and back home. Made a lot of kills with it. I take the Colt from his head.

"Are you giving this to me?" I say.

He shakes his head.

"What do you want for it?"

He makes a throwing gesture. The na'at is just a cylinder

when you're not using it, but when you snap it open it extends up to ten feet. You can use it a lot of ways. Shorter, you can use it as a sword or knife. Longer, a spear or a bullwhip.

He makes the throwing gesture again.

I put the Colt back in my waistband.

"You want me to teach you to use it, don't you?"

He nods excitedly. I look at him hard.

"If I do it, you're going to keep my secret, right?"

He nods.

"You've seen me in the arena, so you know what I'll do to you if you're lying."

He nods again, a little nervously this time.

"Okay," I say. "But not now. I have to go see someone. The next time we camp, I'll show you how to use it."

He smiles, makes a circle with a couple of fingers while moving a finger in and out of it.

"No. I'm not going to fuck anybody. I'm just going to see a friend. You go back to camp, keep your mouth shut, and we have a deal."

He holds out his hand. I go to shake it, but he grabs my forearm instead. I grab his and we shake that way. I guess I did it right because he's grinning from ear to ear when he runs back to camp. Hopefully he's smart enough to keep his lips buttoned up. I'll know when I get back to the dog pack.

Cherry is coming out of the Magistrate's motor home when I'm nearby. No way I want to deal with her kind of crazy tonight, so I duck behind a truck where a group of souls and Hellions are working on an axle. I stay there, staring like a dummy until Cherry is out of sight. Then I make it past the Magistrate's palace to Traven's camper. I knock on the door.

Traven smiles when he sees me.

"Come in. I saw you sneaking over here. Are you not supposed to be here?" He steps aside so I can get in.

"No. I can go anywhere I want. I just don't want the peanut gallery knowing where I'm going. Maybe they'll think you're the one who's been fucking with the gear."

"I see your point," he says. "And thank you for being discreet."

"It was here or the multiplex and I've seen all the movies."

"Yes. I'm sure you have."

I look to where he's laid out holy water, bread, and salt.

"We should probably get started. I don't want to be gone too long. How does this work?"

"It's very simple really. I lay the bread on your body, and sprinkle it with holy water and salt. Then I say a prayer and it's done."

"That's all? It sounds like anyone could do it."

"Anyone could. It's just the desire to rid others of sin that's necessary."

"Is there any particular prayer you have to say?"

"There are several. Do you have a favorite?"

"Yeah. But you don't know it."

"Relax," he says. "You look like you're going to the dentist to have a cavity filled. I promise you, it doesn't hurt."

"It better not."

Traven reaches for the sin-eater snacks, but I get there first.

He says, his smile gentler now, "It's going to be all right. I promise you."

"I know. Sit down and hold out your hands."

"Why?"

"Shut up, Father, and do what you're told."

He sits with his hands out.

"You look like Oliver Twist," I say.

"I feel a little foolish."

"It's going to get worse."

I put the bread on his upturned hands, sprinkle on the holy water, and salt.

"What are you doing?" he says. "This isn't a game."

"I'm not playing. So shut up."

I put a hand on his shoulder and recite the only thing close to a prayer I can think of: the lyrics to Johnny Cash's "Rusty Cage."

When I'm done, I shove the bread in my mouth and chew. It's dry. I'd kill for some Aqua Regia, but I'd even take flounder juice right now. When I finally manage to swallow the last of it, I take a swig of holy water to wash it down.

"There. Done," I say. "You're absolved."

He looks up at me.

"Why did you do that?"

"Whatever you've done down here, including with the Magistrate, it's gone now."

He sits there, looking stunned.

"I don't know what to say. Thank you."

"Someone around here has to get to Heaven, and it sure as hell isn't going to be me."

"You're wrong," he says. "You're a good man."

"I'm a good man who's late getting back. Take care of yourself."

He reaches out and grabs my hands between both of his.

"We'll come through this. We've made it through worse."

"Make me a list of worse and I'll let you know if I agree."

He pats me on the shoulder and I skulk out of the camper, right to where Daja is waiting for me on her Harley.

She gives me a crooked grin.

"You're not getting it on with the father, are you? I'm not sure the Magistrate would approve."

"Then it'll have to be our little secret."

She scoots forward on her seat.

"Get on."

I settle on the back of the bike.

"I guess it's official now. I'm your bitch."

"Now you're getting it," Daja says.

She guns the engine and rides us back to the dog pack.

THAT NIGHT MY dreams are all back in Pandemonium. I'm in a mansion in Griffith Park going from room to room using my na'at, my knife, and my gun to slaughter so many Wormwood members that I lose count. This time, though, I don't just murder them in the mansion. The havoc finds a whole town of them in the Tenebrae. I lead them to the gallows truck and pull the lever to drop them. But I must have done something wrong because I fall, too. I feel a sharp pain in my throat as my neck snaps. Then I'm on the Tenebrae plains. I'm alone. I look at the sky and there are eyes staring down at me. I look at the mountains and see more eyes. There are eyes in the cracks in the road and every crevice of every rock in the wasteland.

I wake up and there's a cold wind coming down from the mountains. When I settle down to sleep again, I can't escape the feeling of all those eyes. The havoc is watching me, wondering if I'm their saboteur. And Wormwood is watching me, too. I can feel it. Between the two groups, I don't know which scares me more.

CHAINS REPLACED AND trucks repaired, we get moving in the eternally dull Tenebrae morning. The Magistrate doesn't consult the map anymore. Before we move out, he gives us a pep talk from the roof of his Charger, waving the rolled-up map like Glinda the Good Witch's wand. I have to stifle a yawn. We used to get pep talks before fighting in the arena. They weren't much different from the Magistrate's. One for all and onward to glory and all that crap. The problem with glory is that it seldom trickles down to the slobs doing the actual fighting. Glory is for generals, popes, and today, the Magistrate.

Before we move out, there's another religious service. Creeps in robes. Burning crosses mounted on a couple of dead cars cannibalized for parts. Unlike the last service, the Magistrate decides to put in an appearance, so the dog pack has to shuffle over and sit through to the magic show. With the Empress and Cherry by his side, he blesses the havoc in so many languages that I lose count. It's like watching TV preachers with my mom when my father was on the road and she'd been drinking. I keep waiting for the Magistrate to lay hands on a sham cripple who can suddenly, miraculously walk, and then pass the hat for donations. It's all I can do not to spit, but the crowd eats it up. I want to hate them for it, but I can't. When you're drowning in Hell, even a cement life jacket can look good.

Finally, he shuts up and heads for his Charger. The dog

pack goes back to our bikes and cars and mounts up while the havoc roars and grinds to life around us. A few minutes later we're blasting down the road, and for the first time, motion feels good. The wind and dust scour the holy bullshit off my skin. It hurts and I like it. I'm already healed from last night's stomping, but I don't want the others to know, so a little scorched skin will help that. But mostly, I enjoy going blank. The total Zen mind of speed, noise, and exhaust fumes. We travel for hours that way. Hell, it could be days, for all I know. I'm a blissful nothing in the center of a holy shitstorm, but it doesn't matter. Nothing matters. I am one with the hot-rod universe, the angel and meat part of me in sync as the road blurs under us. The mountains crawl around us. I could do this forever. I want to do it. But nothing beautiful lasts long Downtown.

A blue flare pops up from the roof of the Charger and the havoc begins to slow. The road is dustier than usual today, so it takes me a minute to see why.

There's a small town ahead. Great. How to go from Zen bliss to a massacre in three easy steps. I don't want to do this today, but there's no backing down while I'm in the dog pack. And now I have a ringside seat.

The Magistrate climbs out of the Charger with his telescope. The Empress, who's riding with him, gets out and he hands her the spyglass. Cherry climbs down out of the ambulance and totters over. Whispers something in the Magistrate's ear. She points hard in the direction of the town. The Magistrate takes another look and sends her back to the ambulance. I get the impression she doesn't love being sent home, but she does it anyway. What's she so anxious to tell him about and what's he so excited about that he practically shoves the Empress back into the car?

A second later a red flare explodes above us. The havoc spreads out across the desert as the Charger speeds off. The dog pack and the others roar off after him. It takes just two or three minutes to reach the town and we spread out in a semicircle out front. There are vehicles by some of the buildings. Mostly soccer-mom and golfer-dad passenger cars. A couple of SUVs. Some of the hoods are up and a lot of the tires are flat. Even with our breakdowns, this bunch is in a lot worse shape than we are. Johnny points out the outlines of other vehicles parked in a half-collapsed garage on one side of town and in the front-booth area of a burned-out café on the other. Probably some of their few working vehicles. Smart move keeping them out of the dust in this shittier than usual area of the desert.

Unlike the other towns, no one comes out to see what all the noise is about. We sit for a couple of minutes until the Magistrate gives the signal to cut our engines. He steps out of the Charger gently, like Dad picking up his little girl at ballet class. He's all smiles and no sudden moves. When he lets the Empress out, they walk arm in arm out in front of the havoc. Daja starts her bike to go up front with him, but he holds up a hand for her to stop.

I go over to her.

"What's he doing?"

"He has to do this every now and then. Some towns are more chickenshit than others. He's good at it. Let him do his job." She looks at me. "And you do yours. Get back on your bike."

I go back to my Harley. Take out the Maledictions and offer one to Gisco on my right. He shakes his head. The twins are on my left. I offer them a couple. One shakes her head and the other waves an admonishing finger. I roll my eyes, but put the cigarettes away.

The Magistrate and Empress stand arm in arm like the monster-movie *American Gothic*.

"Greetings," he calls. "Like you, we are travelers through this strange country. It would be our privilege to meet with you. We'll be dining soon and are quite well stocked. Would some of you care to join us?"

We're in front of a run-down little motel, the kind you see along Route 66, but not the quaint kind you stay in. It's more like the ones where you check in for an hour and come out with crabs or what in gentler times they called a "social malady." It's a series of separate bungalows painted a shit brown as dull and dead as the land. It's the Bates Motel for desert rats and lost souls more afraid of staring at the bruised Tenebrae sky than of knife-wielding mama's boys in the shower.

The motel office door opens and a couple of Hellions in dust masks and bandannas walk out. Then more. It looks like we found a whole damned Hellion town. The dog pack's Mohawked Hellion—I finally learned her name is Lerajie—looks restless.

I lean to the twins.

"You ever seen a town like this before?"

They shake their heads.

"Never," Babetta, the brown and blue one. "But I suppose there had to be one."

"Pandemonium profiteers and politicians sometimes escape the city," says Barbora, the gray and green one.

"Arseholes will commune with other arseholes in times of strife," says Johnny.

"Obviously," I say. "Just look at us."

He smiles, then shakes his head.

"Christ, how long is it going to take to get all these timid bunnies into the street? How many cabins are there?" I ask.

"The town isn't small," says Lerajie. "We could be here all day clearing it."

"Oh dear," says Doris, our knife-happy PTA mom.

"Welcome!" calls the Magistrate. He lets go of the Empress and goes up to press the flesh. He looks like a real politician out there, shaking hands and cracking jokes. I bet the fucker knows every Hellion dialect around.

It only takes him a couple of minutes to zero in on one Hellion in particular. He looks vaguely human, but with bloodred eyes and goofy vampire fangs. His right arm is in a sling. He must be the leader. The Magistrate laughs and jokes with him like they're exchanging muffin recipes. When the Hellion points at the havoc, the Magistrate waves at it dismissively. That's right. Don't mind a bunch of lunatics with a million horsepower's worth of vehicles and enough guns to invade Normandy.

Cherry gets out of the ambulance. She looks twitchy. What's going on with her? I wonder if there are drugs in the ambulance. She always did have a taste for anything speedy.

The Magistrate walks the Hellion bigwig to the Charger. The Empress spreads the map on the hood as he takes a flask from inside his coat. He pours a shot for the Hellion, then takes a pull directly from the flask. The Hellion downs his and the Magistrate pours him another. They look at the map together. The Empress runs her finger across the map from spot to spot. The Hellion gets twitchy. The others by the motel office get restless, too.

When the Hellion tries to walk away, the Magistrate takes his arm and steers him back to the map. He's still smiling, but he's not letting Fang Boy go.

One of the bunch by the office yells something, but I'm too far away to hear. Fang Boy looks at us, then back to his people. The chatty Hellion in the back moves forward. Two more come around from the other side.

Fuck. I recognize the uniforms.

I yell at Daja.

"They're Legionnaires! Deserters."

"So am I," says Lerajie.

"And what if you get caught? Is there a bounty on you?"

She curses in Hellion.

"This isn't good," she yells to Daja.

"Stay put. Let the Magistrate handle it," Daja says.

Which is when he stops handling it.

A gust of wind blows up, tearing the canvas from the sides of the gallows truck. One of the uniformed Hellions points and shouts. Then they're all shouting. The Magistrate waves his hands like it's all a big mistake. Those aren't gallows. That's where we hang our laundry. Fang Boy isn't buying it.

The sling was a gaff. He pulls out his arm and comes out

with a pistol. He points it at the Magistrate's head and drags the idiot back into the motel office.

"Magistrate!" yells Daja. It's the last thing anybody says for a while because the Legionnaires up front pull their own guns and start shooting. So do the snipers hiding on the bungalow roofs. Plus, others from the bungalow windows.

Around here is where Daja shouts "Fire!" though she really doesn't have to. Half of the havoc already has their weapons out and is shooting back.

While the others spray bullets all over the motel, I pull the Colt and take aim. I pop off all six shots and take down two Legionnaires and wound two others. Not my best shooting, but not bad with a shitstorm of lead aimed at my face.

The dog pack falls back behind a line of cop cars that are loaded with weapons and ammo. I reload while the car crew hands out more guns.

The firefight goes on for several minutes without either side getting much advantage. Every now and then I see a member of the havoc go down. But for a bunch of arrogant assholes who ended up on the wrong end of an ambush, we're doing pretty well.

A couple of minutes later it stops going well.

The vehicles in the garage pull out and center themselves in front of the motel. There are five of them in all. Spidery vehicles with heavy guns mounted on the top and sides.

The first wave of fire rips through the front line of the havoc, sending glass, metal, and the occasional arm or leg into the air. A second wave tears into the trucks and other tall vehicles. We fire back, but nothing we have is going to get through the armor on the AAVs.

I look around until I find the havoc's huge, horned APC. Crouching low to keep my head situated on my shoulders, I scuttle back to it. I only get a few steps when someone jumps on my back and presses a knife to my throat.

"Are you fucking running?" says Daja. "Tell me you're running."

I point at the APC.

"We have to get it up front. Nothing else can take the fire."

Daja stays on my back for a few more seconds contemplating the removal of my head. Then she rolls off.

I say, "Do you want the Magistrate in one piece?"

"Fuck you. You know the answer."

"We can't run at these assholes straight on. We have to fox them."

"How?"

"Make like we're coming at them straight. Get the APC and as many running vehicles as we can and charge them. Fill the cars with gas. Set them on fire so they're bombs."

She shoves me.

"Shit for brains. You think that's going to get past them?"

"No. We are."

She looks at me like she might not stab me on principle. I keep going to make sure that keeps not happening.

"We get everyone concentrating up front. Then you and me go around the back and hope the Magistrate is still in the office. Then we just stroll in and take him."

"That's all?" she says like she's getting ready to punch me again.

"More or less," I say. "We get the Magistrate and kill as many of these fuckers as we can. Maybe with the other cars, the APC can punch through the line. I don't know. But we have to get inside. We'll figure out the rest as we go."

"Why are you so willing to die for the Magistrate?" she says. "I see you looking at him. I know you don't trust him."

"I don't trust you. I don't trust anybody. But getting the Magistrate and killing those deserters inside isn't what they're looking for."

"How are you such an expert all of a sudden?" she says.

"How much killing have you done down here? Don't answer. I've done more and a lot of them were Legionnaires. People will tell you all kinds of secrets if they think it means they get to live a few seconds longer."

Daja looks at the front of the line. The havoc is going down fast.

"Fuck," she says. "All right. But if you run I'll bring you back and the pack will peel your skin."

"Charming. You're a charming person," I say. "No one's going to listen to me, so you give the orders. I'll be watching from the side of the motel. Be sure to get back to me before shit starts blowing up."

It's written all over her that she still doesn't trust me, but without any ideas of her own, she gives in.

"Five minutes," she says. "You better be there."

"I've got to get some gear. I'll see you over there."

She takes off and I run back to the dog pack. They're still holed up behind the cop cars, the only ones left that far up on the line. I grab Gisco and pull him close so he can hear me over the gunfire.

"You want to learn the na'at?"

He looks confused, then nods.

"Then give it to me."

He pulls it from his bag and I snatch it away before he can change his mind.

"Keep watching the office door. We might need covering fire."

"Where have you been?" yells Billy.

"With Daja. We're going to do something really stupid."

"Will it help?" says Lerajie.

"Probably not."

Before it turns into a whole quiz show, I take off and move to the side of the havoc. Hunker down by an old woodie station wagon with scenes of Hellbeast orgies carved into the sides. Everyone has their fetishes, even down here. I wait five minutes. Then ten. The gunfire slows a bit, but only because we're losing and the Legionnaires know it. Why waste ammo on idiots in vehicles that would be better off catching *Abbott and Costello Meet Frankenstein* at a drive-in?

Finally Daja dives down next to me. There's an assault rifle slung over her shoulder. She's a lot bloodier than when she left.

"You all right?"

"Fine," she says. "Most of it isn't mine."

"You're going to get messier. We're not using guns. Too loud. It's knives, lamps, staplers—anything but guns."

I slip the Colt in the waistband at my back and point to an old ice machine at the far edge of the motel.

"I've been watching. We can circle around that way. I haven't seen any movement from that side of the motel."

"If you're wrong and we end up in Tartarus, I'm going to eat your fucking guts."

"If we end up in Tartarus, go find a guy named Mason. He'll bring the wine."

We crouch there for another minute before all hell breaks loose again. The APC rumbles forward, flattening everything in the way. The havoc pushes burning cars straight at the AAVs. The moment the first one explodes, me and Daja take off for the side of the motel.

Just like I thought, the Legionnaires were too busy on the run to create an actual fortress. There's a lot of equipment and ammo out back, but only two guards. When the guards are both looking through a window into the motel, I throw a rock at a crate a few yards past them. The moment they turn away, we move.

We're fast, but they hear us coming across the concrete patio.

Daja's guard swings his gun around, but she throws herself on top of him with her knife in his throat. He goes down gurgling and she stays on top, stabbing and hacking until he stops moving.

I get lucky for once. My guard is so distracted by Daja that he doesn't see me until the last minute. I twist the na'at's grip and extend it into a spear. The point goes straight through his chest and out the other side. Another twist on the grip and it turns into a sword blade. I pull it straight up and it slices him in half. It's the first time I've seen Daja look shocked.

"That's a Hellion weapon," she says.

"Is it? I got it in a box of Cracker Jack."

"What is Cracker Jack?"

"I'll tell you later."

She tries the office's back door.

"It's locked," she says.

"Let me see."

I stand in front of it so she can't see me and whisper some Hellion hoodoo. There's no explosion, but the doorknob and its internal mechanism fly apart in my hand.

"How did you do that?"

"Magic."

"Fuck you."

Daja takes a knife off one of the dead guards, so now she has one in each hand. I leave the na'at as a sword for the moment.

There are more explosions out front. More gunfire. A horrendous crash of metal on metal. I gently push the door open and we go inside.

There's no one in the back office. We creep up the hall, checking each of the side rooms. Those are empty, too. Up front by the check-in desk, four Legionnaires are hunkered down. The Magistrate lies on a fake leather sofa. He's gagged and his arms are tied behind his back. The front of the office is peppered with bullet holes. The Legionnaires are all chattering to each other in nervous, guttural Hellion. I don't know if Daja can understand it, but I can and it makes me smile.

The deserters are working out how best to desert the other deserters. Through the window, I see that one of the AAVs is on fire. They jump at each successive explosion from the havoc's cars. These aren't officers. They're all outside in the fight. These are the ones too stupid or useless to do anything but babysit an unarmed man. Only one of them has the brains to actually hold her rifle. The other three have left theirs on the floor. From the way things look, I don't think any of them has ever been in a firefight before.

I tap Daja on the shoulder and point to the Hellion holding the rifle. She's closest to the Magistrate, so I know Daja will go all out for him. Two of the others are on their knees planning their getaway. The fourth one is also by the Magistrate, but couldn't care less about him. He's on the lookout for officers who might blow their escape plans. I point to myself and the two talkers. She points to the lookout. I point to both of us and shrug. Basically, whoever gets there first. She nods.

With her fingers, she counts down: three, two, one—

She springs at the soldier near the Magistrate, getting her in the ribs with both knives. The two talkers turn at the sound and scramble for their rifles. I slice the arm off the one who almost reaches his. Swing the blade around and take off his buddy's head.

There's a shot and all of a sudden my right side is on fire. My leg goes numb and collapses. Not for long, but long enough for the lookout, whose gun jammed, to clear it. However, before he can turn me inside out, the Magistrate kicks out, driving the shooter's head into the wall. His rifle goes off, but the shots are wild and I can roll out of the way. By the time I have the na'at up, Daja is on the guy with her knives buried in his heart.

I limp over to the Magistrate and use Doris's butcher knife to cut his hands free. Daja takes off his gag.

"Thank you both," he says. He puts his hands on Daja's bloody cheeks and she hugs him.

I can feel blood running down my side, but I'm not about

to look at the wound. My leg gets funny again, but I make it to the window before it goes. I kneel down and look outside.

There are a lot of bloody patches on the ground where dead Hellions and souls blipped out to Tartarus. The gunfire from the roof and out front is more sporadic. A second AAV is on fire. There's a whole wall of exploded havoc vehicles burning out front. Smoke slowly drifts down from the ceiling.

"I believe the building is on fire," says the Magistrate. "Perhaps we should go out the back."

I look down the hall.

"Good news. That's the part that's on fire."

Daja looks out the front window. The wall of flame is higher than ever. She turns to me.

"I knew I shouldn't trust you. Big talker. Man with the plan. What's the plan now?"

I look at the Magistrate.

"You're the smart one. What do you say?"

"I am sorry," he says sleepily. "This one hit my head with his rifle. It's hard to think . . ."

The smoke is getting thicker, drifting down with a red rain of ashes.

I hate lying. No, actually I love lying. I just like it to be a good one and this might be the lamest lie I've ever come up with.

I look out the window and say, "I see a break in the fire line."

Daja comes up next to me.

"Where?"

I point to a spot in the fire where a burning cop car and a pickup truck have locked bumpers.

"See? They're about to come undone."

"Are you stupid?" she says. "They're practically welded together."

"Nah. It's fine. Trust me. I'll show you. You get the Magistrate. I'll make sure things are clear."

I stand up and my leg collapses.

"You can't even walk, shithead."

"When the choice is burning or hopping, I'm goddamn Bugs Bunny. I'm going out front and clear a path where the fire's going to break. You wait a second, then bring him."

"You . . ." she starts.

"I trust him," says the Magistrate. "Do what you have to, Mr. Pitts."

I steady myself on the walls with a bloody hand and take a breath. Then I pull the door open and stagger outside.

Fire is hot. Annoyingly hot. And a wall of fire, the kind that melts metal to metal, is even hotter. It's the kind of hot where you have to hold your breath because if you breathe in, the air will fry your lungs. But I took a breath back in the office, so I have just enough air inside me to bark some Hellion hoodoo. And I'm alone, so I don't have to be subtle about it. The other nice thing is this is exactly my kind of hoodoo. Really massive. Really loud. Really destructive.

I barely get the last syllable out when the cop car and pickup truck blow apart in a shower of sparks and flying metal. There's a good ten feet of space in the firewall. Daja starts out with the Magistrate when a Legionnaire who was just on the other side of the cop car sees us. I get the jump on him, throwing out the na'at like a whip and putting it right through the fucker's chest. Before he can blip out, I twist the na'at so that the far end opens into a kind of claw. Then all I have to do is pull and the na'at yanks the asshole's spine clean out.

When he's gone, Daja grabs the Magistrate and runs him through the firebreak. I follow them, getting good and singed as I gimp along on my bad leg.

When I'm clear of the flames, people grab me and drag me away. None of them know that I took a bullet in the side, so they're not quite as delicate about it as I'd like. Still, they get me clear of the fire and I don't faint, so I'll take the help.

When I'm done coughing up smoke, Billy and Doris pour water onto my face and down my throat. It feels good. Someone wipes the water and blood from my eyes. It's Traven. The rest of the dog pack is around me, Daja, and the Magistrate. The broader havoc is spread out around them. Gisco opens my coat and sees the wound in my side. He turns to get help, but I grab him before he goes and hold out the na'at to him. He puts up his hands and shakes his head frantically. Then he runs off to get me a Band-Aid.

I look at Traven.

"What the hell was that all about?"

He looks at the dog pack. He then looks back to me.

"He watched you rip a man's spine out."

"Oh, that."

"And you should see yourselves."

I look at Daja then down at me. It looks like we spent a carefree spring afternoon happily running through sprinklers pumping black Hellion blood all over us.

"Not really springtime fresh, are we?"

"You look fine to us," says Doris.

"But am I still pretty?"

"Ugly as boar's balls," says Wanuri.

I lie on my back and bleed for a while. From this distance, the fire is warm and pleasant. I guess we won. Cherry is staring down at me with some of the others. I wonder what she was talking to the Magistrate about earlier. But I pass out before I get the chance to ask her.

WHEN I WAKE up, I'm wrapped in clean bandages. Someone wadded my shirt and coat and shoved them under my head as a pillow. As I sit up my side hurts like a burning bastard, but it looks like I've stopped bleeding.

I'm surrounded by maybe thirty souls and Hellions in bandages and splints, or in worse shape. Legs or arms gone. Bloody bandages over where an eye or two used to be. The Magistrate moves smoothly from body to body doing triage. Of course he's the havoc's doctor. He probably also wove the bandages and made a chocolate soufflé while I was out. Carefully, I roll over and get to my feet.

"What are you doing?" says Doris. She comes over from where she was kneeling next to Billy and puts an arm around me, taking some of my weight. "The Magistrate wants you to rest."

"What's wrong with Billy?"

"Poor dear. He took one in the belly."

"He going to be all right?"

She shakes her head and helps me turn to see what a fucking disaster we are.

"Maybe," she says. "The Magistrate isn't sure."

"Who else?"

She sighs.

"Lerajie and Babetta are gone."

"How's Barbora taking it?"

"Not so good."

"Anyone else? "

She half laughs.

"Johnny took a shot right along the side of his head. If the little shit had ears it would have blown one off."

"That it?"

"No. We lost the Empress."

I look at the Magistrate. All I can see is his back.

We're basically standing in an auto-wrecking-yard-turned-hospital. Bodies and shot to shit vehicles are scattered at crazy angles in every direction. The havoc looks truly fucked.

I lean away from Doris, taking more of my own weight.

"So much for the crusade."

"Don't lose heart," Doris says. "The Magistrate says we'll be up and around in a couple of days."

"Until we come to the next town. They'll wipe out what's left of us with powder puffs."

Doris looks around, too.

"It doesn't look good, does it? But like Mama used to say, 'Keep a rainbow in your heart.'"

"She sounds like a nice lady."

"Mother? Oh god. She was a monster. But she was a good cook. She taught me proper cutlery use."

The *panabas* and butcher knives tinkle on her belt like slaughterhouse wind chimes. I wonder which blade she used on Mama.

I lean on a burned-out cop car.

"My dad taught me to use guns."

She says, "My daddy used to take my brothers hunting. Did you hunt with Daddy?"

"Sort of. He took me into the woods and tried to shoot me."

She pats my arm.

"Families are complicated. I could have been a better mama and wife myself," she says wistfully.

Now I wonder which knives she used on the rest of her family.

"You're doing all right now, Doris."

"That's sweet of you. Will you be all right if I leave you here? I want to check on Barbora."

"I'm fine. Go and tell her I'm sorry."

"I will. Take care."

Even half dead and bleeding into the dirt, the havoc is busy. Anyone with two legs is looting what they can from the Legionnaire vehicles. Food. Guns. Ammo. Water. They had their own fuel truck. It's shot up, but didn't burn. The camp mechanics and a group of townie conscripts push it to our fuel truck to top it off.

I look around to the flatbeds, hoping they're trashed. That would kill this asshole crusade quick. But I spot the tarp in the distance. It's dusty, but there isn't a single bullet hole.

Cherry totters over, still playing the frail oracle. She pokes me in the side with a finger. I slap her hand away.

"You really are hard to kill, Mr. Pitts," she rasps.

"It's just us, Cherry. You can drop the feeble act."

She leans against the car with me and lowers her respirator.

"I told the Magistrate not to stop here," she says in her normal voice.

"So your oracle act is real, then."

"I told you."

"Yeah, but I never believe anything you tell me."

"We should go behind the trucks and fuck. It might be our last chance."

"Don't start that stuff now."

She pouts.

"You're never fun anymore. Every time I see you you're shot or stabbed or something."

"It's inconvenient for me, too."

She gets in front of me.

"Jimmy, seriously. You can't die. No one else is going to look out for me out here."

I rub the spot where she poked me.

"Relax. I'm not dying anytime soon. The one time was plenty."

"You're a hero, you know. Everyone is talking about how you got the Magistrate out of the motel."

"I seem to remember Daja being there. Isn't she a hero, too?"

Cherry waves dismissively.

"Of course. She's the toast of the town. But it was you everyone saw when you blew a hole in the fire line. Don't deny it. I know magic when I see it."

"So what? I have a cover story."

"Yeah, Daja told everyone that, too. But even she doesn't believe it. You want to stay incognito? You better come up with something better than the car and truck just happened to fall apart at the same time."

"I'll keep my head down awhile. If I fess up who I am, they'll know me and Traven have been lying the whole time."

"And me."

"Yeah. You too."

"Plus," she says, "confessing to a lie that big will almost certainly confirm you're our ghostly saboteur."

"People still think that?"

"Enough that it matters."

"Shit."

I look past her at the camp.

I say, "You know how you can help? You're the local swami. Tell them it's all shit. You read my aura or something and I'm just another lost bastard who got lucky."

She looks back at the camp, too.

"I already did. Some of them believe me. But you know how rumors are. Cool it with the magic and stay away from the trucks."

"Good idea."

"And don't heal so fast. Look hurt. Limp around. You're everyone's favorite wounded puppy right now. Just go with it."

"I'm not good at that."

She pulls some potions from her pocket and hands them to me. I look them over, a little skeptical.

"What are those for?"

"Officially I'm over here to pray and spritz you with some healing potions."

I push her hand away.

"Keep them. I'm sick of the Magistrate's tent revival."

Cherry stamps her foot.

"This is for both our benefits," she says. "Besides, if you're good I have some laudanum."

I lower my head.

"You talked me into it."

She lays a delicate hand on the back of my head and hits me with what smells like rose water and vinegar.

"That stuff stinks."

"Shut up," she says, and hands me a pint of laudanum.

I take the bottle and have a long, deep pull.

She takes it back.

"That's enough for now, tiger. But you know where to come for more."

She winks. I start to say something, but the laudanum kicks in and my brain is very soft and slow and the world is a lovely place.

"Feel good?" Cherry says.

"Like I have a rainbow in my heart."

She rolls her eyes and puts her respirator back on.

"You're ridiculously stoned," she rasps.

She puts her arm around my waist. I drape mine over her shoulders and we stagger back to camp.

"Remember. You're hurt. Play it up," she says, helping me back onto the ground by my coat.

I give her a wave and she totters away.

Wanuri comes over and crouches down next to me.

"How are you feeling?"

Swaying, I give her a thumbs-up.

She frowns.

"Are you high?"

I squint at her.

"Define high."

She looks at Cherry.

"Damn witch and her potions."

"I respectfully disagree."

"Get on your feet. The Magistrate wants to see you."

"I'm not really in shape for a philosophical discussion."

She grabs my arm and pulls me up. Even through the laudanum it hurts.

"Ow. Fuck."

"You big baby. Move your ass."

I look at her.

"You get hurt during the shitstorm?"

She folds her arms.

"Babetta got hit on one side of me and Lerajie on the other. I didn't get a scratch. How does that happen? I don't understand."

I do my sodden best to look her in the eye.

"There's nothing to understand. They died. You didn't."

She looks around.

"What if people think I ducked out? Let them die and Johnny and Billy get shot up."

"You're the last one anyone would think that about."

"Still, man . . ."

"We're just bugs on God's windshield. Don't expect anything to mean anything."

"You know that for sure? How?"

"I'll tell you a secret."

"If you want me to be your valentine, no thanks."

I crook a stoned finger at her. She gets closer.

"I met the Devil. He doesn't have any more of a clue than we do. Neither does Mr. Muninn."

"Who?' she says.

"God."

She gives me a look.

"An asshole like you met God?"

"I told you. None of this shit means anything."

She breathes in and out slowly.

"People are talking about you."

"No autographs, please."

"Laugh it up. Half think you're some kind of guardian angel here to look after the Magistrate. The other want to see you on the gallows truck."

I lean over to pick up my shirt. Wanuri has to grab me to keep me from falling over.

"What do you think?" I ask.

"I'm fifty-fifty."

She doesn't bother letting me reach for my coat. She grabs it and throws it to me.

"You're wrong," I say. "I'm no one's guardian and I'm not your rat. But I can't prove either thing."

Wanuri gives me a shove toward the motor home.

"That's convenient."

"Isn't it just?"

When we get there I say, "If anyone says you ran, point them out and I'll hit them."

She grabs my arm.

"I don't need you to fight my battles for me."

"I'm not fighting for you. I just like punching people."

She lets go and points at me.

"There's another half that thinks you're just crazy."

"Finally. My people."

She nods at the motor-home door.

"Get your ass inside. I'm bringing the others, but the Magistrate wants to see Daja and you first."

"Sounds like a party. I hope there's cake."

Wanuri is already yards away and doesn't hear me.

I start to open the door, but I flash back on the dream. I swear I can hear Wormwood scrabbling around like rats in the walls. If I'm right, someone just made—and someone just *lost*—a pile of money on the shoot-out. Of course, even if Wormwood is still hiding up in some deep dark hole in Hell, what are the odds of them knowing what's going on in the Tenebrae?

"My boy," says the Magistrate.

He comes to the door and helps me inside.

"How is your wound? We are low on some supplies, I am afraid. I did my best with what we had at hand."

"The side's good, thanks. Mimir just fixed me up with laudanum."

"Excellent," he says, and ushers me to the little table where Cherry did her swami act.

Daja is already there, bandages on both hands and her forehead.

"Did you bring any laudanum for the rest of us?" she says.

I shake my head. "I might go back for seconds. You should come along."

"I just might do that."

I look at her bandaged hands.

"You all right?"

"Just a couple of blisters. Some asshole convinced me to run through a furnace."

"He sounds shady. As your lawyer, I advise you to avoid him in the future."

"It's my fondest dream."

The Magistrate pulls a bottle of Hellion wine from a cabinet and sets out three glasses. I've never been that much of a wine guy, but I'm sure it will mix well with the laudanum. But he only pours glasses for Daja and himself. I look at my empty glass.

"If I'm in trouble, why don't you start the yelling now while I'm still high and won't care?"

"On the contrary," the Magistrate says.

He reaches back into the cabinet and comes back with another bottle. He looks at it for a moment.

"We found two cases of this in the Legionnaires' stores. I understand it is something you enjoy."

He sets the bottle in front of me and I recognize the sigil on the wax immediately.

It's Aqua Regia. Who did I tell I like the stuff? Fuck it. I'm too high to care right now.

"Yeah," I say, trying to keep my voice even. "It is something I enjoy. I thought I was never going to see it again."

"There's plenty more where that came from. Of course, you will have to share the rest. But this bottle is for you. A token of thanks."

"Thanks," I say, and for once, Downtown, I actually mean it.

"What is that stuff?" says Daja.

"The greatest invention the Devil ever gave the damned. Aqua Regia."

"What, some kind of wine or whiskey?"

"It's Aqua Regia. It's just itself. Want to try it?"

Her eyes narrow a little.

"You first."

I pull the cork and pour a glass full. Give it a sniff. There it is. The heady bouquet of gasoline and hot pepper. I sip it and shudder a little. It burns just right going down.

"It's that good?" says Daja.

"You tell me."

I hand her the glass. She reaches for it, but then I pull it back for a second. I know I'm going to have to kill her someday, but I don't exactly hate her.

"What the—"

"Go at it easy. Some people find it an acquired taste."

"I don't need drinking lessons from you."

"I'm just saying."

She grabs the drink, takes a gulp, and slams down the glass. Her face curdles like she just swallowed battery acid, which isn't that far from the truth.

"Good?" I say.

She nods and with a heroic effort manages to croak, "Great."

I take the glass back and finish what's left.

"I told you it was an acquired taste."

Daja waves for me to give the glass back.

She chokes out, "I didn't say I was done."

I don't say anything. I just pour another glassful and pass it to her.

Daja takes it and drinks another mouthful. She grimaces, but also nods.

"I think I'm acquiring the taste."

"Have all you want. Just leave me some."

She swallows her wine in one gulp and pours more Aqua Regia in her glass.

I say, "Really, you should go easy your first time."

"You're not Father Traven and I'm not one of your choirboys."

She drinks more. I pour some in my glass.

"Suit yourself," I say.

The Magistrate has been watching this whole thing with the quiet amusement of Mike Brady watching his squabbling TV kids. Only this Mike's kids are killers and Dad's got a messiah complex.

He reaches out and squeezes each of us by the wrist.

"I wanted to thank you both so much for how you risked yourself for my benefit and the benefit of the entire havoc. I knew you were both brave, but not how wonderfully foolhardy."

Daja reaches out for him.

"I'm always here. You know that," she says.

"I do," says the Magistrate.

He turns to me.

"And you, Mr. Pitts. I'll admit it now to your face: I have had grave doubts about you, despite what Mimir says. I see that my suspicions were wrong."

I raise my glass to him.

"Don't feel bad. It was grave doubts all around."

He folds his arms and leans on the table.

Smiling, he says, "You have had your doubts about me."

"Remember the other night in the desert when we played your secrets game?"

"Of course."

"Let's play it again."

"If you wish. Who should go first?"

I look at Daja. She doesn't like my tone or the direction of the conversation.

"What secrets is he talking about?" she says.

"I believe we are about to find out," the Magistrate says.

I take a shot of Aqua Regia and point the glass at him.

"I'll go first. Letting yourself get dragged off like that and trussed up like Thanksgiving dinner. I'm not sure I buy it."

He leans forward a bit more.

"Watch your mouth," says Daja.

I'll admit it. Between the laudanum and the Aqua Regia, my head is swimming just enough that even if she is the dog-pack alpha, I don't care.

"No. It is all right," says the Magistrate. "Go on, Mr. Pitts."

"Mimir told you something out there and you ignored it. What did she say? 'Don't mess with these guys? Drive on?'"

"You think I *engineered* this catastrophe?"

"No. But I think getting caught makes you look weak and you're not the kind of guy who does that without a reason."

Daja starts to get up. The Aqua Regia already has her swaying.

"Get out," she says.

"No, Daja. Please. Sit down. We are just playing a game," says the Magistrate.

He looks at me.

"Are you finished? May I tell you my secret?"

"Sure. Tell me I'm wrong," I say.

"I cannot," he says. "That is my secret."

Daja's eye narrow.

"Magistrate . . . ?"

He turns to her.

"I am not saying that I allowed myself to be captured. What I am saying is that I ignored Mimir for a reason. Would you like to know what she told me?"

I pour more Aqua Regia.

"It's your party."

"Then here is my secret. Before our encounter, Mimir said to me 'When it happens, you cannot trust him.' I did not know what the *it* was that she referred to. However, what is more important is that I did not have to ask *who* she was talking about."

For a second I think about killing both of them and running for the hills, but the Magistrate would have thought of that. A guy like him probably has this moment figured a hundred different ways. So, I sit there and enjoy my drink.

"I don't understand," says Daja. "Pitts helped. I was there. I don't how we would have gotten you out any other way."

"No. You do not. Because Mr. Pitts intervened. But what if there was a separate agenda beyond saving me? It was his idea to burn the cars and charge the armored vehicles, yes?"

"Yes."

Now I lean forward. "Yeah. It was and I seem to remember Daja and me hauling your ass out of a burning building."

He leans back.

"But would the building have burned if it were not for your suggestion to burn the cars?"

Daja looks at me.

"You're saying he tried to *kill* you?"

"I am saying that perhaps his real goal was to damage the havoc so that it could not continue."

He looks at me hard.

"Was that your real motivation, Mr. Pitts? To destroy us and our holy mission?"

Daja gets up and pulls her knife.

She says, "Answer him, Pitts."

I take out a Malediction and light it.

"No. First, you go fuck yourself. Second, if Charlie Manson here is as crazy as I think he is, nothing I say is going to matter, so you two better make your move because we're not all walking out of here."

Daja goes for me, but she's more wasted than she knows. I can take her down before her knife gets close to nicking my pretty face. It's the Magistrate that worries me. He's not counting on her to do his dirty work. She's just a distraction. With the wound in my side, I'm not as fast or as strong as I need to be right now. There's nothing to do but play this out.

I throw myself out of the way as Daja's blade comes down. It hits hard, but all she kills is my chair. I kick her legs, knocking her over backward. By the time she scrambles up, I'm behind her with the Colt in my hand. The Magistrate hasn't moved.

I wrench Daja's arm up behind her and put the pistol

to her head. Whatever stitches were holding me together are ripped to shit. Blood flows down my side and onto my boots. The Magistrate glances down at where I'm messing up his carpet.

"Father?" says Daja.

He holds up a hand.

"It is all right, my dear. Mr. Pitts will be killing no one," he says.

I cock the Colt.

"Actually, I had a bigger body count than that in mind."

He picks up his wine and takes a sip. Clears his throat.

"Let's play another game," he says.

I shoot the glass out of his hand. Someone tries to open the door, but it's locked. They pound on it. From outside we hear, "Magistrate. Are you all right?"

It's Wanuri.

"I'm fine. We are all fine," he says. "Please wait outside while we conclude our business."

He looks back at me.

"One more game," he says. "Obviously, you can kill both of us, but where will that leave you?"

"It leaves me alive and driving this heap out of here."

"And leave the father behind? I doubt that. Besides, unfortunately one of the battery cables has come loose. I doubt you could start the engine."

Yeah. He has this scene figured probably more ways than I can count.

"Then I'll just have to be satisfied with killing you and as many of the others as I can."

"Or you can play the truth game with me one more time. Do it and I will guarantee your safety no matter what happens afterward."

"How are you going to do that?"

He twines his fingers together.

"You'll have to play to find out."

I press the Colt into Daja's ear.

"What do you think, boss? Kill everyone and die or take a chance on Zardoz over there?"

"You can't do this. We're on a holy crusade. God won't let you," she says.

She looks at the Magistrate.

"Will he?"

He ignores her.

"I will go first, Mr. Pitts. What you do after is your affair."

I try to figure the angles, but I know he figured them before I walked in the room. I'm stuck, and I really don't relish the look on Mason's face when I pop into Tartarus.

I nod once. "Talk."

"Here is my secret: Mimir said nothing about you to me. You were right the first time. She told me to pass the town by. I chose to ignore her and, sadly, we have all paid for my arrogance."

"Here's my secret," I say. "I don't believe you. You're a student of psychology. I know we're playing a game, but it's not the one you said it is. What's the real game we're playing?"

He lays his hands flat on the table.

"You're right. There is no secret game, that night in the desert or here now."

"Then what's going on?"

"You think I can read minds, don't you? Or the idea has occurred to you. But you are wrong. Do you know how I know what people are thinking?"

My adrenaline is cutting through the laudanum and my side is burning. Plus, I had a little too much Aqua Regia. I say the first thing that comes into my head.

"It isn't heartbeats. And souls mostly breathe out of habit. That means it's got to be eyes. Micro-expressions."

"Yes," he says, and slaps the table. "I knew you knew the answer. And do you know how I knew?"

"Because I can do it, too."

"Exactly. But you feel weak here, and lost. Why is that?"

Fuck. This guy knows everything. There's no point lying.

"It's harder to read the dead. Without real bodies, the signals aren't there."

"Yes they are," he says. "You just have to recognize them. You have the talent. I can teach you the rest."

"Two minutes ago, you were taking about killing me. Why should I trust you now?"

"Because I know how you really saved me, and I have kept your secret. And I will continue to do so. On this, you have my word."

"What is going on?" says Daja. "Is he an enemy or not?"

"Which is it, Mr. Pitts? I cannot answer Daja's question. You will have to."

I think for a minute. Daja moves. I tighten my grip. Look at the Magistrate.

"Prove you know about me and that you've kept your mouth shut about it."

"Of course," he says. "Sub Rosa."

The prick knows I can do hoodoo. He's probably known all along.

"That thing earlier about Mimir telling you not to trust me. You wanted to see if I'd deny it."

"Yes."

"But if I denied it, I would be telling the truth."

"Yes."

"Then what would it tell you?"

"Enough."

"That doesn't even make sense."

"Not to you, but to me, and that is sufficient for my purposes."

I let the hammer down on the Colt, but I keep hold of Daja.

"Why would you keep my secret?"

"What's Sub Rosa?" says Daja.

"Nothing you need to concern yourself with right now, my dear," he says. "And please do not repeat the phrase to anybody outside this room."

I've lost a lot of blood, enough that I'm not sure if I'm more relaxed with the situation or my blood pressure is dropping. Either way I say, "Even though you knew about me, you still weren't sure about me. With all your tricks for reading the dead, you still weren't sure."

He moves some shiny things around on his desk. Map-reading tools.

"You Sub Rosa are difficult to read. I wanted to trust you, but perhaps I was wrong. It has happened. Not often, but it has happened."

"Like today."

"Unfortunately."

I let go of Daja. She sags against the table, but it's a feint. She throws an elbow back at my head. I move back to avoid it, but end up smashing my head into a cabinet anyway. She lunges for her knife, but I still have the Colt. We're stuck there with her knife to my throat and my pistol to her face.

The Magistrate gets up and comes around the table. Gently, he pushes both of our hands down.

"Children. *Relax*. Everything is all right now. We are all friends, tested in battle and this somewhat convoluted peace."

Daja seems to do whatever he says, and I'm too tired to die right now. Daja puts her knife in its sheath and I put the Colt at my back. My head swims enough that I have to sit down. The Magistrate kneels next to me and opens my coat.

I stare at him a little cross-eyed.

"'Somewhat convoluted'?"

"Trust me, Pitts. I've played games much more tangled than this."

"I need a drink."

I hold Daja's empty glass out to her.

"You need one, too."

She smacks it out of my hand.

"I don't want to drink with you."

"Of course you do," says the Magistrate. "After tonight we know one thing: if there is anyone in the havoc we can trust, it is him."

"I might still be whoever's messing with your equipment," I say. "Or partnered with them."

"But you are not."

"How do you know? You know who it is?"

"No. But I know you enough to know that while you may be a killer, you are not nearly subtle enough to be a spy or a saboteur."

"I think my feelings should be hurt."

"My apologies."

"I'm supposed to trust this prick?" says Daja.

"Yes, my dear," says the Magistrate.

"But I don't have to like him, right?"

"Of course not. That is your choice. But trust in these times is more important than affection. Do you not agree, Pitts?"

"Trust isn't my greatest asset."

"I think we can all say that. But here we are. Any combination of us could have killed any other combination and yet we are still alive. That must count for something."

Daja sits.

"I want a drink after all."

The Magistrate pulls off my bandages.

"Unfortunately, tonight became a bit more physical than I had hoped. I will have to restitch your wound."

"Does that mean I get more laudanum?"

"All you want."

"Then hack away."

Daja picks her glass up off the floor and pours herself some wine. I guess the Aqua Regia isn't her favorite after all.

"Everyone is outside," she says. "What are we going to tell them happened? The gunshot? All this blood?"

The Magistrate goes and comes back with a medical kit.

"The gun was a misfire because Mr. Pitts has been drinking. He ripped his stitches during his stupor."

"Sure," I say. "Blame it all on me."

"As you said yourself, Daja is the boss and I am the Magistrate. Who else should we blame?"

I try to think, but I'm drunk and in a lot of pain.

"Fuck it. No matter what we say, they're going to take one look and blame me."

"Unquestionably." The fucker smiles. He starts threading a surgical needle. "Daja, please let the others in."

"I will, but one last thing. What's a Sub Rosa?"

"A guardian angel," I say.

"Guardian asshole," she mumbles, and opens the doors.

AFTER GETTING MY second set of stitches, Aqua Regia, and more laudanum, I sleep hard.

In fact, the whole dog pack sleeps late. I only wake up when someone drops a shot-up transmission as they're raising it out of a truck and it shears off the side of the engine housing. Apparently there was a memorial service for everyone who died in the firefight. I don't like preachers and a few of the dead didn't deserve it, so I'm glad I missed it.

An hour later, I'm sitting on my bike staring at Daja and the wreck of the camp behind her.

It's going to be a few days' work to get the havoc on its feet and moving again. The mechanics strip every part from every dead vehicle. Then they start on the Hellion AAVs. One of them is still running, but there's a few inches of Hellion blood inside that need to be swabbed out. It's times like this that I'm glad I'm in the pack. I don't know how to fix car engines. I don't want to haul supplies in and out of trucks like the conscripts. And I sure don't want to be on blood cleanup duty.

When the whole pack was in the motor home last night, the Magistrate laid out our post-getting-royally-fucked orders. One, do a recon run up the road and scout for other towns and potential ambush points. And two, look for a landmark the dear departed Empress told the Magistrate about. An obelisk with instructions to whatever magic beans it is we're looking for. Fortunately, they're both in the same direction, so yay for small favors.

Billy is still laid up with his belly wound, but at least he's not dead. Lerajie, Babetta, and the old toothless guy are dead (I never could remember his name, but with the white power tats on his knuckles I didn't try very hard). The rest of us are bandaged and stitched together, but basically functional.

"We're short on people, so this is going to get complicated," Daja says. "We need people on the run, but we need to leave enough behind to protect the Magistrate."

"Why not just do four and four?" says Wanuri.

"I thought of that, but with shit the way it is, I'd like one more to stay here as guard."

"That leaves three of us for the run. We can make do with that," Johnny says to the group.

Daja shakes her head.

"That's thin if anything goes wrong out there. Even if it's just a breakdown when you're far out. Two on one bike might not have the fuel to make it back."

I raise my hand.

Daja gives me a look.

"This isn't kindergarten. Say what you have to say."

"Get Traven to help stand guard. That will give us four for the road."

The pack laughs quietly.

"No offense, dear, but he looks like he's afraid of moths," says Doris.

"I used to work with him back home. He put the fear of God in a lot of bad people. And I watched him kill an Inquisitor with his bare hands."

Medea Bava was the grand high executioner for the Sub Rosa in L.A., and she had a real thing for me. She might have taken me down, too, if it wasn't for Traven.

"An Inquisitor? How old are you?" says Barbora.

"Not that kind of Inquisitor. More like an enforcer for a group of underground power brokers."

"Father Traven?" says Daja. "Mr. Bookworm Librarian? You saw him *kill* someone."

"With his bare hands. And he's damned more souls than Hooters. He could do a trick called the Via Dolorosa. Whenever he wanted, he could fill a soul full of so much sin it was a one-way ticket to Pandemonium."

The pack isn't impressed. Lots of shaking heads and nos.

"Look, mate, I respect loyalty to a friend, but you've got to be fucking joking," says Johnny.

"Maybe we shouldn't be so quick to judge," says Doris, which raises a few eyebrows. She's not used to speaking up. Her hands absently play with the knives on her belt.

"Care to explain?" Frederickson says. He scratches his scalped head.

"Back home, people didn't think much of me either. I cooked and cleaned for my family. I had a cat and a book club and I baked cookies for the school fund-raisers. Then I had my little . . . well, incident with the in-laws."

People laugh. Wanuri makes a chopping motion with her hand.

"The first trial was a hung jury and the second one acquitted me. Why? Because I was nothing. A harmless little housewife who wouldn't hurt a fly. Maybe Father Traven is a bit like me. Hiding his talent under a bushel."

Daja gives me a hard look.

"If I trust Marian the Librarian and something happens, you guarantee he won't wilt like a flower?"

"You can trust me."

The Magistrate said so, remember? Or are you still mad enough to hold a grudge?

She looks at me and around the camp.

"Fine," she says impatiently. "Johnny, Frederickson—get him over here."

"You can't be serious," Frederickson says.

"Do I sound like I'm kidding? Get off your ass and bring him to me."

He goes to get his bike, a Hellion-style BMW cruiser. The tank wraps over his knees like the flared head of a cobra. Instead of chrome pipes and forks, they're made of some kind of thick bone. The pipes glow green when he hits the throttle.

"Assuming that the padre works out, that leaves four for the road. Volunteers?"

Doris says, "I'll go."

Gisco raises his hand.

"How about you, Wanuri?" Daja says.

"I'd rather stay and keep an eye on the Magistrate."

"I'd rather have you on the road."

"Why?"

"'Cause he's the fourth."

Everyone looks at me.

"Oh, goody."

Daja says, "Wanuri, you ride point with the map. Everybody else takes orders from you."

She looks at me.

"Everybody."

"Got it, boss."

"You know no one here thinks you're nothing, right, Doris?" says Barbora.

"I know, but it's still nice to hear," Doris says. "And I know they know back home. By now, the house will have been sold and the new owners will have dug up the garden. Oh, the things they'll find down there."

We smile along with her and pat her on the back because sometimes a little revenge is all you can squeeze out of one lifetime. And besides, it's Doris. Her family. A nasty neighbor or two. The guy at the local market who parked his sports car across two spaces. Local dog owners who were mean to her cat. Anyone she planted in that garden, you just know they had it coming.

WANURI FOLLOWS THE map and we follow Wanuri. Four people. Four bikes. The usual flat road and hills. We ride an hour from camp before Wanuri signals to slow. We turn off the ley line we've been following for days and head a short way into some low, stony hills. From there, Wanuri uses the

Magistrate's spyglass to check out a small town a quarter of a mile away. She doesn't seem interested in giving anyone else a peek, so I light a Malediction and hold out the pack to Doris. She shakes her head. Gisco takes one and I light it.

"Getting comfortable, are we?" says Wanuri.

"Having a cigarette picnic. Want one?"

"No and neither do you. Mount up. We're moving on."

I finish as much of the Malediction as I can and we head back to the map route.

It's the same routine at the next two towns we come to. Up a hill. Crouch in the rocks like bashful lizards. Then back to blow down the Magistrate's Yellow Brick Road.

At the second town, Doris gets on her bike but doesn't start it.

"What's wrong?" says Wanuri.

"I have a confession to make. I'm not exactly sure what an obelisk is."

"Then why did you want to come on the run?"

"Camp is so depressing right now. I thought I could be more helpful out here."

"Looking for something you don't know what it is?"

Doris gives Wanuri as fierce a look as I've ever seen.

"In case there's trouble."

Wanuri leans on her bike. Before she can say anything, Gisco gestures, holding his arms a length apart like he's measuring something from the ground.

Wanuri frowns.

"Now, what the hell are *you* saying?"

I say, "He's saying an obelisk is a pillar."

Gisco nods. I look at Doris.

"It's a kind of pillar with a little pyramid on top."

"Thank you both," she says.

Wanuri looks us over.

"Are you done? Can we just do our job?"

"Back off," I say. "Doris asked a legit question."

"If I don't back off are you going to shoot us up like the Magistrate's trailer?"

I get off the bike and go to her.

"Is that going to be your excuse?"

Doris looks from Wanuri to me.

"What do you mean?" she says.

"For when she shoots me in the back. Tell me. Is this your idea or did Daja put you up to it?"

"What?" Doris says. "He's wrong. Tell him he's wrong, Wanuri."

She doesn't say anything.

Gisco gestures violently.

I say, "If you think I'm going down easy . . ."

"Hush!" says Doris. "Both of you."

She yanks the *panabas* off her belt and gets between Wanuri and me.

"We don't do that kind of thing to each other," she says. "Whatever personal problems you have with Pitts, you need to deal with some other time because if something happens to him out here I will be very cross."

Gisco goes to stand with her.

Wanuri looks over our tawdry little mutiny and gets on her bike.

"Let's move out," she says, and points to a nearby peak. "We're heading there. The map says we might be able to see the obelisk from the top."

No one says another word as we get on our bikes and head out.

IT'S A HALF hour's ride down to the base of the peak. There's no road or even a path. The rocks are too loose and it's too steep to consider taking the bikes, so we leave them behind a couple of large boulders and start up on foot. My side hurts from the long ride, but I don't let on. I'd like another taste of laudanum or at least a shot of Aqua Regia. Instead, I have to suffer with water and a couple of aspirin Cherry gave me.

We trudge up the goddamn hill. Slipping and sliding the whole way. The hill isn't that high, but the loose rocks we found at the base get looser and bigger the higher we climb. We practically have to crawl up the last few steep yards to keep from sliding all the way back to the bottom.

The Tenebrae sky is dim and the shadows are long, but the Magistrate was right. From here we can see for miles. Too bad there's nothing to see. No one says anything, but you can feel it hit like a punch to the gut. We've come miles and climbed up the highest peak in the area for a crystal-clear view of the same shit wasteland we've been traveling through for how long? I don't know anymore.

"Come on," says Wanuri. "Let's look at the other side. Watch your step."

The way the rocks shift and slide, it's like roller-skating on marbles up here. Halfway around, I slip and Gisco helps me up. Then it's Doris's turn. There are a few dry trees up here and she grabs one, but can't get her footing. I help her up.

After I get her on her feet, she grabs me.

"A pillar?" she says. "With a pyramid on top?"

"Yeah."

"Like that?"

She points into the distance.

I squint.

"Well, goddamn."

I yell to the others, "Doris just got employee of the month."

They look to where we're pointing.

It stands there in murky half-light, straight, white like marble, and at least fifty feet tall. And it's behind us. We probably passed it fucking hours ago. Our tire tracks run right alongside it, but the obelisk itself is in a divot at the bottom of one of the anonymous hills, surrounded by high rocks that block it from ground-level view.

Wanuri gets out the spyglass.

"Fuck, Doris. Fuck."

She slip-slides over to us and gives Doris a big hug.

Gisco makes a sound and shakes his hands at the spyglass.

Wanuri says, "Sure. Take a look, kid."

She tosses him the telescope, but it goes a little wide. Gisco jumps to catch it, and promptly disappears over the far side of the peak. All we hear is the sound of falling rocks.

We scramble over the treacherous footing as fast as we can. Near the top of the peak, we start shouting.

"Gisco!"

It's a couple of minutes before we hear anything.

"Down here," shouts Wanuri.

The three of us slowly make our way down the steep hill, sharp rocks streaming around us like a river of razors.

Gisco is only half conscious when he get to him. Me and Wanuri grab his arms while Doris grabs him around the waist. He doesn't budge.

"It's his leg," Doris says. "It's wedged under a boulder."

The three of us get around it and push. On another day, in another place, I'm sure I could move the goddamn rock myself, but I'm only on one cylinder. Between the three of us, we manage to rock the boulder up a few inches, but not enough to move it off Gisco.

I say, "Doris, Wanuri and I will push the rock. You try to pull him out."

She nods and grabs his arms.

Wanuri and I push. The rock shifts.

"It's not enough," says Doris. "A few more inches."

We let the rock down carefully.

"Shit," says Wanuri.

I kneel and slap Gisco a couple of times. He moans.

"Don't fade out, kid."

I look where the rock has crushed his leg.

"We need a car jack."

"We need a lever," Doris says.

"Either one of you have one? 'Cause I'm fresh out," says Wanuri.

Doris points up the hill to where a couple of the gnarled trees stand.

"What about those? Maybe we can make one."

"Got your *panabas*?" Wanuri says.

Doris says, "Always."

Wanuri turns to me.

"Stay here with him. We're going up."

I get up.

"I should go."

"Why?"

"One of us should talk to Gisco and he barely knows me. He'll know your voice."

Doris unhooks her ax.

"He has a point."

"All right," Wanuri says. "Make it fast."

We half run, half crawl up the hill. When we reach the tree, I get on the low side and put all my weight on it. Doris gets on the other side and hacks at the roots with her *panabas*. Each blow vibrates through my whole body. But the wood is hard and Doris has to hack a lot longer than either of us wants. I move farther up the trunk and lift my feet off the ground, hoping the extra weight will help. Hanging there as useless as a shriveled peach. I have a clear view of the Tenebrae on the far side of the mountain. In one second, I'm excited. In the next, I'm queasy with tension.

Everywhere mortals exist in the world has an echo in the Tenebrae. A fragile phantom version of the real thing. Squatting ugly, dark and filthy, barely a shadow of the real thing, is the Tenebrae ghost of L.A. And it's only a few miles away. From there, I know how to get into Hell. It ain't salvation, but it's where Traven and I can disappear and never think about this traveling carny show ever again.

Wood splinters. A shudder runs through my body as the

tree trunk splits from the roots. I drop a couple of feet, taking the weight on my shoulder. Doris grabs the other end of the tree and we haul it down the hill as fast as we can.

Wanuri is still with Gisco. He's awake and she's giving him sips of water. While Doris pushes a smaller rock underneath so we can balance the trunk, Wanuri and I get the end of the tree under the rock.

"Get ready," Wanuri says. "Haul him out the moment he's clear. This shitty wood might not hold long."

Doris says, "I can do it."

Wanuri and I lay our weight on the tree trunk. The boulder moves. Gisco screams.

"Just a little more," says Doris.

We push harder. Gisco screams. The tree cracks.

"Got him!" Doris yells.

The trunk snaps in half and the boulder thuds back into place. But Doris has Gisco out and propped against a pile of rocks nearby.

That's the good news.

The bad news is his right leg. The lower part is bent at almost a ninety-degree angle. There's no bone sticking out, though.

That's the other good news.

The bad news, though, is that it means whatever bone is left is probably pulverized.

"Should we straighten it?" says Wanuri.

"No. We splint it like that," I say. "Get him back to camp before we start fucking with it."

"You sure?"

"I've dealt with a lot of these injuries over the years."

"Don't lie to me."

"Look at my face. I didn't get these scars in pillow fights."

That seems to convince her. Never doubt the power of ugly.

"Okay," she says. "We can chop up the tree. How do we secure him to it?"

I shove the na'at into my boot and take off my coat. Hand it to Doris.

"You've got the knives, cut this up into strips."

She unhooks one of her butcher knives and starts slicing.

"Wait," I say, and take a flask from an inside pocket.

"Where did you get that?" says Wanuri.

"It was in a pile of dead Hellion junk."

I unscrew the top.

"What is it?"

"Aqua Regia."

"You're going to drink *now*?"

"No. Gisco is. Everything from here to camp is going to hurt like a motherfucker."

She looks at him.

"What do you say? You want to drink his poison?"

I hold the flask out to him.

"It tastes like dragon piss, but it's about two hundred proof. It will help with the pain."

Gisco takes the flask and tries a taste. Then coughs and spits a fair amount of it on his shirt. I hold him upright while he sputters.

"This isn't sipping whiskey. Just hold your breath and swallow as much as you can."

He makes a face, but doesn't hesitate as he upends the

Aqua Regia, taking three long pulls. Coughing and gagging, he shoves the flask back at me.

"Feeling any better?"

He breathes in. Lets his head fall back. He gives a thumbs-up. I push the flask back into his hand.

"You hold on to this. You might need more in a minute."

Doris has my coat shredded in no time. Wanuri uses the *panabas* to cut the tree trunk into smaller segments. When they're done, I grab Gisco by the shoulders and he grabs on to my arms. Wanuri and Doris splint his leg as fast as they can, but the next few minutes are all screams and a lot of fumbling, punctuated by curses and more screaming. Gisco isn't a big guy, but it's all I can do to hold him.

Finally, it's done. Gisco isn't moving.

"Is he all right?" says Doris.

I lay him down flat on the hillside.

"He's fine. He just fainted."

We use the rest of my shredded coat as a rope to lower him down the hill. When we reach level ground, I offer to ride with Gisco back to camp.

"No," Wanuri says. "He's my responsibility."

We maneuver him onto the back of her bike, and me and Doris use the rope to secure him against her back.

I say, "You got your balance with him on there?"

"I'm fine," she says, but I can tell she's struggling. Still, Gisco is as safe with her as he'd be with any of us. And I know Wanuri would rather die than let anything else happen to the kid.

We abandon Gisco's bike and ride back to camp flat out the whole way.

They must have heard us coming for miles, because there's a whole reception committee when we reach the havoc. The Magistrate takes one look at Gisco and he and Johnny cut him free of Wanuri's back. They use the drop door from a pickup truck as a stretcher to carry him wherever the messiah will lay hands on him.

Me and Doris get off our bikes, but Wanuri sits unmoving on hers.

Doris pats her back.

"Are you all right, dear? You did all you could," she says.

Wanuri shakes her head and watches them carry Gisco away.

She says, "On top of everything else, I lost the Magistrate's telescope."

I hand it to her. She turns the telescope over on her hands. Looks at me.

I say, "I saw it before we started down, so I shoved it in my back pocket."

"Is that dried blood all over your shirt?"

I look down at myself.

"Mine and some Hellion. I'm hard on clothes."

"You're disgusting. Go get something from the ice cream truck over there."

She points into the distance.

"Thanks."

She holds up the spyglass.

"Thank you," she says again.

I head for the ice cream truck, stopping to throw my shirt into the bonfire. It breaks my heart a little. If we were in Pandemonium, I could wash the blood out of the thing. But it doesn't work that way traveling in the desert. I watch the last Max Overdrive T-shirt I'll ever see shrivel up and turn to ash. And my coat is gone, too. Two more connections to the world gone forever.

These days, when I think of Candy, she's at the end of a tunnel a million miles long, and it gets longer every day. I can barely make out her face. Sometimes she waves. Mostly, though, we just look at each other until one of us looks away. This time it's my turn, not because seeing her is like dying all over again but because I saw a way out of here. All I have to do is get Traven and make it through the L.A. ruins. From there I can find a way home. I know it.

Now I know things are starting to go my way when I get to the ice cream truck. Sure, the shirt is bile green, the lettering on the front is in Hellion, and it's two sizes too big, but I grab it anyway. There can't be that many Skull Valley Sheep Kill T-shirts in Hell.

With a little more searching, I find a frock coat made of basilisk leather. My bike pants are a little stiff with blood, too, but there's no way I'm giving up those or my boots. Nothing else that reminds me of home gets away, no matter how fucked up.

I lost my flask back on the peak, so I track down the Aqua Regia crate and help myself to a bottle. Cherry totters in and out of the ambulance a couple of times bringing medical supplies to the Magistrate. Gisco isn't screaming anymore, so maybe he got some of the laudanum. I walk by the motor home looking for Traven, but he isn't there. I find him with a handful of other people watching the Magistrate doing open-heart surgery on Gisco's leg. I've seen enough bodies cut up for one lifetime. I go over to the father and say, "We need to talk."

"Right now?" he says.

"Now."

We head back to the bonfire, taking our time, not staying in any one place where people can hear us talk.

"I found a way out."

He gives me a puzzled look.

"Out of where? The havoc or the Tenebrae?"

"Both. I found L.A. Ghost L.A. From there, I can navigate us into Hell and away from these lunatics."

"That's . . . astonishing."

"From Pandemonium, we can go anywhere or just stay in the city until we come up with a plan. The point is, we'll be free."

He rubs his chin.

"I wish it were that simple."

"What do you mean?"

I look around and spot two meat mountains, a bandaged soul, and a Hellion in a Legionnaire military coat full of bullet holes. They're both carrying rifles.

I turn back to Traven.

"I never pictured you as the entourage type."

"It wasn't my idea. The Magistrate arranged it. Now that we're this close to the crusade's first goal, me, Mimir, even the head mechanics . . . we all have bodyguards."

"Or surveillance."

"No. I believe the Magistrate is sincere in wanting to protect us, but I'm afraid that for now protection and surveillance amount to the same thing. I can't go anywhere without an armed escort."

"Fuck."

He looks me over.

"That's a nice coat."

"You like it? I lost my other one. Also my cigarettes. Do you have any?"

He stops and takes out a couple of Maledictions. Lights mine.

"I'm sorry things have become complicated," he says. "But think of it this way: in the mess and confusion here, there's no better time for you to go. I might even be able to help. Create a diversion of some kind."

I shake my head, blowing smoke in the direction of his goon squad.

"Thanks, but no thanks. I'm not going without you."

"I appreciate that, but you might not get another chance."

"I won't. We won't."

I uncork the Aqua Regia and take a nice pull. Turning, I hold it up in the direction of the meat mountains. They both shake their heads.

"That means that wherever the Magistrate's rolling this shit show, we're going to ride it through to the end."

"I'm afraid you're right."

I look down at myself.

"You really like the coat? I don't look like a kid thinking about shooting up his high school?"

"You always look like that."

I have to laugh. I can't help it, we are so truly fucked.

Me and Traven sit by the fire. I drink and smoke his cigarettes. I don't rush the bottle, but eventually it's gone. I toss it into the flames.

"Are you all right?" says Traven.

"Never better. But I'm in the mood to kill someone. Who don't you like around here?"

"Please don't talk like that."

"What about your bodyguards? Which one should I do first? The one on the left looks extra stupid."

"They're as much my responsibility as I am theirs, so please don't try."

I get up.

"You're right. They're too obvious."

I stagger a few steps away from the fire.

"Where are you going?" says Traven.

"To pick a fight."

"With who?"

"Anyone."

Instead, I fall into a drunken sleep in the cab of a half-dismantled backhoe.

I WAKE UP with a bad headache, a sore back, and aching stitches. But I'm all right.

I didn't pick a fight last night, but I am keeping my other promise. My mind is a complete blank. No memories. No sorrow. No more bad dreams for me. This is Day One. Just like when Mason Faim first sent me to Hell. Only this time, I'm not the scared, privileged little shit who fell into a world of monsters. I'm Sandman Slim. The monster who kills monsters. And I'll kill every one of these road hogs if it gets me an inch closer to home.

REPAIRS TAKE FOUR days. It gives the havoc time to heal, but it also gives them time to become restless and bored. Hunter-gatherers need to hunt and gather. Sitting around, people drink too much and shoot off their mouths, enough that fights break out all over camp. Even the conscripts, usually a pack of passive little bunnies that keep to themselves, form a few gangs that prey on the weaker ones. The camp is about to explode. There's practically no one at the next religious service.

On the third day of sitting on our asses, the dog pack runs the Magistrate out to see the obelisk. Gisco can't ride a bike anymore, but with some trucker speed and Cherry's potions, he's okay enough to drive a car. Daja scores him a silver Hellion chop-top convertible that looks like the love child of a giant squid and a torpedo. The Magistrate rides with him into the desert.

When we reach the obelisk, he's the first to get to it, gently running his fingers over the thing like it's made of parchment and not marble.

"It is stunning. Even more beautiful than the Empress said it would be."

"It's wonderful," says Daja.

Wanuri, Johnny, and Frederickson mumble "Yeah" vaguely in a way that sounds more like "This is what we killed and died for all this time?"

"So that's an obelisk," says Doris. "It reminds me of the marker on Tootsie's, my cat's, grave. Though it's a bit taller, of course."

I wash the dust out of my mouth with some water and hand the bottle to Doris. She drinks and passes it on.

I call to the Magistrate, "What does it say?"

"I have no idea," he says brightly. "It is very old. The markings are an early, degenerate form of Hellion that I do not know."

"Then what the fuck good is it?" says Johnny in a tone that visibly annoys Daja. I don't say anything, but I definitely agree with his sentiment. "You brought us all this way and almost killed Gisco, and for what?"

"Calm down, Johnny," Daja says.

"No. It is all right," says the Magistrate. "I knew all along that there was a chance I could not decipher the markings. That is why we have a specialist."

Now I understand the bodyguards.

"You mean Father Traven," I say.

The Magistrate turns to me. "Of course. While I have some facility with languages—"

"No shit."

"—he is an expert in ancient mystical tongues that even I am not acquainted with."

"Then let's fucking get him out here and be on our way," shouts Johnny.

Daja walks over and gets right in his face.

"Not. Another. Word. I mean it."

He holds up a hand and makes a gesture by his mouth like he's turning a lock.

"All in good time," the Magistrate says. "You have noticed the tension among the havoc. We will bring the father out here quietly and at a discreet hour. Should anything go wrong—if, for instance, he does not have the proper reference books or needs time with a proper translation—we will deal with it among ourselves and no one else. We must do nothing to further damage morale. Does everyone understand?"

We nod and grunt grudging affirmatives.

"Good. When we return to the havoc we will smile. We will be cheerful and optimistic. But we will reveal nothing else for now. Leave all revelations to me."

Everybody agrees, but it's a bullshit plan.

I say, "Shouldn't we give them something? Otherwise they're going to be suspicious."

"I hate to admit it," says Wanuri, "but he's right. There's bad talk around camp. That we're lost. That the crusade itself is a kind of punishment."

The Magistrate thinks about it for a second, then says, "Since you brought it up, do you have any bright ideas, Mr. Pitts?"

I point back the way we came.

"In one of those towns we passed, there was a roadside store. Let's see if there's anything left. It isn't much, but everyone likes candy and presents."

"That's pretty fucking optimistic of you," says Daja.

"I know. Maybe the place is picked clean. Maybe there was never anything at all. But it's worth a look."

"Indeed it is," the Magistrate says. "And since you noticed the shop, you will lead us there."

"Okay."

Fuck. There better be something there. M&M's. A pecan log. Some goddamn bubble gum. *Anything*.

The Magistrate gets back in the car with Gisco and yells, "'Lay on, Macduff, and damned be him who first cries "Hold!"'"

"What?"

"It's a line from *Macbeth*."

"What does it mean?"

He beams at me.

"It means lead the way, Mr. Pitts, to sweets and glory."

Wanuri shakes her head. Johnny gives me a *"don't blow this"* smile. Doris winks. Gisco gives me a thumbs-up.

I don't bother looking at Daja.

Gisco guns the convertible. I kick the bike to life and take off. Hit the throttle and take point.

I look cool and keep my eyes peeled for the right town, but inside all I'm thinking is *Give me one damn box of Tootsie Pops*.

A half hour later I spot the shop. An hour after that, we pop the trunk on Gisco's convertible and it's goddamn Christmas day in camp. You'd be surprised how much handfuls of stale chocolate, bubble solution, stupid hats, and cotton candy can improve the moods of even the most psychotic killers. I'm not saying it's a party in camp that night, but it's the most relaxed night in the havoc since we looted the casinos.

I find a couple of dried-out fortune cookies in plastic wrappers. As Traven walks up, I hand him one. We crack them open.

He says, "You go first."

I hold the fortune up so it catches light from the fire.

"'Your smile will tell you what warms your heart.'"

"Dear God," says Traven. "I'm an optimist and even I think that's awful."

I agree. "What's yours?"

"'With a cheerful demeanor, career opportunities abound,'" he says.

"Aren't we the luckiest assholes in Hell?"

"Without a doubt."

I take a bite of my cookie.

"Thank you for not saying 'in bed' at the end. I always thought that was a stupid joke."

"Me too," says Traven.

The cookie is terrible. It tastes like sugary dust. I eat every bite.

INSTEAD OF WAITING to sneak Traven out to the obelisk, we move camp the next day while people are still on a sugar high . . . and of course the chains on the flatbeds break just a few miles down the road. Later in the day, a semi boils over and needs to have its radiator replaced.

Just like that, everybody's mood goes black again. The evil gremlins are back at work. A cut here. A slice there. And the whole crusade dies in its tracks. At least no one is looking at me anymore. Especially Daja and Wanuri. I'm still not sure what would have happened the other day if Doris hadn't called Wanuri out. I doubt I'd be around to worry about it. That leaves the sixty-four-dollar question: If I'm not the rat, who is?

And why?

After we make camp for the night, the Magistrate, Traven, and the rest of the dog pack pile into Gisco's car and drive to the obelisk. Traven moons over it almost as much as the Magistrate.

"It's amazing. I've never seen anything like it," he says.

The Magistrate stands next to him.

"But do you recognize it, Father?"

Traven nods, not taking his eyes off the marble.

"It's a proto-Hellion script. Pre-Pandemonium, I'd guess."

"Guessing is not good enough, I am afraid. Can you translate it?"

"Yes," says Traven. "But I'll need my books and a day or two. Some of the figures are worn and I'll have to work out what they are by trial and error."

"But you *can* do it?"

"I can."

The Magistrate claps his hands, and for the first time in days, you can feel the pack relax. Doris hugs Barbora and Wanuri.

Daja goes to the Magistrate.

"You did it. You've brought us through the first step of the crusade," she says. "Thank you."

He puts an arm around her and gazes at the obelisk.

"Thank you for believing in me."

He turns to the rest of us.

"Thank you all for believing. The next two days will be momentous for us all. It is time to tell the others."

I still think the Magistrate is crazier than a clown car full of rats, but I keep that to myself. As the others head back to their vehicles, I hang back with Traven.

"You sure you can do this?"

"I'm positive."

"Does it say anything about why we're lugging a howitzer through the Mojave?"

"With luck, I'll be able to tell you soon."

"You're going to need more than luck. If these lunatics don't get some good news, they're going to tear each other apart."

He looks at me.

"Isn't that what you want? For the havoc to destroy itself?"

"Not when we're in the *middle* of it. A riot is like a tire fire. Only fun if you're seeing it from a great distance."

"Shake a leg, lovebirds," shouts Wanuri.

On the way back to camp, I take out the butcher knife Doris gave me and slice off my bandages. Toss them in air and let the breeze carry them away.

Daja looks at my bullet wound.

"It didn't heal up so bad."

"One more for the collection."

"You should learn to duck."

"No one tells me these things until it's too late."

She gets up and dusts herself off.

"I've decided not to kill you," Daja says.

"Why's that?"

"You helped with Gisco and haven't been entirely useless around camp."

"When were you going to do it?"

"Tonight. Now that we know the father can do the translation."

"That's funny," I say.

"Why?"

"I was going to do the same thing to you and make it look like Wanuri did it."

We look at the other woman. She frowns at us.

"Let's just keep that between us," says Daja.

"Yeah. It's probably for the best."

I get out the water bottle I filled with Aqua Regia. We both have a drink.

Wanuri is still looking at us. I offer her the bottle. She sniffs it and hands it back.

To Daja she says, "I told you this one is crazy. Don't let him make you crazy, too."

"We're celebrating," Daja says.

"What?"

"It's our anniversary," I say.

"Anniversary of what?"

"Not murdering each other."

Wanuri shakes her head.

"It's too late for you, girl. He's dragged you into his madness."

Daja takes out a chocolate bar and gives it to her.

"Relax," she says. "It's going to be all right. Everything is going to be all right now."

Wanuri looks at the obelisk, not entirely convinced, but she gobbles down the chocolate anyway.

WE MOVE CAMP the next day and set up the havoc around the obelisk. A paddy wagon takes some conscripts back to the roadside store. They drag a desk and chair from the manager's office and set it up by the obelisk for Traven. He lays out his old books and begins copying the symbols from each side of the obelisk. The damned thing is so tall he has to use the Magistrate's spyglass to copy the highest carvings. This isn't going to be a quick job.

The Magistrate knows it and is a one-man pep squad. He wanders around the havoc with his map, pointing out to anyone who'll hold still where we were, where we are, and, maybe, where we're going. It's pure hustle, like those celebrity bus tours of L.A. Dumb as they are, they make people feel warm and special and closer to their TV gods. It's the same thing here. He points out the thrilling sights, the exciting points of interest, and hints that maybe if we're lucky, the ghost of James Dean will swing by to give us all rides in his Porsche Spyder.

Traven has been working for around eight straight hours when a storm blows up in the distance. He's sketched all four sides of the pyramid and copied all the symbols from one. Everybody stops what they're doing to watch the approaching clouds.

"Is it a sandstorm?" says Doris.

"It sure isn't rain," says Wanuri.

"Do you think it ever rains in the Tenebrae?" says Barbora, who's hardly said a word since her sister died.

I say, "Nothing happens out here because nothing is supposed to be here. That's why it's so boring. It's the Fresno of damnation."

"That doesn't mean it never rains," says Johnny. "Back home, even the deep desert gets the occasional monsoon."

"Have you seen any wallabies down here? This isn't back home."

"What makes you such an expert on the Tenebrae?" says Daja.

"Maybe God told him. Or the Devil," says Wanuri.

"Who's been with the Magistrate the longest?" I say.

Daja and Gisco raise their hands, along with a couple of grease monkeys who were wandering by.

"How long have you been with him? Months? Years?"

Gisco and Daja look at each other.

"I don't know," she says. "Time is funny here. But I'd say a few months."

Gisco nods in agreement.

"In all that time have you ever seen anything like that?"

Gisco mutters something like "Nuh," and shakes his head. Daja shakes hers, too.

"Never."

"It's a funny bugger, don't you think?" says Johnny. "It keeps changing size and shape."

Frederickson says, "More like a swarm than clouds." He looks puzzled. "They don't have locusts down here, do they? I hate those wiggling bastards."

This chatter is pissing me off. I take a drink from the water bottle.

"I told you. There's nothing alive out here."

Doris shields her eyes and stares into the distance.

"I have to agree with Johnny. It's more like a swarm of bees or flock of birds than storm clouds."

Barbora says, "Maybe it's a sign from God."

"If it is he isn't happy to see us," I say. "Where's the Magistrate's telescope?"

"Your boyfriend has it," says Wanuri.

"Wait here. I'm going to fucking settle this."

Traven is copying symbols on the far side of the obelisk, so he doesn't even see me take the spyglass. I bring it back to the others, holding it over my head like a war club.

I point to each of them.

"It's not rain. It's not locusts. It's not sand. And it sure as shit isn't the Almighty."

Daja folds her arms.

"So, what is it?"

I extend the telescope and hold it up to my eye.

And just about piss myself.

"Where's the Magistrate?"

Daja hears something in my voice.

"What's wrong? What did you see?"

"Where's the fucking Magistrate?" I yell.

"He's over in the motor home. What's wrong?"

I speak to her as quietly and calmly as I can.

"Round up everyone and get them in the center of camp. Make sure they have guns and ammo."

"What the hell did you see?" she says.

"The worst thing you can imagine."

Before she can ask another stupid question, I run to the motor home and bang on the door.

The Magistrate opens it and says, "Pitts. What is wrong?"

I climb up a step.

"Do you have any Spiritus Dei?"

"Of course. It's with Mimir."

"A lot?"

"Gallons," he says.

"Good. We need to pour it on all the ammo."

"What are you talking about. What is wrong?"

I hand him the telescope.

"Look."

He peers in the direction of the cloud. Adjusts the glass several times, then takes it from his eye.

"Are those angels?"

"Damn right. And those aren't bouquets they're carrying. They're swords."

He comes down from the motor home and we run to Cherry's ambulance.

"Mimir will be able to tell us if you are right," he says.

"I am."

"What if you are? Perhaps they are angels of the Lord, come to aid us on our mission."

We reach the ambulance and I slam open the door. Cherry is lying on the floor, twitching with convulsions and foaming at the mouth.

"I don't think they're coming to help us."

The Magistrate swallows and nods. It's the first time I've ever seen him truly spooked. He grabs a couple of gallon jugs of Spiritus Dei from the ambulance. As he climbs out he says, "With this on our bullets, will we be able to destroy them?"

"Spiritus Dei will kill pretty much anything, but I'm not sure about angels. But it *will* slow them down until we come up with a better idea."

He heads out with the jugs to the center of camp where they're handing out weapons.

"You stay with Mimir," he says. "I will rally the havoc."

Right. Great. This is exactly what I wanted. We're about to be overrun by flying armored assholes with flaming swords and I'm on babysitting duty. I look down at Cherry. She makes choking sounds, so I roll her on her side and use a rag to wipe the spit off her face. The ambulance is full of medical supplies, but I don't know what 90 percent of them are for. I was never great at healing hoodoo, but we're all about to die and there's no one around to see me, so I improvise a quick spell.

Cherry does one more big convulsion and coughs up a lot of white spittle. She opens her eyes and looks at me blearily.

"What the fuck is happening?"

"Congratulations. I actually believe you're an oracle, but you're a shitty one with bad timing."

"What are you talking about?"

I help her sit up and point to the approaching cloud.

"That was my vision," she says. "Angels."

"Do you have anything more helpful to say?"

"Yeah. They're going to kill us and it's your fault."

"Why is it *my* fault?"

She sits up and I help her out of the ambulance. She looks at the angels, and then looks at me as if I'm the stupidest person in Hell.

"Who do you think they're looking for, Shit-for-Brains?"

They're close enough that I can see individual angels in the swarm. Their Gladiuses—their flaming angelic swords—crackle with power and flash like lightning.

"Well, go ahead," says Cherry. "Save us."

"What? How?"

"Give yourself up."

"Yeaaaaah . . . I'm not doing that."

"Are you going to do *anything*?"

"Yes—I'm going to go out there and fight them."

"By yourself?"

"If I have to. Do you have any better ideas?"

"Yeah. Let's run. This ambulance is gassed up. Let the Magistrate and the Lost Boys distract them while we get away."

"Right. I'm sure no one will spot that and then we'll have angels *and* the havoc after us."

"How are you going to fight them?"

That's right. Cherry doesn't know that my angel half can manifest its own Gladius.

I say, "Like this—"

—and nothing happens.

I look at my hands and there isn't the slightest flicker of flame.

"Anytime now!" Cherry screams. The swarm is right over the havoc.

I think about screaming, too.

So, let's see. I'm still fast and I'm still strong. Check. And I still heal quick. Check. But I didn't think about taking the Gladius out for a test drive. In retrospect, I should probably have checked on it earlier.

Without warning, the mass of angels dives and tears through the camp like a tornado, knocking aside vehicles and blowing members of the havoc into the air, where they smash to the ground like sacks of meat or are sliced in half by fiery swords. The remaining havoc pours automatic gunfire up at them. It doesn't kill them or even penetrate their golden armor, but it drives them back into the sky. The murder cloud climbs out of the range of the rifles. But one angel descends and hovers above the camp, his wings wide and his sword high.

By the time he starts jabbering, I'm already on the roof of an eighteen-wheeler with a plastic bottle I stole from the ambulance. When I get to the top, I slice my wrist with the knife Doris gave me.

The angel bellows, "We have no quarrel with you. Give us the Abomination and you may pass in safety."

It's no big surprise when no one in camp has a fucking clue what he's talking about. I pull the Colt and fire off a couple of shots into the air.

I yell, "Hey, space monkey. I'm right over here. Come on over and let's have a drink."

I wave the jug at him and pretend to take a swig.

He doesn't need to be asked twice. Flyboy shoots down at me like a meteor, but stops just before he hits the top of the eighteen-wheeler, drifting down for a gentle landing.

Show-off.

He drops his Gladius down to his side and we walk toward each other. We're only about three feet apart when he stops.

"I didn't think you possessed enough honor to show yourself."

"I never could resist an asshole in uniform."

He looks around.

"Still, you did let some of your compatriots die for you."

"Don't kid a kidder. We both know you're going to kill everyone here whether they gave me up or not."

"True. But now I have the pleasure of killing you face-to-face."

"What's your name?"

"I am Simiel of the Thrones."

"A throne. Mr. Muninn's furniture movers. What are you doing here?"

"We no longer serve the God who would allow damned souls to pollute the Heavenly presence."

"You're spoiled brats who don't want kids from the wrong side of the tracks drinking in your malt shop."

He looks me up and down.

"You're less than I thought you'd be. Not much more than the pathetic creatures you hide among."

"You angels always did like the sound of your own voices. What are we doing here? Are you going to take me Upstairs so you can kill me in front of your frat pals?"

He slowly raises his Gladius.

"I have led the army that found you, so it will be my privilege to destroy you."

I hold out the bottle.

"At least have a drink with me first."

"I will not drink with the Abomination."

"Just one," I say, and flick my wrist, splashing liquid from the bottle onto his face.

His free hand quickly comes up to rub his eyes.

"It burns! What have you done to me?"

"Don't worry. It's just bleach," I say. "And some of my blood."

I hold up my bleeding wrist and he staggers back, letting his Gladius go so he can use both hands to wipe my blood from his face.

"What have you done to me!" he yells. "Unclean!"

Thrones are all morons and they sure as hell aren't fighters. I grab the ceremonial golden dagger from Simiel's belt. Still blinded, he tries to shoulder-butt me away, but I'm almost as strong as he is.

"Let me help you get clean."

I slash the dagger across his throat where his armor doesn't quite reach. And slash him again, making a real mess of both of us. Pearly-red angel blood splatters my new shirt and coat.

I told you I was hard on clothes.

He throws his arms and wings wide, trying to scream. But all he can do is gurgle a bloody prayer as I shove the knife into him up to the hilt. I'm normally a lot more efficient at killing things, but I want to make sure every soul, Hellion, and winged creep know exactly what I'm doing.

When he's just about dead, I pick him up and throw him off the top of the trailer. I guess he dies on the way down because he never hits the ground.

There's a moment of silence, then a shriek from above. I look up, expecting to see every fucking angel in the sky speeding down at me. Instead, the angelic swarm bursts apart like a Fourth of July fireworks display. Angels fly apart in every direction, their Gladiuses flailing uselessly as they spin out of control. The swarm explodes again, but this time the fireworks are fainter as some head back up into the sky and others fall, dying.

It takes me a minute to figure out what the hell is going on.

Turns out a second group of angels dive-bombed through the center of the first and are happily ripping them to shreds. They're a smaller group, but they're faster and they look better armed. Whatever it is about them, Simiel's group backs off fast, fluttering away into the dim Tenebrae sky with their tail feathers between their legs. But before they disappear, they have time for one final fuck-you.

A group swirls past the obelisk with their Gladiuses raised, and smash it to pieces.

Besides being morons, Thrones really carry a grudge.

As the second group of angels settles to the ground near center camp, I climb down from the truck. I'm still holding the golden dagger and dripping with Simiel's blood when I make it over to them. The Magistrate, as cool and calm as ever, is chatting amiably with the tallest angel, a woman with cascading red hair. His smile fades a little when he sees what a mess I am, but he beckons me over.

He says, "Mr. Pitts, you have visitors. And, it appears, benefactors."

The redheaded angel bows her head at me slightly and I do the same to her. She's scarred, and her armor is dented and scratched. So are the other angels with her. They're fighters, no question.

"Thanks for stopping by."

I reach out to shake her hand, but when I get a look at my filthy mitt, I pull it back.

"We're friends of Hesediel," she says. "I believe you knew her."

I sure did. I watched her kill herself to destroy Black Milk, a drug that might have prolonged the war in Heaven forever. I don't respect many angels, but she was one I hated to see go.

I wipe Simiel's knife clean on my pants and put it in my pocket.

"I knew her. She was the only angel I ever liked."

"That's what I understood. Perhaps, though, we can change your attitude."

I shake my hands, trying to get the blood off.

"I seriously doubt that."

An angel from the back of the group steps forward. She's shorter than the others.

"For fuck sake, Jim. Stop being such a dick."

I blink to make sure I'm not seeing things.

"Alice?"

She rolls her eyes.

"No. It's Veronica Lake. Now clean yourself up so I can hug you. We have a lot to talk about."

THE MAGISTRATE'S MOTOR home is big, but it's not this big. He's at his table with Daja next to him, and Traven and Cherry next to her. Most of the dog pack—including Billy, who's finally back on his feet—are crammed together at the far end of the motor home like rush hour on a Tokyo subway. I'm at the other end with Alice and Vehuel, the redheaded angel. The other four angels she brought with her are standing guard outside, like anyone is going to bother us after what just happened.

"That was quite the performance you put on out there, Mr. Pitts," says the Magistrate. "Do you have anything to say for yourself?"

I take out Simiel's blade.

"Yeah. Anybody want to check out my cool new knife?"

"I do!" says Doris.

I give it to Traven to pass back to her.

Alice says, "I think what your friends want is to understand how you were able to take an angel's knife in the first place."

"And why an army of rebel angels was after you," the Magistrate says.

"That too," Alice says.

I look around. Not a lot of friendly faces right now.

"That wasn't an army. It was more like a street gang come to shake us down for being in their territory."

"I doubt that," says the Magistrate. "I was under the impression they were looking for you in particular."

"Yeah. It kind of looked that way, didn't it?"

"Yes," the Magistrate says dryly. "Especially when you said, 'Here I am.'"

"Right."

"And why did that one call you an Abomination?" says Wanuri.

I look at Alice. She squeezes my hand and for the first time in a long time I don't feel quite so alone.

"*The* Abomination is what he said. If you're going to call me that name, get it right."

The Magistrate says, "And what sort of Abomination are you precisely, Mr. Pitts?"

Doris passes the golden blade back to me.

I catch Traven's eye, and he gives a little "*I'll back your play*" shrug. I shake my head. "Hell. I'm tired of this. My real name is James Stark. My father was an angel, which makes me a nephilim. That's why he called me Abomination."

"You told me your father tried to shoot you," says Doris.

"Different father."

"I see."

The Magistrate says, "It's my understanding that 'nephilim' is plural. I believe that 'niphal' is the singular."

"Thank you, Mr. Rogers."

Gisco is propped against the wall on crutches. He grunts

a few syllables at me. I recognize them from the other night. The Magistrate looks at him.

"I don't understand, Gisco. What are you trying to say?"

I put the knife back in my pocket.

"He's saying that my other name is Sandman Slim."

A couple of mouths drop open. A few eyebrows go up. The Magistrate sits up a little straighter. Johnny looks around at everybody, then at me.

"Sandman what? What the fuck kind of name is that? Some kind of TV cowboy?"

The Magistrate half turns in his chair.

"Sandman Slim was a rather renowned killer in Hell. But he disappeared. I take it that is who you claim to be?"

"No. The angels that just kicked your ass and the one that I killed with his own fucking knife. *That's* who says I'm Sandman Slim."

The Magistrate turns to Vehuel. She's smiling to herself, amused by the tension among the mortals.

"My dear lady celestial, can you shed any light on this? Is this man, our Mr. Pitts, the half angel called Sandman Slim?"

"Oh yes," she says. "He's Sandman Slim and James Stark and the Abomination. All these names are his."

"And why do you smile at him like that?"

"Because he's every bit as ridiculous as I was told he would be."

"And who told you this?"

"God," says Alice.

The mouths go open. The eyebrows that had settled down go back up. You get the idea.

Johnny is still the holdout.

"God doesn't know this waste of space. It's a trick. He's a con man." He points at Vehuel. "How do we even know you're who you say you are? You could be in on it with him. You're just a bitch on wings to me, sweetheart."

I almost feel bad for Johnny.

Faster than anyone can see, Vehuel's arm is up and her Gladius is aimed right between Johnny's eyes. When she speaks, her voice rattles the walls.

"You are a fool and an offense to the Lord and his emissaries. You will not speak again or you will be silenced."

Johnny holds up his hands, scared but trying to save as much of his face as he has left.

"All right now. No offense meant. I'm mostly mad at that wombat standing next to you."

Alice prods me with her elbow.

"I think he means you, wombat."

The Magistrate laces his fingers together. Takes them apart.

"Mr. Pitts, Mr. Sandman, Mr. Stark—and any other names we do not know . . ."

"Those about cover it."

"Good. Of all the places in Perdition you could have been, why did you come to us?"

"I told you: I don't know. I was on that mountain, I walked down, and there you were."

He nods, thinking.

"I thought we had reached an understanding, a state of trust between you, Daja, and myself," he says. "Why did you not tell us of your other life?"

"Did I mention I was fucking murdered? Even when I first landed in Hell, I wasn't this off balance."

"Still. It's disappointing."

"I watched you massacre whole towns because they annoyed you. It made me wonder what's this guy going to do if he finds out I'm an Abomination."

"*The* Abomination," says Vehuel.

"Thanks for the reminder."

"You raise a fair point," the Magistrate says. "But from now on, no more secrets."

"I'm fresh out of those right now."

"I am glad to hear it."

"Hello, Alice," says Traven. "I'm Liam."

They shake hands.

I say, "Besides the Magistrate, Father Traven is the only one around here with any brains. I knew him back in L.A. after you, you know . . ."

"Died," she says. "I won't be offended if you say it. You're dead, too."

"Yeah and it's weird."

Alice looks across the table.

"Hi, Cherry," she says.

"Hi, Alice," rasps Cherry through her respirator.

"Love the fur coat. Or did you just stop shaving your back?"

"You're not fooling anyone with that armor. You look like you're trick-or-treating for UNICEF."

"Cherry?" says the Magistrate. "Mimir? How many names do *you* have, my oracle?"

She puts her hand over his.

"I am your Mimir."

"Shit, Cherry. Take off that stupid mask so we can understand you," I say.

The Magistrate reaches over and pulls the mask down off
her nose and mouth.

"This, too, was a lie?"

She puts both of her hands over his.

"I had to disguise myself. I was afraid of people from my
old life. People like him," she says, looking at me. "Cherry
was my name in the mortal world. Before I knew my powers
and my true calling."

Alice cocks her head.

"Did she tell you that back in the mortal world, she used
to sell overpriced Hello Kitties and teddy bears?"

"They weren't overpriced," snaps Cherry. "They were
imports."

"And the great power she's talking about? Back on Earth
she used it to turn herself into jailbait, not to see the future,"
says Alice.

"Fuck you, bitch!"

Cherry takes a swing at her, but the Magistrate grabs her
and pushes her back into her chair.

"We will talk later, Mimir."

"You still believe in me, right? I'm still your oracle. Even
Jimmy believes in me and he hates me."

"I don't hate you. Okay, sometimes. But I do believe you're
an oracle."

"I will keep your endorsement in mind, Sandman Slim. As
I will the fact that she lied to me about you."

The threat hangs there, but for once it's not aimed at me,

so who cares? So I say, "Please don't call me that. It's a terrible name."

"Strewth," mumbles Johnny.

"You raise an interesting point," says the Magistrate. "Beyond your name, what are we to tell the havoc about you?"

"Just tell them that I got lucky. Or that I'm crazy. Most of them already think it. Besides, they don't care about me. There are four angels having a smoke outside and two in here. I think people are a lot more interested in them than my ugly ass."

"I thought I was finally getting a handle on you," Daja says angrily.

"And I was trying to stay out of Tartarus."

"Was anything you said true? Starting with you up on that mountain?"

"Everything about the mountain is true. Someday I'm going to find Death and dance on his balls to thank him."

"I still maintain that Death sent Stark to us for a reason," says Traven. "And I think the presence of these angels proves it."

"You knew who he was this whole time, too, didn't you?" says the Magistrate.

"Yes. I did."

"You were friends in the mortal world?"

"Yes."

"So, your chief loyalty was to him and not to me, who saved you, or to our cause."

Traven runs his fingers along the edge of the table.

"Speak freely," the Magistrate says.

Traven looks into his eyes. "Very well. The thing is, I was

happy in Blue Heaven. The havoc appeared from nowhere and burned my home to the ground. You slaughtered my friends in front of me. Except where it comes to Stark, I've been loyal to you. But it was mostly out of fear."

"I see. Thank you, Father. That is food for thought," the Magistrate says. "Since this seems to be a day for secret sharing, I will share with you one of mine. I'm sure all of you are curious as to what it is that we have been carrying with us all this time. It is a weapon. A weapon that could turn the tide of the war in Heaven."

He looks at me.

"But, of course, you knew that already, didn't you, Mr. Stark?"

"Just the weapon part. I didn't want you to point it at me, so I never mentioned it."

"Naturally. But the truth is that I could have pointed it at you all day and all night and you would have been perfectly safe because the gun lacks one key component."

"The Lux Occisor," says Traven.

"Exactly," says the Magistrate. "The weapon could blow apart the gates and walls of Heaven or dispatch its enemies to oblivion. But it is a dead thing without the Light Killer."

Something occurs to me.

"Let me guess: the light the gun wants to kill . . . it's Lucifer, isn't it?"

"It was at one time. The weapon was built for a final assault on Lucifer and his army. But it was never used because God sent the great betrayer over the walls himself with a sword fashioned from a thunderbolt."

"And you need the sword to work the gun."

"Very good, my boy. You have a good head for these things."

"I killed a lot of generals over the years."

"I only wish that our crusade were that simple. We had completed the first task. We found the obelisk. It would have led us to the Lux Occisor, but now it lies in ruins," the Magistrate says. He drops back in the chair exhausted. "I must admit, at the moment I am at a loss as to what to do next. Do we wander from town to town forever, hoping for more scraps of information, while above us, armies of darkness seek to destroy God and all his works?"

"I've copied one side of the obelisk. I might still be able to figure it out," says Traven.

"There's no need," says Vehuel. "I believe we can help you on your search."

"You know what the obelisk says?"

"No. But we believe that we know the whereabouts of the sword."

"That's wonderful. Can you take us there?"

Vehuel takes a step closer to the Magistrate.

"Perhaps. But I need you to swear an oath that the weapon you carry will only be used against the enemies of the Lord and will be returned to him once we have put down the rebellion."

"And open Heaven to all these losers," I say. "Don't forget that part."

"Of course," says Vehuel.

"What does opening Heaven mean?" says Wanuri.

I say, "It means you get to choose. You can stay Downtown, live in a shit hole like Pandemonium or the Dust Bowl out here, or you can ride your Harley straight through the pearly gates."

"We could leave Hell and go to Heaven?"

"Or stay. The whole point is you get to choose."

"And this was your idea?"

"Sort of."

"Of course it was his idea. He's really not as dumb as he looks," says Alice.

"I agree to all of your terms, Vehuel," says the Magistrate. "We, too, want the war ended as quickly as possible."

"Very well. We have a bargain," she says.

"How far away is the sword?"

"It isn't far, but it's not wise for you to travel in the open anymore. We will take you there through the secret channel. An underground river that is known to very few in Perdition."

"Excellent. When can we begin?"

"Soon. The river isn't far, but it's over a set of high hills and many of your vehicles are damaged. We will help repair them."

"Since when are angels grease monkeys?" says Frederickson.

"Since forever," I say. "Angels built the fucking universe. I think they can strip a diesel engine."

Daja says, "Magistrate, things aren't good in the havoc. Morale is low. People are beginning to doubt the crusade. I don't think the attack today is going to help the situation."

"I will speak to them. Now that we have angels sent directly from the Almighty on our side, they will see the value of our work."

"I hope so."

"Trust me."

Johnny clears his throat.

"Excuse me. Now that there's a plan and everything is right with the world, can I have a word with this drongo?"

I look around, and realize he's pointing at me. *I'm* the drongo?

What the fuck is a drongo?

"You may address him, but not me," says Vehuel.

"Much obliged, ma'am."

He looks at me.

"If I understand things right, you're some big-time killer. Murdered Hellions and generals and such?"

"That's right."

"And there's talk you met Lucifer along the way."

I look at Wanuri. She's the only one I told about meeting him.

"What's your point?"

"My point is you cut up that angel easy enough today. Why didn't you kill Lucifer?"

"He's not exactly a regular angel."

"Did you even try?"

Before I can come up with a way to answer, Vehuel says, "I believe you knew Lucifer well at one point. Even called on him as an ally."

"You're not helping," I tell her. "And that was later. When I was in L.A."

"Having tea and cakes with old Scratch, were you?" says Johnny. "That must have been cozy."

"It's called a strategic alliance. And I was trying to save the world."

"What about saving us down here?" he shouts.

"If it makes you feel any better, I stabbed him once when he pissed me off."

"But you let him live? Bollocks to you, mate. From now on, just keep your distance."

"I wouldn't order the Abomination around," says Alice. "Not if you want to make it to Heaven."

"Fuck Heaven and fuck him."

I don't need to read micro-expressions to see that Frederickson, Billy, and Barbora are with Johnny on this. Gisco seems all right. Hell, I think he's the only one having a good time. I'm not sure about Wanuri and, especially, Daja.

Vehuel looks at the dirty pocket where I put the golden knife.

"I take it that you intend to keep Simiel's dagger?"

"That's exactly what I intend."

"Be careful," she says. "Some angels won't appreciate you having it."

"You mean a dirty Abomination?"

"I mean someone who, until very recently, was as much our enemy as the rebellious angels."

"But now you and me are on the same side, so relax."

"Angels aren't exactly kick-back-and-relax types. But you know that," says Alice.

She looks at Vehuel.

"I'll talk to him."

"I don't need a talking-to," I say.

"You sure do, dummy," says Alice.

The Magistrate says, "I think that we should end our meeting for now. As Daja said, the havoc will be getting restless. If our angel guests will join us outside, I will address the camp and tell them the wonderful news that you will lead us to our next stop on the crusade."

"What are we supposed to say about *him*," says Daja, giving me the evil eye.

"Nothing. He remains Mr. Pitts for now. A lost soul crazy enough and lucky enough to trick an angel into destroying itself."

The Magistrate leads Vehuel outside. Alice goes next and I follow her.

Traven claps me on the back and nods to Alice before going back to his camper to write everything down. Always the record keeper.

Daja shoots me a look as she goes past. Johnny spits by my feet. Barbora and Billy don't look at me. Gisco says something to Alice and she says something back that makes him smile.

"Great. Now that you have your wings, you can understand languages, too."

"Yep. Every one ever spoken."

"Show-off."

"Jealous."

Doris comes out and pats me on the cheek.

"I knew you were a good boy."

Wanuri stops in front of us. She looks at Alice.

"So, you're an angel."

"That's how I got the wings."

Wanuri hooks a thumb at me.

"You knew him from before. Back on Earth."

"We used to sleep in the same bed. Getting to know him was inevitable."

"Your *boyfriend*? You're a brave woman. Fifty times a day some of us have plotted his tragic demise."

"Trust me, I know how you feel."

I look at them both.

"You know I'm standing right here, right?"

Wanuri says, "I suppose if an old love comes all the way to Hell to fight for someone, that person must have some redeeming qualities."

"No I don't."

"Yes he does. He just can't control what comes out of his mouth," says Alice.

"But he really tried to open Hell for us?"

"He really did."

"All right," Wanuri says. "I hereby declare you not entirely useless."

"Does that mean you're not going to shoot me in the back?"

"We'll see. Can't speak for Johnny, though. He's mean when he gets like this."

"I got that impression."

"Take care, Mr. and Mrs. Pitts," says Wanuri, heading back to center camp.

Before I can say anything, Alice pulls me down to sit on the steps of the motor home.

"I'm sorry you're really dead," she says.

"Me too. Now I know what all these poor saps feel like. When I was alive and in Hell, I always thought I'd find a way home. Later, when I had the Room of Thirteen Doors, I didn't think about real damnation much at all. Was Heaven hard, too?"

"At first. I missed you. I missed our friends. I missed burritos and sashimi. But I got used to it. There's a lot to do and a lot of very interesting, very nice people."

"It sounds horrible."

"It really isn't. How's that girl of yours? Candy?"

"Candy. I don't know how she is. I wasn't exactly rational when you were killed and I wasn't even there. Candy saw me get murdered, so I have a feeling she's not in good shape."

"I'm so sorry."

"She killed the guy who stuck me, though. I keep hoping I run into him down here. That would be fun."

"See? That's exactly the kind of thinking that gets you in trouble. Focus. One war at a time. You have forever to find him. Or forgive him. That's an option, too, you know."

"If you're recruiting for Heaven, I'll pass. Tell me about your wings."

"You know how it is in Heaven these days."

"I'm dead. I don't get the newsletter anymore."

"But you can guess. Anyway, a lot of angels went all Lex Luthor. A lot on our side have been killed. When I found out that they were letting souls take some of their places, I said why not? I even have an angel name now: Penemue."

"I'll stick with Alice."

"Please do."

I take out the Maledictions. Alice shudders.

"I heard you smoked those things these days."

"I don't have to if it's going to bug you."

"No. Go ahead if it's going to calm you. That's what you need to be for a while. Calm and boring. Let this whole angel murder episode fade from people's memories."

I light up and take a puff.

Alice waves the smoke away.

"Oh God. It's like you're smoking a pig's ass, and the pig isn't well."

I blow smoke in the other direction, and then say, "Not that I particularly care, but how do people feel about me Upstairs? I suppose in some ways the war is my fault. I thought opening Heaven would fix things, but it just made everything worse."

"You're right about that," she says. "But you're also not Einstein."

"What do you mean?"

"It means you're hardly the first one who thought about opening Heaven. It means the war would have happened sooner or later."

"Then everyone doesn't hate me?"

She waggles her hand up and down a few times.

"That's what I thought."

"I thought you didn't care."

"I don't. And most angels can still kiss my ass."

"Say that louder. I'm not sure Vehuel heard you."

"I always wondered, do you have movie nights in Heaven?"

"All the time."

"Damn. Good ones or just Shirley Temple stuff?"

"Every movie ever made. And some new ones. We have a lot of actors, writers, and directors up there. I got to be an extra in Sam Fuller's new movie."

"Samuel Fuller? How did he end up in Heaven?"

"A lot of artists make it. Contributions to humanity count for a lot."

"So everything would be different if I'd listened to Mom and took accordion lessons."

"Yes. Your life would be completely different and you'd be fluttering around a cloud jamming with Django Reinhardt."

"See, now I think you're fibbing."

"We are who we are, Jim. There's no changing that, back in the mortal world or here."

"You mean there are miserable, depressed assholes in Heaven, too?"

"Of course."

"A lot?"

"Enough."

"And they piss everyone off?"

"They sure do."

"Good."

She bumps her shoulder into mine. "It's nice to see you."

"You too. You look good with a couple of scars."

"By the time this is over I might look like you."

"I'll make sure that doesn't happen."

She puts her hands on her knees and leans back.

"*You're* going to protect *me*? The guy who couldn't even manifest his Gladius a few minutes ago?"

Shit. "You saw that?"

She pats me on the arm, a mischievous grin on her face. "It's okay. It happens to guys sometimes. No one thinks any less of you."

"Oh, man."

Alice stands and brushes off her armor.

"Come on. Bring your stupid cigarette and show me around this Popsicle stand."

THE REPAIRS GO quickly with five angels working wrenches at light speed, but the work still takes all night. Alice doesn't know a damned thing about engines, so she's a kind of unofficial angel ambassador to the havoc, answering people's questions about Heaven, God, wing maintenance, and settling bets over whether or not angels shit (apparently, it's their choice, which is weird even for angels). Traven, on the other hand, tries to quiz her on obscure theological arguments. French hermits in caves versus traveling German Flagellants versus a day trader from upstate New York who had a vision of the Virgin Mary at the Strawberry Panda strip club in Vegas. She took all his money, but later at his hotel he found a gram of coke in the back of a Gideon's Bible and declared it a miracle. Alice answers each of his questions with Groucho's lines from old Marx Brothers movies I made her watch.

"Either he's dead or my watch has stopped."

"I once shot an elephant in my pajamas. How he got in my pajamas I'll never know."

By the time she starts singing "Hooray for Captain Spaulding," he catches on that she's not revealing any deep, dark secrets and settles for trading stories about their favorite L.A. bookstores.

Cherry has been keeping a low profile since Alice blew her cover. All the windows in the ambulance are covered and smoke curls from a vent in the roof. She's locked herself up doing her swami bit, trying to get back in good with the Magistrate.

But even with the angels' help, the havoc loses more vehicles. When I came along, there were twelve semis and several pieces of construction equipment towing the flatbed. Now there are four semis, a dump truck, and the AAV we took from the dead Legionnaires. Members of the havoc and the conscripts have to squeeze into buses and the smaller trucks together, which puts everyone in an even better mood.

Before we move out, the Magistrate leaps on top of his Charger and addresses his increasingly restless flock.

"My friends, as we move out today, we embark not on a new journey, but a renewed and more powerful one. We are blessed with the presence of six angels who will guide us in these next steps. Despite all that we have been through, all the losses and dark moments, the crusade has always moved forward, and today it will move forward again. We will reach the second step of our holy campaign in just a few days, and once there, I tell you now: we *will* possess the Lux Occisor, the sword the Almighty used to strike down Lucifer and his rebel angels. With the weapon and the help of our angel companions, we will enter the third and final stage of our crusade, and join in the battle for Heaven itself!"

The Magistrate pauses for dramatic effect. I think he's waiting for a roar of approval, but what he gets are a few whistles and a smattering of applause. I've said it before: Hell is a tough room.

"Now, before we move out, I think we should thank our new companions for their presence and support."

He stretches out a hand to Vehuel, Alice, and the other angels.

There's more applause this time and even a few cheers. Lucky Magistrate. The angels might be about the only thing holding his crusade together at this point.

The angels pile into the Charger with the Magistrate. How they manage to get in there with their wings and armor is more mysterious to me than anything in Traven's old books.

Alice gets in last, putting on a little show for the crowd, making a big deal of trying to squeeze into the car. People laugh, and as engines start around us, you can feel the havoc begin to relax.

I've just settled on my bike when Daja comes over. She looks worried.

"Are you planning on riding up front with your angel pals?" she says.

"First off, they aren't my pals, and second, I was planning on riding where I usually ride. Unless that's going to be a problem."

I glance at the rest of the pack. Johnny, Frederickson, and Barbora, a few others won't even look at me.

"It's no problem by me," Daja says. "In fact, I was going to ask you to stay. After seeing what you did to that angel . . . well, it would be good to have your help looking after the Magistrate."

"I'm here and I'm ready to ride."

I don't say the other thing I'm thinking, which is that despite all his charm and brains, I think the Magistrate is the worst kind of Holy Roller motherfucker. He's a genocidal bastard with a gallows truck and a gun big enough to blow holes in Saturn's rings and he'll use it on anybody who disagrees with him. And now he thinks his divine destiny is proven by a gaggle of angels.

No, I don't say any of that. I just start my Harley and pull a bandanna up over my nose because the road ahead looks soft and powdery.

Daja says thanks, but it's drowned out by the thunder that's the havoc waking up. She goes back to her bike, and as the Charger peels out, we take off after it, not a dog pack anymore. Just a lot of bikes and one car that all happen to be going in the same direction.

We follow the Magistrate's ley line for a few miles before turning off on a winding road that leads into a jagged mountain pass of shining black stone. The higher we climb, the steeper the road becomes. I can hear the semis grinding gears even over the sound of my engine. Everyone slows so the trucks don't get left behind, but the road just keeps getting worse. When the trucks get stuck, members of the havoc lead conscripts to the rear so they can help push them free. I wonder if every crusade has its own slaves. It wouldn't surprise me. If they'd decided I was an "unworthy," I could be back there pushing with the rest of them. And what's going through the heads of those angels? I thought friends of Hesediel's wouldn't be the usual angel bastards, shitting on mortals and their oh-so-boring suffering. Yet they just sit in the car, doing nothing.

Just when I'm ready to write them off, the Charger stops and the doors pop open. All six angels take off into the air and settle down at the rear of the convoy. Each angel takes a vehicle and pushes with the conscripts. With all that angel horsepower, it doesn't take long for the trucks to start rolling again. I want to go back and help, but I promised to stay with the pack. Plus I'm not sure I want to give up all my secrets to the havoc yet.

The last couple of hundred yards of steep road are hard, even with the angels' help. Most of the havoc waits at the top of the hill as the semis crawl forward a few feet at a time. It's over an hour before the flatbed crests the hill, and when it does, people cheer like they haven't in a long time. The applause continues as the angels fly back to the Magistrate's car. Before she squeezes in, Alice makes a muscle in my direction and sticks her tongue out at me. I give her the finger. And we move out again.

There's actually some scrubby vegetation on this side of the hills, rare for the Tenebrae. The air is clearer, too. I pull down the bandanna and can feel dampness in the air. After two more hours winding down through the hills, we come to a dead end and stop.

We're at another of the shining black stone mountains. At the base of the peak there's something I've never seen in the Tenebrae before: a small pool of water.

From nearby I hear Johnny say, "If this magic river of theirs has dried up, I swear I'm slitting them."

There are grunts of agreement. Even Doris, the steadiest person in the pack, looks like she's ready to turn Vehuel and her pals into chicken pot pies. I have my na'at in one pocket, the golden blade in another, and the Colt at my back. I know that Alice can take down any of them, but that doesn't mean I'm going to give them the chance to try.

All the tough talk and bad thoughts evaporate in the next few seconds as Vehuel gets out of the Charger and says a few words.

The mountain begins to rumble and split open. Massive doors of black stone swing wide, opening to reveal another road leading under the mountain itself. The doors are still moving when the Charger slowly enters the passage into the mountain. Gisco in his convertible goes in second, with the rest of us on bikes on his tail. The rest of the havoc follow us underground. For a long time. When the mountain doors slam shut behind us, every vehicle with a working headlight turns it on.

The road going down is almost as steep as the one coming up. If someone has fucked with the chains on the flatbed and they break, a lot of cars are going to get pancaked. I stay close to the Charger in case I have to pull Alice out.

I haven't been in this kind of dark since I was in Tartarus and I don't like it. The big difference here is that the longer we move down, the cooler and wetter the air gets. Which isn't to say it's a fucking picnic tunneling under the Tenebrae's shitty skin. The noise from all the vehicles reverberates off the stone walls and gives everybody migraines. Shadows snake and slide along the walls, thrown at crazy angles by the jagged, shiny rock formations. After the Hellion and angel attacks, you can feel everybody tense, expecting the worst. But the shadows are just shadows and it's hard to stay scared forever. After a while, they're just another part of the scenery.

Just like it was easy to lose track of time in the Tenebrae, it's just as easy here, crawling at a few miles an hour in pitch dark. Eventually, though, the road turns from a steep slope to a gentle grade, and finally eases into a flat, straight line. Better than that, there's light up ahead. The Magistrate must have seen it, too, because the Charger roars forward. We gun the bikes to chase the car's receding taillights, finally catching up just as the road opens into a cavern that looks to be a mile wide and just as tall. That's not what gets everyone's attention, though.

It's the three large ships floating nearby on a rushing river. The Charger stops by a pier extending out a few dozen yards into the water. As the Magistrate and angels get out of the car, we kill the bikes and go over to them.

"Welcome to the Styx, the first and oldest river in Hades," says Vehuel.

I go to the side of the pier.

"It doesn't really look like a Hellion river."

Vehuel gives me a look.

"Excuse me?"

"Most of the rivers I've seen in Hell are a lot more *Hell-y*. You know. Rivers of shit or blood or fire."

"No. There's none of that here. The Styx is merely water, though few know of this tributary's existence."

"And that's the way I like it," says an old man who'd been hiding behind one of the pier supports. His eyes narrow at us, but they turn to slits when he looks at the angels. "Greetings, Vehuel," he says.

"Charon," she says, a hint of surprise in her voice. "I thought you'd retired."

"You mean you thought I'd *been* retired. They tried it. Lucifer and his minions. They could pull me off the main part of the river, but I'm still the Styx's boatman. No one gets past me without paying."

"But you're alone down here," Vehuel says. "Doesn't that defeat the point of being a boatman?"

"Not at all. I am as patient as the river. And as for being alone . . ."

He looks at the long line of vehicles beginning to fill the tunnel.

"I don't seem to be alone anymore."

"Very well," says Vehuel. "We'd like—"

"Shh," he says, holding up a hand. "I'm trying to count."

"Of course," Vehuel says in a tone that makes it pretty obvious she's not used to getting shushed.

The Magistrate steps forward.

"Hello. I am—"

Charon holds up a finger.

"You made me lose count. Now I have to start over."

"I can tell you how many are in our party, if that would help."

"It wouldn't. I have to count. You might try to cheat me."

"We travel with angels, sir. We would never cheat you."

"Shh."

Charon waggles his finger as he counts people or vehicles or maybe both. Whatever he's counting, it's clear it's going to take a while. I get out the Maledictions. Daja and Wanuri take one. I bring one over to Gisco and start to light it.

"There's no smoking," says Charon sharply. "Read the sign."

I look around.

"What sign?"

He looks at the wall over my head.

"Oh yes. I thought I hadn't seen it for a while. It must have rotted away in the damp. Anyway—no smoking. Now quiet or I'll have to start over again."

Everyone gives me back their cigarettes. Alice hops onto the back of the Charger and I sit down next to her.

"He's fun. One of yours?"

"I'm not sure," she whispers. "He could be an angel, I guess. He's kind of a prick if he is."

"Then he's more like most of the angels I've met. Your bunch are the weird ones."

"I'm glad we could broaden your horizons. You don't want to know what a lot of angels say about you."

"No. I don't."

"No. You don't."

"How do all of you fit your wings in the car?"

"We tuck."

"You can tuck your wings?"

"Oh yeah. They fold up real small. I'll show you sometime."

"Quiet!' shouts Charon. "You people and your noise. I should charge you double just for the aggravation."

Vehuel shoots Alice a look. She mouths "Sorry" back at the boss.

A few minutes later, Charon finishes counting and goes to the support where he'd been hiding earlier. When he comes back, he's holding a long ash staff.

"I am Charon, boatman of the Styx—"

"We know who you are, Charon," says Vehuel.

"Don't interrupt. Now I have to start over. I am Charon, boatman of the Styx. All may pass, but all must pay."

"Of course," says the Magistrate.

"In gold," says the old man drawing out the O.

The Magistrate reaches into his duster and pulls out a dove. As it flies away, he's already shooting playing cards from hand to hand. He fans out the deck and says, "Pick a card."

"No," says Charon.

"Oh, come on. You want to be paid, do you not?"

Charon makes a sour face and points to a card. With a great flourish, the Magistrate tosses the rest of the cards into the air, where they burst into flame and disappear. With another extravagant flourish, he turns over Charon's card for us to see. There's a picture of a gold coin in the center. People applaud. He shows the card to Charon. The old man takes it and throws it into the river. He shakes his staff.

"Do you see this staff which I hold? With it, I bar or open the way to the river. With it, I command the ships and the tide. But without gold, I'll do nothing at all and you can all bugger off the way you came."

"Of course, dear sir," says the Magistrate. He snaps his fingers and there's a gold coin there, like he plucked it out of the air. People applaud politely.

Charon takes the coin and tosses it into the river.

"Not enough," he says. "Gold for all of them. Every soul. Every Hellion. Every one of your pretty little angels." He smiles sourly at Vehuel. She smiles sourly right back. "And gold for your transports. Double gold for those big bastards at the back. What're they?"

"Trucks," I shout.

"Trucks? Funny word," Charon says. "Yes. Double for them. And double for him. He has a big mouth."

Everyone looks at me.

"You're not helping," says Alice.

The Magistrate looks back at the havoc and the angels, then back to Charon.

"Dear sir, if we had known that we would need so much gold, we could have prepared for it. As it is, you have thrown all of our gold into your lovely river."

Charon slams his staff into the pier.

"Then you can go back the way you came and take those nosy angels with you."

"But, sir—"

"No!"

Charon crosses his arms, clutching his magic staff tight.

Vehuel says, "Be reasonable, Charon. We must pass. We are on a holy mission."

"Tough. Gold or you can rot on these banks like my sign."

The Magistrate starts talking. The other angels go over and they start talking. All you can hear coming from the mob is Charon saying, "No. No. Never. Forget it. Nope. No . . ."

I go to the pier and push a couple of angels out of the way. Charon says, "What do you want, Mr. Bigmouth?"

I take out the Colt and smack him on the head with the butt. Before he falls into the river, I grab his staff and toss it to the Magistrate.

"You're smart. You and the halo polishers figure out how to make it work."

I go back to the Charger and light a Malediction. Toss the pack and matches to Wanuri, who lights one for herself and gives out smokes to anybody who wants a cigarette. Even Johnny takes one.

"Smooth," says Alice. "You realize that's not going to do your reputation in Heaven any good."

"Then you'll just have to stick up for me."

"Believe me, I've tried. But it's five of them against one of me."

I hold out a hand to where the other angels and the Magistrate are examining the staff.

"You're warriors. You've seen worse than that in battle."

"You mugged an old man!" says Alice. "That kind of thing gets around."

"He called me a loudmouth."

"Bigmouth, actually." Alice cranes her neck, looking where I pushed in Charon. "I hope he's all right."

I point about twenty yards downstream.

"Ask him. He's right over there."

The old man shakes himself like an angry cat, but keeps his distance. In a few minutes, the three ships waiting upriver begin to move toward the pier. The Magistrate and the angels smile.

"Are you satisfied now?" says Alice.

"I'll be satisfied when this is over."

"What are you going to do then?"

"I have no idea. I don't even know what 'over' means. The Magistrate will have his gun. To tell you the truth, I don't trust him with it."

"Me neither."

I look at her.

"I thought you were here to help him."

"Who told you that?"

"You saved the havoc."

"We saved *you*. You're why we're here."

"What the hell does that mean?"

She points a finger at the ceiling.

"You have friends in high places."

"Mr. Muninn?"

"I'm not at liberty to say."

"Fuck me. I thought he'd checked out completely."

"Nope. Just busy. You might not have heard, but there's a war on."

It never crossed my mind that anyone in Heaven or Hell remembered me or cared. Especially Mr. Muninn. Talk about a bigmouth. I popped off at him a couple of times. It didn't occur to me until later that being snotty to the ruler of the universe might not be in my best interest. But now here we are.

"Does the Magistrate know?"

"Hell no," says Alice. "And we're going to keep it that way, right? The Almighty doesn't want to look like he's playing favorites, especially with an Abomination."

"*The* Abomination."

"Stop showing off."

The Magistrate signals for the flatbed to be moved onto the dock. Once it's on board the first ship and secured, the second ship floats up. With the angels directing traffic, they load all the vehicles. We get on the third ship with the havoc and the conscripts. Vehuel seems to have figured out how the staff works, so she directs the ships to move farther into the channel and heads them downstream.

As we pass Charon, the Magistrate walks to the side of the ship and calls to the old man.

"If only you had asked politely."

He throws out his arms. Gold coins pour from his sleeves onto the deck.

Vehuel walks to the stern of the ship and shouts, "We'll send your staff back to you when we've reached our destination."

Charon shouts something that I'm pretty sure it isn't "Sounds great. Catch you later."

I THOUGHT THAT with the angels around and finally knowing our next destination would calm people down. No such luck. We're on the river for maybe an hour before the first fight breaks out. Some of the conscripts forced to work on the trucks jump one of the mechanics and try to throw him overboard. There's a mini-riot between a mob of souls and a handful of Hellions over a case of beer looted from one town or other. The case is caked with dirt and rattier looking than Karloff in *The Mummy*. The swill is probably flat and has been that way since before the invention of fire.

At least two people end up in Tartarus over it.

The Magistrate spends the first hours of the trip doing nothing but putting out emotional tire fires. Johnny, Frederickson, and a couple of other idiots even heckle the angels. Vehuel and the others bunch together in the prow of the ship, clearly horrified by the emotional mortal meltdowns. I keep my distance, but can see Alice doing a lot of explaining and hand waving trying to calm them. The poor bastards were sent here to cover my ass and now it looks like they're going to need pepper spray just to keep their feathers on straight.

I think part of the problem is being underground. The Tenebrae might be a desiccated wasteland of shit and ruins, but at least you can see the sky. Down here, we're bugs floating on leaves along the river of the dead. The only things you can see in any direction are the cave walls and stalactites overhead, any one of which could sink our asshole armada if it came loose.

A whole group of geniuses abandons ship and swims for the dock. They're in the water maybe thirty seconds before they're torn apart by a swarm of something that are all tentacles and sharp, hatpin teeth. I knew Charon was bullshitting us. Maybe the river isn't a torrent of puke or full of blood rapids, but it's as depressing and dangerous as any other body of water in Hell's little punishment carnival.

I head up to the prow of the ship to talk to Alice, but she waves me off. When I go to the dog pack, half of them walk away.

"Did I eat the last donut in the box?"

"Yeah, you did, comfort-wise," says Wanuri. "All those people who used to think you were crazy? They still do. Now, though, all the people who thought you were a guardian angel are starting to think that maybe you're the cause of all our problems."

"I didn't ask to join this circus. I was drafted as much as any of those slobs who were out pushing trucks up the hill today."

"Don't shoot the messenger. I'm just telling you what I hear around. Plus, now that people got a look at real angels, and watched you practically saw one's head off, they're a little spooked by you."

"Johnny's probably going around telling everyone I'm a wombat. I've never even *seen* a wombat."

"They're adorable," says Doris. "I took the grandkids to the zoo for Tristan's—my little grandson's—birthday and there was a whole enclosure full of wombats. They look like little piglets crossed with teddy bears."

"I've been called a lot of things, but never a piglet bear."

"I don't think he meant he thought you were cute," says Wanuri.

"Why don't you ask him?" says Daja.

"No. He might ask me to be his valentine and I'm already seeing someone."

"Speaking of seeing someone, your little angel is quite something," Wanuri says.

"Alice? She's great."

"The few angels I've ever seen were all so stuck on themselves. Better be careful or I'll steal her away from you."

"There's nothing to steal. She's my ex."

"Dumped you, did she?"

"No. A shit named Parker was going to murder her, so she killed herself just to spite him."

"Damn," Wanuri says. "I'm sorry."

"Yeah."

Still on crutches, Gisco rattles off a few syllables and signs with his hands.

"What does that mean?"

"I think he's wondering the same thing I am," says Doris. "How does a suicide get into Heaven? I thought there was a rule about that."

Gisco nods.

"If there's anything I've learned about Heaven, it's that the rules are subject to change without fucking notice. That's the one good thing about Hell: at least it makes sense."

"If she put up with you," Wanuri says, "then she was destined to be an angel."

Daja puts out a fist so Wanuri can bump it, but before she does, an arrow goes through Daja's wrist.

"Fuck!" she yells, holding her bleeding arm.

I push her to the ground as a volley of arrows arcs high

overhead and plummets down on the ship. Another volley flies up from the opposite shore. All around us, members of the havoc are getting skewered. Pinned to the ground, where they lie, or stuck to one of the masts or a hatch door. Others have it worse. They take shots through the throat or skull.

Then, as quickly as they started, the arrows stop. The wounded lie all around us, but before anyone can get to them, jets of fire erupt from each shore, their streams crossing downriver. We're sailing straight into a firestorm.

The angels split into two groups of three and fly off, their Gladiuses blazing. The gouts of fire ahead break apart and move upward, trying to catch them in flight. Fat chance. Whoever is operating the flamethrowers is way too slow. When one of the streams gets within fifty feet of Vehuel, she dives for it . . . and catches the flames on her Gladius. The fire arcs back to where it came from, frying everyone on that side of the river.

It doesn't go any better for the fry cooks on the opposite shore. Alice and a tall blond romance-novel-cover angel named Johel come at that flamethrower from two sides at once. They dive-bomb the shooters. One of their Gladiuses must have hit the flamethrower's fuel source, because their whole side of the river goes up in an orange ball of fire that rolls all the way to the top of the cavern.

I yell, "Alice!" But I'm being melodramatic. She and Johel swoop out of the flames a second later and land back on the ship. I run over to her, but she puts out her hands for me to keep back. Waves of heat shimmer off her armor.

"I'm still a little hot to the touch," she says.

"Can I at least light a cigarette off you?"

"Fuck you. I was being heroic and all you want is a smoke. Typical."

"You cool off. I have to check on someone."

By the time I get back to Daja, Doris has cut off the tail end of the arrow right at her wrist. Wanuri holds the end with the arrowhead. Gisco and Johnny hold on to Daja's arm. I crouch down with Billy and grab her shoulders.

"You ready?" says Wanuri.

Daja grits her teeth and nods.

On three, Wanuri rips the business end of the arrow out of Daja's wrist. Blood spurts from the wound, but Barbora binds it tight with a piece of cloth, stanching the flow.

"Where's the Magistrate?" Daja says. "Is he all right?"

Wanuri says, "I'll find him," and runs into the chaos of the walking wounded and the dying.

"Who the bloody hell was that?" says Johnny as Alice comes over.

"I don't know," she says. "We didn't see on our side, and they ran off into tunnels before Vehuel's group could find them."

"Fat lot of good the angels have done for us."

Alice ignores him and takes Daja's wrist.

"I can't fix you, but I can make you feel better. Is that all right with you?"

"Yes. Please," says Daja through gritted teeth.

Alice puts a hand on either side of Daja's wrist and speaks a few words. Some of it sounds like one of the High Hellion dialects, but I'm guessing it is the angels' original language that Hellion came from. I can't understand a word of it. I bet Traven could.

Fuck. Where's Traven? I get up to look for him when Alice pulls me back. Daja's eyes are closed and she's more relaxed.

"Better?" she says.

"Much better. Thanks," Daja says.

Alice looks at me.

"Help take care of her. Keep her hand elevated. I have to go help others."

Before I can say anything, Alice disappears into the crowd, going from one wounded body to another.

"Has anyone seen the Magistrate?" says Daja again.

"Wanuri is looking for him," Doris reminds her.

She comes back a couple of minutes later, out of breath and bloodier than before.

"Did you find him?" Daja says.

"Yes. He's hurt, but he's all right," says Wanuri.

"I want to see him."

Daja grabs Frederickson's shoulder and tries to pull herself up. He takes her good arm as Wanuri gets on the other side. Alice wouldn't approve, but Daja isn't going to be talked out of it.

We guide her through the mess on deck and down into one of the ship's holds. On a bare bunk in a dim stateroom, the Magistrate is on his back with quickly wrapped bandages across his chest. Traven is in the bunk next to him. Cherry is tying bloody rags around his right thigh. I ignore her as I go to him.

"How are you doing?"

"I've been better," he says. "Check on the Magistrate. He's more badly injured than I am."

That's the best news I've heard in a while. If the Magistrate snuffs it, we can shove the big gun into the Styx and all go our separate ways. Unless the angels want it for the war. That hadn't occurred to me until now. That might be the real reason they're here. Maybe Mr. Muninn told them to see if they could keep me in one piece, but I bet if they had to choose between my ass or a weapon that could change the war, they'd drop me off on the nearest corner with a dollar and a bus map.

When I look over at the Magistrate, he's sitting up in the bunk with his back braced against the wall. He's pale, but doesn't look like he's going to check out tonight. The angels probably aren't down for doing any cold-blooded murder themselves, but I wonder how they'd feel if I held a pillow on his face for a few minutes?

I'm snapped out of that merry thought when he says, "How are you, dear Daja?"

"I'm fine. It's just a little cut. It doesn't even hurt."

"Are you sure? Your head is clear?"

"I'm positive."

"Then, until I'm better, I want you to take command of the havoc. Continue the crusade with the help of our angels."

"I will. I promise."

She doesn't say "Father," but you can hear it in her voice. If I killed the Magistrate, I'd probably have to kill her, too, and at this point I don't think I'd like that.

"I don't understand how anybody could find us down here," says Doris.

Wanuri moves up next to her.

"She's right. The angels said that almost nobody knows about the river. How did they find us?"

I go to the foot of the Magistrate's bed.

"That's easy. One of us told them."

Everybody looks at me.

Wanuri says, "How do you know that?"

"It's the only thing that makes sense. There's still a traitor in the havoc. While you geniuses were measuring me for a noose, the real saboteur has been having fun and now has us trapped underground."

"I am afraid he is right," says the Magistrate. "We must be on our guard from now on. Besides the angels, we can trust no one outside of this room."

I'm pretty sure I know exactly what's going on, but they wouldn't listen to me because they don't know what I know. A setup this complicated and devious, involving a Heavenly weapon, do-gooder angels, and a whole army of lunatics . . . there's only one group I can think of with the resources and the greed to try and stop it.

Wormwood. There isn't just a cutthroat in the group. Someone is working for Wormwood and has been long before I got here. It could be any of these clowns. Aside from Traven, there's no one I want behind me with anything sharp. And this time I know I'm not just being paranoid.

"Magistrate, may I say something?" says Cherry.

But before he gives permission, Daja is in Cherry's face, stabbing her finger at her with her good hand.

"Like hell you can. Why didn't you see this coming, oracle? What good are you?"

Cherry rubs her temples like she's trying to push her skull together.

"I didn't see this attack because I was blinded by the real

one. The arrows and fire were just a test of our defenses. The real attack will begin in a few minutes."

The Magistrate pushes everyone away.

"Hurry. You must defend the ship. Do not let them get the Lux Occisor."

Daja is out of the door first, but the rest of us are right behind her. The weapons and ammo are all stashed belowdecks, where they're hard to get at because we weren't supposed to fucking need them. And even if we could get them and hand them out, how many are left on deck willing and able to get into a firefight right now?

We head on deck and run to the bow of the ship. There are sails in the distance, spread out across the width of the river.

"Fuck me," says Wanuri. "It's a whole goddamn army."

"Technically it's a navy," I say.

"Shut up," says Daja.

"Whatever the fuck they are, we're not going to fight them off with a few rifles," says Billy.

"We have to," Daja says. "Start handing them out." There's a moment of hesitation, so she yells, "Now!" and people start moving.

Billy, Johnny, and Frederickson go belowdecks to start getting together the weapons everyone knows will be useless. I don't. I look back at the flatbed.

I say, "Billy is right. A few bullets aren't going to stop—what, a dozen ships? Maybe more?"

"What else are we going to do?" says Daja.

Her hand is bleeding again.

"We put up a scarecrow."

"What?"

"We scare the shit out of them."

"How?"

"You want to use the weapon," says Wanuri.

"Exactly," I say.

"But it won't work without the Light Killer," Daja says.

"Then we make them *think* we have it."

"How?"

I pull her and Wanuri in closer so people can't hear us.

"You heard these winged clowns. I'm as big an Abomination as there is. And Abominations can do tricks. Big ones. I can make these assholes think that your popgun back there works."

"How?"

I'm starting to get tired of Daja saying that. "Let me show you."

"What have we got to lose?" says Wanuri. "We give everyone else the guns we know work and let the lunatic try his tricks."

"Fine," says Daja. "But if you hurt the weapon I'll kill you."

"It's a date."

Wanuri and I head for the bow.

I say, "Get some people on the ship with the flatbed. I need them to pull the tarp off. We'll only scare these bastards if they can see the gun. I'll be there in a minute."

I look around for Alice and find her with the other angels near the mast. Vehuel has conjured a map of the river in the air between them. It floats, transparent, showing our ships and the ones heading for us. She moves her hand back and forth across the map, laying out a battle plan. When she's done, the map vanishes and the angels head to the side of the ship. I run and catch up with Alice.

"Be careful, you," I tell her.

"You too." She looks at me, confused. "How come you're not armed? Where's your gun?"

"They're getting it ready for me."

"Keep your head down."

"You too. Things are going to get loud."

But she's already in the air with the other angels and doesn't hear me. I jump from the front of the ship onto the one holding the vehicles, weave through and onto the ship with the flatbed. It's almost completely uncovered when I get there.

I head for the breech. Wanuri and a few other people are waiting.

She says, "How exactly do you plan on using an unloaded gun?"

"It doesn't have to be loaded. They just have to *think* it's loaded."

"All right. How are you going to do that?"

"I'm not a hundred percent sure. I'm making this up as I go along."

"I don't believe it. Daja was right about you."

I take out the plastic bottle of Aqua Regia and have a pull.

"I'm going to try something. You might want to move back in case I don't get it right."

"Faith is dwindling in you, Mr. fucking Pitts."

I pull open the breech and get down on my knees. I can see the other end through the barrel. It looks a mile away.

"Well?" says Wanuri.

"I don't think it's going to work from this end. I'm going up front."

"Make up your damned mind!"

She follows me up to the muzzle. The ships are still a good distance away, but closing fast.

"If you're going to do something, do it," she says.

I watch the ships for a minute.

"We should wait until they're closer."

"Why?"

"'Cause I'm not sure how far I can do this."

"Do fucking *what*?"

"Give me a minute."

As the big ships crawl our way, a group of smaller attack boats moves out in front, speeding toward us. They send out long streams of fire over the water as they come.

"Right. You're an idiot," says Wanuri. "I'm going back to the real fight."

"If you do, you're going to miss it."

"What?"

"This."

Crouching by the barrel, I shout Hellion hoodoo as loud and long and pissed off as I can.

Fighting Hellbeasts in the arena isn't a subtle job. I used the na'at as much as I could on the smaller ones, but the big ones I had to use hoodoo. The bigger the beast, the bigger the hex. It left me rusty when it came to small spells, but an expert at eviscerating house-size fuckers. But those were mostly close battles. I've never tried killing something as big as a ship and never anything this far away. I have no idea what's going to happen.

But I know it's going to be pretty fucking spectacular.

There's an explosion by the muzzle and the gun rolls back a few feet. Over the attack ships, the air catches fire and blows three boats in the middle right out of the water. I shout hoodoo again. The air explodes. This time I miss, but a couple of the outer ships slow. I shout again, switching the hoodoo around a little.

This time the water beneath the remaining ships explodes, tossing them into the air. The blast also tosses a whole school of the tentacled underwater bastards upward with them. The ships and sailors that survive the blast are pulled into the churning water in a writhing mass of teeth and tentacles. I try shouting one more time, but nothing comes out. My voice is fried.

I sit down with my back against the gun, suddenly exhausted. Get the Aqua Regia and drink a big mouthful. It burns my raw throat like acid, but it's worth it.

Wanuri sits down next to me. I pass her the Aqua Regia and she passes it right back.

"Keep your swill and tell me how you did that."

I make a rasping noise and point to my throat.

"You can't talk? That's one blessing at least."

The rest of the crew that uncovered the gun come up to where we're sitting and stare out over the water. Nothing to do now but wait and see what happens next.

A lot of nothing occurs over the next few minutes. Eventually, though, one by one, the big ships turn and head back upriver away from us.

A cheer goes up a couple of boats back as the peanut gallery sees that they get to die tomorrow instead of right now.

Our bunch cheers, too, but Wanuri and I just sit there. I know she's thinking exactly what I am: We got lucky once, but what happens next time?

We head back to the ship, where the havoc is already breaking out drinks.

Daja is waiting for us.

"What did you do up there?"

I point to my throat.

"He's gone mute, the poor dear," says Wanuri as unsympathetically as possible. "What he did was what he's best at. He talked them to death."

Daja says, "Whatever that means, good job. The Magistrate wants to see you."

I point to myself.

"Yes. Just you."

There's a party going on belowdecks. As I push through to the Magistrate's stateroom, people clap me on the back and offer me drinks. I shake my head and keep moving. At the Magistrate's door, I knock and go in.

Traven isn't there anymore. I point to his bunk.

"Do not worry about the father," the Magistrate says. "He just moved to the adjoining room to give us some privacy."

Grimacing, he sits up a little higher in bed.

"I heard the blasts from here. I take it those were your doing?"

I nod and point to my throat.

"Shouted yourself hoarse, did you? That is all right. I know about the Sub Rosa and the things they can do. And I know about the nephilim. More perhaps than you think. Help me take my shirt off."

He unbuttons himself and I help him get out the rest of the way. With some effort, he turns around.

"If you will, look at my back."

There are two deep scars, long and ugly, running from his shoulders almost to his waist.

Fuck me.

He's an angel.

I was not expecting that.

He turns back around and falls against the hull of the ship. Pearly blood dots the bandages on his chest.

"I can tell that you recognize the scars. And that you are perhaps a bit shocked. Is it my wound? Yes, it is worse than it should be, but I do not heal the way I used to. I lost some of my power when I gave up my wings."

All I can do is croak out a word.

"Why?"

"That is a story for another time. What is important now is the weapon. It was clever of you to use it as you did. But niphal tricks will not bring down Heaven's wall or restore order to Creation. That is why we must continue the crusade."

"You. Captured."

"When I was taken by the Legionnaires? Yes. Your first guess was right. I allowed it. I needed to speak to them. I hoped that as fallen angels, they would understand an angel who lives in exile voluntarily. Unfortunately, they did not. They had no information of value and they would not join the havoc. There was nothing left for them but to be destroyed."

"Does Daja know?"

"No. And please do not tell her. Her faith is strong, but her heart is fragile and there is still so much left to do."

I shrug.

"We must find the Lux Occisor. We must arm the weapon and take it to Heaven. That is our mission. Nothing must stop it."

I try to say something, but nothing comes out. I take a shot of Aqua Regia and try again.

"Why tell me?"

"Because you have something that I do not have, nor do our angels. You have a friendship with Death."

I frown at him. Where is he going with this?

"You must find him. Convince him to help us. How many attacks have we endured and the second part of our journey has barely begun? We cannot continue on like this. Death is one ally none of our enemies can overcome. He must be brought to our side."

"Don't know where he is."

"Then you must find him. We will bring the ships to shore and, like the saints of old, you will go into the wilderness and meditate until he appears."

The Magistrate is ten times more deranged than I thought, but what if he's right? He's a wreck. The havoc is barely holding together. I'm sure the angels want the gun, but it's no use to them unless it works. They should just steal it and get the Light Killer themselves, but angels aren't supposed to steal. And maybe they need the havoc to get the sword. It's entirely possible that they're not telling us something and stringing us along.

Then there's Wormwood. I know they're involved somehow, but I can't figure out how or why. The Magistrate has more secrets, too, I bet. Goddammit. I don't know what to do. I want off this crazy train, but there's nowhere to jump and people I care about will get hurt if I go. Maybe even Alice. I got her killed once. I won't let that happen again.

"Okay," I croak. "I'll try."

"You must do more than that," says the Magistrate. "Help me up. We will go to shore immediately."

I help him onto the deck, where he uses Charon's staff to steer the ships out of the deep water to shore.

Alice comes over.

"Nice trick back there," she says.

"Thanks," I rasp.

"Oh, you poor thing. You've ruined your voice. Let me see if I can help."

She puts a hand on my throat and mumbles a few words.

"How's that?"

The pain is gone.

I look around at the havoc. People seem happy that we're heading to shore. Without me making half of them uncomfortable, the dog pack seems happy, too. Cherry lifts her respirator enough to sip a beer as she talks to the big blond angel.

I take Alice aside.

"Have you ever heard of Wormwood?"

"No. What is it?"

"Mortals. Very bad people. They make money on everybody else's misery. They might be arranging these attacks."

"Are you sure?"

"Pretty sure. I need you to keep an eye on things. Angels are good snoops. If anyone acts strange—well, stranger than a bunch of idiots on a mission from God—let me know."

"Okay. Do you know why we're heading for shore?"

"I'm going bowling with Death."

"No. I mean, do you really know?"

"Seriously—I'm going to meet Death. We're sort of friends."

"I'd like to think you're lying, but I know you aren't."

"Nope."

"Do I have to tell you to be careful?"

"I'll be fine."

"Be careful anyway."

We stand by the side of the ship watching the shore get closer.

She says, "Do you ever wonder what it would have been like if you didn't go to Hell and I didn't die?"

"Only a few thousand times."

"We would have made funny old people."

"We would have."

"Candy is a lucky girl."

"Not so lucky at the end."

"No one is lucky at the end."

Alice holds my hand until we reach shore. A lot of confusing feelings are coming back to me, but like my memories of Candy, this isn't the time or place for them. I push them all away. For now.

When we reach shore I pick a tunnel at random and go inside to look for Death.

THE PASSAGE IS made of the same shiny black stone as the rest of the mountain. It reflects light from the opening a long way in. I don't have to use a match until I come to a sharp right turn. By the time I use two more, the tunnel ends at a smooth wall. I light another match and look around. I suppose if I was looking to die, this might be a nice, dramatic location. I'm sure it would look great in a forensic photo and on the dust jacket of a bestselling true-crime exposé. But all that will have to wait. I'm not looking to die. I'm looking for the prick that *makes* people die. But this seriously doesn't feel like the place. I'm about to back out the way I came when I look up and see a patch of dirt. Dry roots hang down a few inches. I stand on a rock outcropping and touch it. The dirt crumbles in my hand and a few inches of sky lights up the cave. Probing a little deeper, my hand lands on what feels like the lip of the hole. I jump from the outcrop and shove my other hand up until it finds the edge. Then I pull myself up.

I swear climbing out of the ground feels exactly like the first time I escaped from Hell. I half expect to come up in Hollywood Forever cemetery. But no such luck.

I'm back on that little slice of parched Heaven we call the Tenebrae. Right back where I started from again. The story of my life. I look around at where I came out.

I'm at the base of one of the spiked mountains that the Magistrate insists are rocks. There's nothing between me and the next set of mountains but the remains of an old fifties-style gas station with a general store attached. The roof of the store has collapsed, but it's better than nothing.

I use the golden blade to dig a big X in the ground so I can find my way back, then head for the store. Being back in the desert feels funny after being on the river just a few minutes ago. I can feel the water being squeezed out of my system with every step. My boots crunch on pulverized rock, so that each step sounds like I'm walking on snow. I wonder if it ever snowed in the Tenebrae. This place might not be so depressing with a few flurries coming down. I remember a funny little movie, *CQ*. There's a scene toward the end where it's snowing on the moon. It was weirdly pretty. If Mr. Muninn can make this place such a brain-numbing shit pit, he should be able to turn it into something a little less stifling. I'll have to mention it the next time I see him.

I reach the general store in about twenty minutes, give or take a decade. I've given up trying to tell time out here. The X is good and clear from the front of the store, so I go in.

The place is as much of a wreck as it looked from the mountain. However, after just a few minutes of looking, I find an unbroken bottle of Moxie cola and a box of very stale chocolate donuts. I take them outside under the gas station's carport and use the golden blade to draw a magic circle in the dirt. Nothing elaborate. Just some simple summoning hoo-doo. Then I sit in the middle with my bounty and wait.

I start on the donuts first and use the Moxie to wash down the rock-hard nuggets. Even stale they're good, though nothing like the ones at Donut Universe back home.

Donut Universe. I hadn't thought of it until this moment. One more thing maybe lost forever. If I remember right, there was a donut shop a mile or two from Lucifer's old palace in Pandemonium. It's where I found Cindil, my Donut Universe angel who was murdered by some piece-of-shit demons just to piss me off. I got her out of Hell, but never went back to check on the Hellion donut emporium. All right. That's the first place on my bucket list when I get back. It's good to have priorities.

Thinking about Cindil, Donut Universe, and L.A., I almost fall into the trap of thinking about home. I try to force the thoughts from my head, and when they won't go, I take out Doris's butcher knife and cut my arm lengthwise from the elbow to the wrist. Let the blood flow and the pain sink in. Then I have another donut.

I finish the Moxie and toss the rest of the donuts back into the store. That was a good and useful way to spend my time. How long have I been waiting for Death? How long does it take to eat six stale donuts? Probably not that long. Maybe I should have paced myself. Not only am I sitting alone in the most monotonous place in the entire universe, but I'm full of sugar. Didn't think that one through.

I get out a Malediction to calm my nerves only to find that I used my last match back in the tunnel. I could use some hoodoo to burn something, but there's nothing in the circle I can burn except me. I shouldn't have thrown the donut box away. I could have used that. I can still go get it. I mean, I can see it from where I'm sitting, but I'm new to this saint-meditating-in-the-desert bit and I'm afraid that if I leave the circle it will reset whatever magic clock determines how long I have to wait and I'll have to start all over again.

In an act of desperation, I put a Malediction on the ground and whisper some hoodoo to see if I can light it.

It explodes like a firecracker.

Yeah. I need to work on those little spells. God knows I have time for it now.

I try shouting at the mountain to see if I get an echo back, but what little voice I had left I used up talking to Alice.

I might have lost everything else, but at least I got to see her again. That's pretty good. One check mark in the Not

Entirely Dismal column. I'm going to have to come up with a lot more of those to even out that column with the Are You Fucking Kidding Me one.

Now how long has it been? Another five minutes? Ten? I shouldn't have had all that sugar.

After all the time I spent in Hell, I should probably have looked up my parents. I know my father is here. He tried to kill me and Upstairs they're not big on trying to kill your son. That said, I'm not even sure my mom is down here. Her only sin was being sad and lonely. Okay, she fucked an archangel and gave birth to me. And I'm guessing giving birth to an Abomination might not get you in good with the Heavenly membership committee. Right. Second thing to do when I get back. Look up Mom. She hated being alone, so she's probably with the refugees at Heaven's gates. I think about my father some more. Consider letting bygones be bygones and all that crap they tell you in magazines. Hell, I'm knee-deep in angels ready to murder the universe over daddy issues. Maybe it's time to let mine go.

Still, it might be fun to sneak up behind him and yell "Bang!" just once.

Is Death here yet?

I take a long drink of Aqua Regia. It burns my throat, but not as much as before. Still, it makes me dizzy. Or am I dizzy because I cut myself? I think I lost a lot more blood than I meant to. Oh, man. If I die here and someone finds me, my headstone is going to read HERE LIES SANDMAN SLIM, HE DIED OF DONUTS AND SELF-PITY.

Happy eternity, everybody. Good night and be sure to tip your waitresses.

I jerk my head to the side and come up with a mouthful of dust. I'm not sure, but I think I might have passed out for a while. At least I'm not bleeding anymore.

Man, I want a cigarette.

I try shouting at the mountain again and sound comes out of my mouth. And it didn't even hurt.

Wait. If my throat's healed it probably means I really was unconscious for a while. I wonder for how long.

Maybe I should just go back and lie. Tell them that Death said hi and that they should say their prayers and remember to floss. I mean, how would they know I wasn't telling the truth?

A calm, smooth voice says, "Lies make the baby Jesus cry. Didn't your mother tell you that? You don't want to make the baby Jesus cry, do you?"

I look up at Death. He's every bit as sharp and perfect as when he was Samael.

"Nice suit."

"I like your coat," he says, coming around in front of me. "What is that? Basilisk? The cut's a little dated, but you make it work."

"Don't worry. *GQ* called. The shoot's off. They don't use dead models."

"It depresses the readers."

"Exactly."

"I see you cut yourself. Be careful about that kind of thing in the Tenebrae. You don't want to get an infection out here. They don't go away."

"It seemed medically necessary at the time."

"Like so many of your bad decisions."

I try standing, but my legs are cramped and stiff. I must have been out for a while.

"Here's something fun. I'm on a crusade with a psychotic angel and a mob of lost boys and slaves. We're following the Yellow Brick Road to where God dropped a sword that knocked you and your pals out of Heaven. But why am I even saying it? You knew all of that, didn't you?"

He adjusts his sleeves.

"Some. With all the death your Magistrate is drumming up, business is very good these days."

"Is there anything you can do about it? By the time we find the Light Killer, I'm not sure there's going to be anyone left to save."

"*Lux Occisor*. I haven't heard that name in a long time. What memories."

I take out the Maledictions.

"I don't suppose you have a light, do you?"

He tosses me a lighter. There's a solid gold phoenix wrapped around the body. It's heavy.

"Very pretty."

"Please be careful. That's an S. T. Dupont Tournaire Red Ligne. It's worth more than your soul."

"So, about six-fifty?"

I spark the cigarette.

He holds out his hand for the lighter back. I take a step to hand it to him, but my foot comes down on the Moxie bottle. I fumble the lighter and the damn thing goes down in the dirt. I grab it and rub it on my sleeve, brushing and blowing off as much grit as I can.

"I'm really sorry, man."

I hold it out to him. He just stands there.

"Why don't you keep it?" he says. "I was thinking about getting a new one anyway."

"Seriously. I'm sorry."

"I know. Somehow, I think it was destined for you."

"Is it really expensive?"

"You don't want to know."

"I kind of do."

"What was it you were saying about a crusade?"

"Right. That."

I manage to put the lighter in my pocket without dropping it again.

"The fucking messiah I'm riding with thinks he can end the war with this big gun he's hauling around. He wants me to get you to help us. I keep wondering should I kill him? Should I help him? I don't know what to do anymore."

"Relax," says Death. "Or don't. Here's the thing. This crusade of yours is a lot more complicated than you think. I knew the Magistrate in the old days. Back when he was still Raziel, the bitchiest of the archangels. Always complaining. Always knowing more than anyone else."

"Gee. That doesn't sound like anyone we know."

"Touché. The thing was, he was even more radical than me. I merely rebelled against God. Raziel rebelled against the whole concept of any guiding force in the universe."

"I don't know what that means."

"Raziel reasons now that Father has become both God and Lucifer, killing him will free the universe of what in his mind is tyranny. That's the real reason he wants me on his side."

"He's wants you to help him kill Mr. Muninn? Why? So he can take over?"

"Not at all. He rejects all leadership."

"But he's the most goose-stepping vicious asshole do-what-I-say-or-else leader I've ever met. He plays twenty questions with whole towns, and if they lose, he kills everyone. You were a tight ass when you were Lucifer, but nothing like this guy."

"Isn't that how it always is? We become the thing we despise. And I was never a tight ass."

"If you say so."

He puts out his hand.

"Let me have a Malediction. I'm all out."

I give him the package.

"Keep it. We have crates full."

The pack is covered in dust and dried blood. He handles it with his fingertips. As soon as I light his cigarette, he tosses me back the pack.

He says, "Thank you. I'll pick some up later."

"What are we going to do about the Magistrate? You want me to kill him?"

He raises and lowers his index finger a couple of times.

"The problem is that his argument against Father isn't a bad one."

That I didn't expect.

"You *want* him to kill Mr. Muninn?"

"Of course not. But there is a logic to it. Things have to change. Even if we win this war, there will be another. And another."

"Then what's the answer?"

He puts up his hands.

"I have no idea. That's why you have to continue the crusade. Besides, there's another complication. I'm not allowed to take sides."

"Not even for your father?"

"Not even for him."

I smoke for a minute.

"Okay. I'll kill him and finish this thing right now."

"Then you'll have to kill the entire havoc," he says. "Are you ready to do that? I thought you were miffed about Raziel's massacres and here you are proposing your own."

"Then you want me to go on like nothing happened."

"There's the weapon itself to consider. Especially if he finds the Light Killer. If you murder Raziel, who knows who will end up with such a destructive force? At least now you have some control over it."

"I still have a hard time believing this whole thing is about a gun."

"Believe what you want about the weapon. Raziel is dangerous and the weapon is important."

"Why don't I just dump it in the river? Or destroy it? I bet I could do it, especially with the help from the angels."

"Can you destroy every scrap of it? Every atom? This is a celestial weapon. Any angel or Hellion knowledgeable and powerful enough could resurrect it from the smallest fragment."

"And we're right back where we started."

We just stand there smoking for a while. He looks a lot more comfortable in the wasteland than I do.

I point to his feet.

"You're getting dirt on your shoes."

He gestures to my jacket.

"Check your left lapel. There's a tiny spot that isn't completely covered in filth."

"What am I going to tell the Magistrate when I go back?"

"Tell him I'm with you. That I'll do my best from my end to see that you succeed."

"But you're not going to, right?"

"Right."

I guess that's it. I came all this way, bled in the sand, and apparently a stupid little white lie is all I'm going back with. Come on. There has to be something else.

I say, "Maybe you can't take sides, but you can throw a little chaos into the system."

"Go on."

"Let people know you have your eye on them. Miss a few pickups. You know. Death stuff. Throw the universe off a little. You don't like the job. Maybe you'll get fired."

"I do enjoy a bit of chaos," he says quietly.

Death reaches into his pocket and takes out a delicate amber blade.

"This is the knife I use to sever souls from their earthly bodies. What a lot of people, even in Heaven, don't know is that there's a little side benefit to it. It will kill *anything*. Angels included."

I take out the golden blade.

"I already have a knife that kills angels. I got it from an angel I killed."

He flicks the tip with his finger. It rings like a tiny bell.

"Very pretty. The problem is it won't penetrate an angel's

armor," he says, pressing the amber knife into my hand. "This will go through armor like water."

I turn the blade over and over. It feels like it's vibrating.

"What's going to happen to you without your knife?"

He drops his Malediction and crushes it under his million-dollar shoes.

"I have no idea, but I'm sure it will be interesting."

He rubs his hands together.

"And chaotic."

I put the amber knife in the inside pocket of my coat.

"I'll get this back to you as soon as possible. By the way, do I have to keep calling you Death?"

He thinks for a few seconds.

"Go back to Samael. As you said, I might not have the job much longer."

"Thanks. I owe you a drink when this is over."

"At Bamboo House of Dolls? I'm afraid that's a bit far for you these days."

"Nope. I'm going to get home."

"The eternal optimist."

"What else have I got?"

He says, "What if you can't go home? Not all deaths are equal, but this is the most dead you've ever been."

"Are you saying I can't go home?"

He doesn't say anything, which says a lot.

Finally he says, "There are some things you can't trick or punch your way out of. I'm sorry."

My guts feel like they've been dropped down an elevator shaft.

"You're wrong. I'll find a way."

"If you need to believe that to carry on, then believe it."

I'm getting woozy again and I don't want to fall on my face in front of him.

"I should probably be getting back."

"I'm sorry I can't give you better news."

I wave it off.

"Don't sweat it. Oh yeah, in the future, don't bother with the 'I don't take sides' line. You knew the havoc would find me when you put me on that mountain. This whole thing was your idea."

He puts a hand to his chest. "Me? Devious? I'm hurt by that."

"I'll get our angels to pray for you."

"What a horrible idea."

"I'll see you later for that drink. In L.A."

"Of course." He wipes some dust off his slacks. "The next time you want to meet, try to find someplace less desolate. Maybe the surface of the sun."

He walks away and I'm alone again.

I break the magic circle with the toe of my boot. Kick dirt over the rest and follow the big X back into the hole.

The tunnel is cool and wet. It eases my urge to throw up. Samael is wrong about me being stuck here. He has to be. It's another of his tricks. He loves his games and jokes. That's it. He's playing another angle. He fucking well better be.

By the time I make it out of the tunnel, I'm calm again.

I wave to the ship. No one waves back. They all look at me like I have baked hams on my feet. Finally, Alice comes over and smiles. I walk up the gangplank and she hugs me.

"Why is everybody looking at me like that?"

"We thought you were dead. Some people thought you might have run off, but I knew that wasn't true."

I look over and see Doris and Gisco. Both wave. Okay. Someone else remembers me.

"How long was I gone?"

"Eight days."

"Damn. That was a long nap."

"You took a nap?"

"It was a long walk to the gas station."

"I'm not even going to ask about that. Did you see Death?"

"Yeah."

"And?"

"Everything is going to be all right."

She grabs me and drags me to Vehuel, who seems a little put off by my current caked-in-filth look.

"He says that Death is on our side," says Alice.

The boss angel looks at me.

"Is that true?"

"I saw him like a half hour ago. Everything is going to be fine."

Vehuel frowns.

"I'm surprised. That doesn't sound like Death."

"Hey, if you want to go out there and eat stale donuts and sit in the fucking dirt for a week, be my guest. I'm telling you what he said and if you don't like it—"

Alice pats me on the back.

"Okay, tiger, ease off the throttle a little."

Vehuel is standing very tall, very upright. I don't think people talk to her like that too often. But I'm a gentleman. I know what to do.

I take out the golden blade and hold it out to her.

"Here. Why don't you have this back?"

She looks at me like she's waiting for a punch line or a trick. When she doesn't get either she takes the blade.

"Thank you. A number of angels will rest easier tonight," she says in a low melodious voice.

That wasn't the nicest way anyone ever said "fuck you" to me, but it sounded the prettiest.

"Did I miss anything while I was gone?"

"Lots," says Alice. "Do you want the good news or the bad news first?"

"Good."

"Lots more people ran away. Some into the tunnels, others went upstream."

"That's good? What the hell is the bad?"

"The ship with all the trucks and cars sank."

Being dead just keeps getting better and better.

FREDERICKSON SAYS, "LOOK what the cat dragged in."

"Mr. Leisure Time," says Johnny. "Have a nice walkabout, did you?"

"I did. The donuts were great. I would have brought you back one but, you know, fuck you."

Barbora, Frederickson, and Billy surround Johnny with the other assholes I never really got to know behind them. Daja, Wanuri, Doris, and Gisco are a few feet away. I get the distinct impression that while I was gone the dog pack split into the kind of factions that aren't ever going to kiss and make up, even if they're supposed to be on the same crusade. Great. Another bunch I don't want getting behind me.

I go to where Daja and her group are bunched up.

"Where's the Magistrate? I have some news for him."

"Good news?" she says.

"He should be happy."

"You saw him, then?" says Wanuri. "You saw Death?"

"That's why I went out there."

She cocks her head, more than a little skeptical.

"What does Death look like?"

"He's not a creep with a robe and a scythe scaring little kids on Halloween, if that's what you mean."

"Then what does he look like?"

"Picture the handsomest guy in the world. Now put him in the most expensive suit you can imagine. Now put a lot of dirt and scratches on his shoes."

"Death wears shitty shoes?"

"No. They're really nice. Probably custom. But we met at a gas station in the Tenebrae and they got kind of fucked up."

Wanuri shakes her head.

"I think nothing happened out there and you're pulling all of our legs, Mr. Pitts."

"Yeah? If he wasn't there, where did I get this?"

I'm not about to show them the amber knife, so I hand her the lighter.

"He said it's Tournaire Red Ligne made by P. T. Barnum or someone."

Doris looks over Wanuri's shoulder.

She says, "Did you mean S. T. Dupont?"

"Yeah. That's it. How did you know?"

"My husband's dear departed father, Jeremiah, had a Dupont."

Wanuri gives it to her. Doris looks it over carefully.

"It's a bit dirty."

"I dropped it."

"Of course you did."

"Death said it was expensive."

"I've seen other Duponts similar to it. Jeremiah's cost twenty thousand dollars."

"You're not serious," says Daja.

"Completely. He tried to bribe me with it. Wouldn't shut up about the damned thing. I cut his head off to shut him up."

Maybe I should let her keep the lighter.

I say, "Knife or ax?"

She looks at me.

"On Jeremiah? Lord, he was huge. It's always hardest getting through the spine. I had to use Grandpapa's old ax in the garden shed."

"I've taken a couple of heads myself. I know what you mean about spines."

"Thank you. Most people just don't understand the amount of work involved."

Wanuri gives me a look and cuts in. "Were you rich, Doris?"

"Obscenely," Doris says. She smiles. "That's why there was a garden big enough to do my special planting."

Johnny reaches for the lighter, but Doris snatches it away and hands it back to me.

"That doesn't mean anything," he says. "He could have had that all along."

"He's been bumming lights and matches from people since he got here," Daja says.

"Bollocks."

I flick the Dupont on and off a couple of times. Point it at Johnny.

"That's it, pal. You're off my Christmas-card list. It was going to be a good one, too. Kittens pulling Santa's sleigh."

"Stay away from me and my people," he says.

"Your people? You're a joke. A handful of cretins and scaredy-cats doesn't make you John Dillinger or the Magistrate. They'll dump you at the first sign of trouble."

"Come on," he says, and his puppy pack trails behind him, tails wagging for their master.

"That was fun. Can I go see the goddamn Magistrate now?"

"He's downstairs in his room," Daja says. With a week full of healing, her hand is looking a lot better.

We follow her to the hatch belowdecks and down the ladder.

"Is he still fucked up?"

"No. He's mostly better."

Mostly. The fucker is faking it. Archangels heal even faster than I do.

"That's good to hear."

Daja knocks on his door and we go inside.

Sure enough, he still has a big bandage wrapped around his chest. I bet he does it himself. Won't let anyone help him, not even Daja. They all think he's such a strong, brave soul when he's just exactly the kind of winged asshole I've been dealing with for years. I'd like to rip the bandage off and show everyone what a liar he is, but I stay cool. Samael was probably right. Hang on and find the Light Killer. Then make sure this clown doesn't play with it like a ten-year-old with the combination to Daddy's gun locker. He looks up from the map in surprise when I come in.

"Mr. Pitts. You have come back to us. I'd almost lost hope."

"I was out of Moxie."

He comes over and gets me in a big bear hug. For a guy who's supposed to be hurt, he's got a pretty good grip.

"Come. Sit down. Do you bring good news?"

I sit on one of the bunks while the remaining pack crowds in. I say, "Where's Traven?"

"The good father is going through what books he could save from his library. Vehuel and her companions have pinpointed the location of the Lux Occisor. We planned on sailing there tomorrow, with or without you."

"Glad I made it back for supper."

"You better eat up while you're on board. We're not taking any supplies with us when we go for the sword," says Wanuri.

"Why?"

"We cannot carry them," says the Magistrate. "Without the vehicles, we will have to move the weapon ourselves."

I look around the room. He's serious.

"We've gone from a crusade to pack mules? Why not just leave the gun, get the sword, and bring it back?"

"With whom should we leave it? Who can we trust at this point?"

"You saw Johnny and his bunch," says Daja. "He isn't the only one with a gang at this point."

I say, "What about the angels? Can't we leave the gun with them?"

"Then who would lead us to our goal?" says the Magistrate. "Who would protect us if there was another attack?"

I shake my head.

"I don't believe you people. I'm gone a few days and I come back to the end of *The Good, the Bad, and the Ugly*."

Everybody stares at me.

"It's a movie. There's a standoff in a graveyard at the end. Everybody is going to shoot everybody else."

Gisco says something and signs. I don't need a translator to know he wants to hear how it comes out.

"Clint Eastwood is the star. You do the math."

He gives me a thumbs-up.

"That is all terribly interesting, but what about the larger issue? Did you find Death?"

"Actually, he usually finds me. But yes, I did."

His eyes light up. At least someone around here believes that I know interesting people.

"And what did he say?"

"He's with us. He's not going to run around killing everybody who looks at us cross-eyed, but when the time comes, he'll be there."

"Is that all? Did he give you anything to bring back that might help us?"

I wonder if he knows about Death's hoodoo knife? He's an archangel. Of course he does. He was probably on the budget committee that approved it.

"There's this."

I hand him the lighter.

He holds it up to the light and looks it over.

"What does it do?"

"It lights cigarettes."

He hands it back to me.

"I was hoping for a more tangible symbol of his support."

"What did you want? Team jackets? He's Death. Death doesn't lie. He just kills you. Or the other guy. In our case, it's going to be the other guys."

The Magistrate sighs.

"You are right. Death is a celestial being and celestials do not lie."

Well, that's a goddamn whopper of a lie right there. Well done, Raziel.

"There you go. It's settled. Everything is going to be fine."

The Magistrate rolls up his map and heads for the door.

"Have you told Vehuel about this?"

"Not much. I only saw her for a second."

"Come. We must confer with her and prepare for tomorrow."

"Can I get something to eat after that? All I've had in a week is six stale donuts."

"What kind were they?" says Wanuri.

"Chocolate."

"Ooo. I love those. You could have brought some back for the rest of us."

"I was alone out there. I could have died, you know."

"Which doesn't alter the fact that you ate all the donuts."

"I promise. Next vision quest, everybody gets snacks."

She seems satisfied, but I don't mean a word of it. The next box of desert donuts I find, they're all mine. I think about going to Traven's cabin and telling him what Death said about me not being able to go home, but I don't do it. Either he was telling the truth or he was lying. I'm calm now. I have a handle on things. Talk about it is just going to throw me off balance again and I've been like that for too long. It's time to let things go and deal with it.

I'm stuck here. Just another sucker in a kingdom of suckers.

WE SAIL FOR a day and a half before heading back to shore. Knowing what's coming, I eat the whole time. No way I'm hauling a doomsday gun to who the fuck knows where on an empty stomach. I also want to avoid Johnny, so I don't come up on deck until we're docking.

"You're done," says Alice.

"For the moment."

"Are you proud of yourself? Are you proud of packing away as much food as a blue whale?"

"Which is bigger, a blue whale or a sperm whale?"

"Blue whales are the biggest animals ever."

"Then yes. I'm very proud."

PEOPLE WHO KNOW how to use rope and tie knots use every single inch of the ships' ropes tying lines to the double flatbed with the Light Killer. Even with all the desertions, there's still quite a mob of people left in the havoc. Still, I'm not sure it's enough to move Big Bertha. And I'm right at first. But then the fucking angels jump in like the helpful little elves they are and the flatbed slowly starts to move. Imagine my glee.

Luckily, unlike when we entered the river tunnel, there aren't any big hills going out. The side of the mountain opens for us and we grunt and curse like angry plow horses, but we get the gun moving out into whatever hellhole Vehuel and company are leading us to. The Magistrate takes Traven and Cherry up front with him and some of the angels.

The good news is that there are roads here. The bad news is that they're old and rutted. Wherever we are, it isn't like the Tenebrae. No desert monotony. No spiked mountains. It's more like forest land after a nuke attack. Bare, mossy skeleton-like trees and tough tangles of gray and green weeds sprouting on low rolling hills. Pretty much everything but the weeds seems dead here. I can't be sure about the trees. They're thick and their branches twist at strange angles. Spirals, circles, and triangles. At points, some of the branches break into so many smaller branches that they look like clusters of nerves.

We trudge onward like morons, one foot in front of the other, ropes straining on our shoulders and backs. I wonder if Samael knew about the vehicles sinking and that we'd end up like this, army ants dragging the carcass of an elephant back to our mound. Bet he did. It seems like the kind of thing he'd find hilarious. Of course he wouldn't let me in on the joke ahead of time. Where's the fun in that?

Alice walks beside me, a length of rough, grassy rope pulled tight over her armored shoulder. My legs hurt and I'm sweating like a hippo in the middle of a triathlon. She, on the other hand, looks like she's carrying a basket of daisies to Grandma's house.

"This isn't fair," I say.

"What?"

"You angels have all this Incredible Hulk strength. Why do the rest of us have to pull at all?"

"Isn't there an old saying about idle hands?"

"I wouldn't know. The only sayings I can remember are old Iggy and the Stooges lyrics. See? All this pulling is bad for my health. I think I'm having an aneurysm."

"Do you even know what an aneurysm is?"

"A little furry thing. Like a wombat."

"Right on the money," she says. "If you're having such a hard time pulling, why don't you use some of your hocus-pocus to float the gun where it's supposed to go."

"You'd like that, wouldn't you? I'd probably blow it up and let you angels off the hook."

"Seriously, why don't you at least make it easier for yourself?"

"I can't take any chances on hurting the gun."

We pass a pond of hot, bubbling shit. The smell is excruciating. Welcome back to Hell. You whined all this time about being in the Tenebrae and now you're on home turf. *Happy now, asshole?*

"Did Death tell you something about the gun while you were out there?"

"Yes. But I can't talk about it here. The only thing that's important is getting the Light Killer."

"Then shut up and keep pulling, Bessie."

"Bessie?"

"Isn't that what you call cows?"

"Bossie."

"Trivia. I knew we kept you around for something."

"Keep pulling, Supergirl."

The Magistrate calls a cigarette break at midday. Everyone in the dog pack that's still speaking wants a light from a 20K gold lighter.

Afterward, I sit with Alice by one of the nuke-blasted trees.

"I want to show you something. I got it when I was with Death."

"You're not going to trick me and show me a spider, are you? I hate spiders."

"It's not a spider."

"It better not be."

I take out the amber blade, but keep it hidden under my coat.

"It belongs to him. He uses it to cut souls from their bodies. He says it'll kill anything."

"That's spooky. What are you supposed to do with it?"

"He wasn't specific on that part, just that I should have it for now."

"Why are you showing it to me?"

"If I should mysteriously snuff it, you need to get it before anybody else. I don't even want Vehuel having it."

She looks at me.

"Nothing is going to happen to you."

"How are you so sure?"

"Do you see this armor? I'm kind of a warrior now. I'll kill them."

"Thanks."

"Don't mention it."

"But just in case."

"I know. Get the knife. Got it. Now let's change the subject."

"Okay."

"If you could go to Heaven, would you?"

"No."

"Don't be so glib."

"I'm not. I'm not built for Heaven. I'm built for killing things and Hell is where killers go."

She picks up a dry twig and waves it in the air like a conductor's baton.

"You're the one trying to open Heaven to all the souls in Hell, killers included."

"Still."

"Fine."

"Don't be mad."

"I'm not mad. I knew exactly what you were going to say and you didn't disappoint."

"I'm sorry."

The Magistrate calls for us plow horses to get back to work.

Alice tosses the twig away.

"I think I'm going to go in the back and walk with Vehuel and the others for a while."

"If that's what you want."

"It's what I want."

"See you later."

She doesn't say anything. I go back to my rope feeling like the biggest idiot in Heaven, Hell, or Earth. Alice isn't dying and I'm not being dragged away anywhere, but it feels a lot like I lost her all over again. It's confusing and I don't like it.

We pull the flatbed for another slow, tedious, agonizing day and a half through mud, streams of shit, waterfalls of blood, and over a road paved with bones. People collapse and have to be tossed on the flatbed, making it even heavier. Others run batshit into the wilderness. A couple of people die in gang fights.

I don't see Alice again the whole time.

AT THE END of the second day, and with everybody at the breaking point, it rains. I don't know if it's water. I'm just grateful it isn't any bodily secretions. Except, of course, the road turns to a swamp and the flatbed bogs down. The angels come up front and pull while us puny types push from the back. It doesn't help. Neither does getting them to push and the rest of us to pull. The Magistrate meets with Vehuel, some of the mechanics, and other people who seem to have a fucking clue and they come up with a plan. A really bad one.

We need to get something under the wheels for them to grip and the only things around are the skeleton trees. A contingent of the Magistrate's goons and conscripts drags their asses up a hill and starts chopping down the forest. They have to clear a whole hillside to get enough wood for the twin flatbeds' wheels. It takes hours to get the wood into place because a lot of the first batch sinks with the wheels and a second crew has to cut up the opposite hill. Eventually, we get enough wood, but we get something more, too.

At first it looks like a landslide down the bare, muddy hill, but it's too slow and too regular. It doesn't rush down toward us as much as it skitters. Vehuel and Johel manifest their Gladiuses to light the hillside.

I'm only here because I'm dead. I didn't sign up for this shit.

It turns out what's coming down the hill isn't an *it* at all. It's a *they*. About a million of them. Each about the size of my hand. The beetle colony must have nested under the trees and took exception to a bunch of strangers stealing their homes.

The insect mass is a solid carpet of writhing legs and

ripping jaws. Turns out that not only are these particular beetles ill-mannered, they're also carnivorous.

They hit the part of the havoc still coming down the hillside first, swarming over them until they've disappeared under the beetles' bodies. By the time the insects move down to the road, anyone who was alive a couple of minutes earlier is stripped to the bones and blips away. The havoc panics. Most of them rush up the opposite hillside, but a handful of souls and Hellions freeze in place or get bogged down in the mud. The first wave of beetles covers them while others swarm around their bodies headed farther onto the road. Even the angels look lost. They're used to fighting other angels, not chasing roaches when the lights come on.

People scatter, but there's nowhere to scatter to. The bugs are everywhere. Muffled screams under piles of beetles as souls and Hellions try to claw their way out. Flashes of bones as bodies are stripped of their flesh. People scramble onto the flatbed, but the little bastards are going to swarm that soon, too.

No way I'm going out as bug food and neither is Alice.

I can't think of anything else to do, so I bark some Hellion hoodoo at the front of the beetle wave. They explode into flames. The fire burns from the vanguard of the insects, spreading out across the hillside. Beetle bodies smoke and explode like monster popcorn, tossing their guts into the air.

The rain keeps falling. The angels look at me and I look right back at them.

"Great plan. Nice fucking road."

When we finally get the flatbed moving again, the rain changes. People scream as tiny objects from the sky slash their skin. Some people hide under the skeleton trees, but most of the havoc dive under the flatbed as a razor storm cascades from the skies. The weird part is that it sounds nice. Like a million little bells tinkling overhead.

A few minutes into the deluge, Alice runs over and slides under the flatbed next to me.

"Are you all right?" she says.

"I'm fine. Do you know what's going on?"

"Unfortunately yes. It's the war. Things are getting worse. Do you know what celestial spheres are?"

"Yeah. They're big glass globes that hold the light Mr. Muninn uses to make stars."

If she's impressed by my knowledge, she doesn't show it. "Not anymore. That's them breaking into a million little pieces."

"You're losing, aren't you? The ones loyal to Mr. Muninn."

"We weren't supposed to say anything. Please don't tell anyone."

"I won't. But are *you* okay?"

"Yeah. I guess."

"Just stay here. It can't last forever."

Turns out I'm not as good a swami as Cherry. The glass falls through the night and the next day. The good news is that it does stop, and when it does, the rain stops, too. We shovel as much glass as we can from around the wheels and push the flatbed free. The Magistrate stands up front with the angels. His map was torn to shreds in the glass-fall. Good. Disgusted, he throws it onto the side of the road. I think everyone is expecting one of his Holy Roller pep talks, but the only thing he says is, "Let us get moving."

Not exactly Dale Carnegie material.

We throw the ropes back over our shoulders and start pulling again. No one has eaten in over two days and the only water we've had is what fell from the sky. The angels better pull a miracle out of their saintly asses soon or there isn't going to be anyone left to care who wins or loses their goddamn war.

AFTER ANOTHER DAY of pulling, and people collapsing or running off, we come to a crossroads. Strange, skeletal trees line both sides of the road and the hills. The branches look like they're the bones of snakes woven around each other and posed to look like a forest by a very bad gardener or a very good taxidermist.

Vehuel and the Magistrate march to the front of the flatbeds. Vehuel's red hair is stringier than when I first saw her. She and the other angels are as caked in mud and filth as the rest of us. It's quite satisfying. On the other hand, except for his muddy boots, the Magistrate looks like he just got back from two weeks in Cabo. I hate him more by the minute.

Vehuel says, "Loyal friends, I have good news for you all. We have reached our destination. The weapon needs to be pulled no farther. In an hour or two, we will have the Lux Occisor in our possession and the weapon will be ready to return to Heaven so that God may use it to destroy his enemies."

The Magistrate gives her an enthusiastic round of applause, but everyone else is too exhausted and sore to even pretend they're excited. A few relieved groans is all she gets.

Someone up front yells, "Where is the bloody thing?" It's Johnny. Ever the gentleman.

Vehuel points up the road to her left.

"In a nearby stronghold called Henoch Breach."

Now. That's weird. I swear I know that name from somewhere. It's on the tip of my tongue. Why does something in an area this obscure, even by Hellion standards, seem so familiar?

The Magistrate says, "We might need assistance in retrieving the sword. I wonder if Daja and Mr. Pitts would care to join us?"

We join him and the angel crew. Daja stares up the dark road. She looks nervous. I don't blame her.

"You have six armored angels," I say. "Why do you need us?"

"It was Vehuel's idea," the Magistrate says. "Is that not right?"

"It was," Vehuel says. "Let's get started and I'll explain along the way."

I tilt my head toward the havoc.

"What about them? What makes you think they're not going to run off or kill each other while we're gone?"

The Magistrate shakes his head. "Let them. There is little use for the havoc anymore."

"What do you mean?" says Daja. "Those are our friends. Members of the crusade."

"And God will remember the worthy ones. The others will have to fend for themselves." He takes Daja by the shoulders and says, "Try to understand. The crusade itself is what is important. Not the crusaders."

And there it is. The voice of a true believer. Nothing matters but him and his obsession. The people that followed him for how long through the desert don't mean anything more to him than the slaves he captured in the towns he burned along the way. I met freaks like this everywhere. Everyone has. Not just in Hell and not just in wars. They're people you pass on the street. A preacher, a grocery-store manager, a parent. Anyone with a vision and enough of a vicious streak to make it come true no matter what they have to destroy or who they have to chew up and spit out along the way. Even Mr. Muninn was like that in the old days. There were older gods than him, but he tricked them out of this universe and then locked them out forever. That was the plan, but they found their way back and almost destroyed Creation. And sometimes that's the only small satisfaction you can hope for with someone like the Magistrate. Sometimes there's something they missed, or something they thought was dead, or someone they were sure was on their side, but they were wrong. That one small mistake can bring them down, but not until they've burned and ruined everything around them. I wonder if Vehuel understands that about him? He'll kill her angels, too, if he doesn't get what he wants. I touch my coat and feel Samael's amber knife where I left it. I won't use it on him if I don't have to, but if I *do* have to, I'm going to enjoy every second of it.

Daja says, "You can't mean that about everybody. What about Wanuri and Doris? What about Gisco?"

"The Almighty will look after them."

"What about me?"

He pulls her close and says, "You are different, Dajaskinos. You will always be with me."

I want to tell her, *Until you're inconvenient or ask the*

wrong question so that the messiah questions your faith. Then we'll see how different you are from the rabble he's throwing on the fire.

I shake my head and look at Alice. She sees exactly what I see, but she stays quiet and for the same reason as me. The Light Killer is too important.

"I don't understand what's happening," says Daja.

"You will," says the Magistrate. "Soon. But for now, we must make this last, short journey to the sword. Once we have it, our real work begins."

"All right, Father."

"Good girl."

He keeps an arm around her as Vehuel leads us to Henoch Breach. It's almost painful to watch Daja so manipulated, and it's all I can do to not plunge Death's knife between the Magistrate's wing scars.

Instead I just grit my teeth and keep walking.

IT'S NOT LONG before we come to a deserted town. It's old, as old as anything I've seen Downtown. No one has lived here in a long time. In places, the buildings are so overgrown with the skeleton trees and tough weeds that they look like something that sprouted from the dead soil. The style of the buildings looks Hellion, but not quite. Simpler. Less ornate than the elaborate Hellion designs on the buildings and vehicles in Pandemonium.

I don't notice that Vehuel has fallen back to walk with me until she says something.

"You're staring."

"It's a ghost town. Why shouldn't I look? Besides, maybe there's something valuable in the houses. Maybe something to eat. Or smoke. I'm almost out of cigarettes."

"You won't find any Maledictions in these buildings."

"Yeah? Why not?"

"I've read about this place," says Traven from a few feet away. "Maledictions didn't exist when Henoch was built. They didn't exist until centuries later in Pandemonium."

Traven is limping, but he keeps pace with us.

"You sound like a tourist brochure, Father. Is there a souvenir shop? I might need a snow globe."

Vehuel smiles when she looks at me, not taking anything I'm saying personally. It bugs me. What does she know?

"None of this looks familiar?" says Vehuel. "Maybe you saw it in a dream?"

"Some of it, I guess. But all old, dead towns are the same, don't you think?"

"I wouldn't know. There are no ghost towns in Heaven."

"I get it now. It's a real-estate scam. You take us to the middle of nowhere and we can't go back until we sit through a time-share sales pitch."

The angels all laugh, all except for Alice and Traven. They look worried, but not because I refuse to kiss the boss angel's ass.

"What do you know about the first war in Heaven?" Vehuel says.

"Lucifer rebelled. God threw him out. End of story."

"When you say Lucifer, of course you mean Samael."

"Of course. Who else?"

"I'm talking about the *first* war in Heaven. The one led by Maleephas. Samael's petulant conflict was the second."

Maleephas.

There it is again. That annoying feeling that I've been here and heard that name before.

"It's frustrating, isn't it? To be so close to remembering, but unable to make the connections?"

"Please, Vehuel. Just tell him," says Alice.

"Tell me what?"

Vehuel says, "You've been here before."

"No. I haven't."

"You were here and you killed an old man. The angel Maleephas. The first Lucifer."

I stop in the road.

"Samael was the first Lucifer. I was the second."

Vehuel shakes her head.

"Samael was the second to hold the title of Lucifer. You were the third. *Maleephas* was the first."

"Henoch Breech. I wasn't sure it was real," says Traven. "This is where the first war in Heaven ended. This is where Hell began. Not Pandemonium."

Something scratches at the back of my skull.

"That's a nice bedtime story, but I don't believe it."

"Wait a minute," says Daja. "You're Lucifer?"

"*Was* Lucifer. Past tense. I was tricked into the job. I was lousy at it. And I didn't do it long. That's why Mr. Muninn—God—took over."

She looks at the Magistrate and Traven.

"Is any of this true?"

Traven nods.

He says, "Yes, my dear. You see, the ways of Heaven and Hell are more complex than most realize. Lucifer is merely a name. A title that can be handed down to anyone as qualified or unqualified as Sandman Slim here."

"Then he's not the Devil anymore."

"No he is not. He was barely the Devil when he held Lucifer's title."

"I was Lucifer down here for one hundred days and not a second more. Look it up. It's probably in a history book somewhere, right?"

I look at Vehuel.

"It's amusing that you should mention history," she says. "Yours is missing a few days, isn't it? The memories of them, I mean."

"If I don't remember them, how should I know?"

Vehuel stops. I stop with her. She looks at me with a mix of amusement and pity. It's not a look I enjoy.

"Trust me—you've been here before. And not that long ago," she says. "You killed Maleephas and burned his palace, such as it was. You did all these things, but the memory was taken from you."

"Why?"

"Because even among the Hellion, the myth of Lucifer was strong. By the time Samael fell, few among the angels even remembered Maleephas. The only way the fallen could build a new Perdition was to believe that they were the true rebels, the glorious first ones."

We continue up the road and come to a large, burned-out mansion. I can't do anything but stare.

Bits and pieces are coming together for me.

What did Samael say in the desert? Something about how things had to change or there would be another war in Heaven and another after that? Is Henoch Breach what he was talking about? He'd already lived through one war, started one himself, and was now caught in a third. He was trying to tell me about this, but with the same twisty logic that he always uses, he couldn't come right out and say it. He probably thought I needed to see it to believe it and understand. And now I do.

"They poisoned me, didn't they?"

Vehuel nods.

"Yes. So you'd forget Maleephas and this place. You had to kill him to make Hell secure, but you weren't allowed to bring the knowledge of the first Hell back to the current one. It would have destroyed it."

Alice comes over to me.

"Are you all right?"

"Yeah. I think so. I don't know."

I give Vehuel a look. She's enjoying tormenting me just a little too much for my taste.

"Why are you telling me all this? What does it matter if I remember Henoch Breach or not?"

"I think they need you," says Traven. "You can't get the Light Killer, can you?"

Vehuel nods.

"It's not for angels of the Lord to retrieve the Lux Occisor. It's Lucifer's job."

"I'm not Lucifer anymore," I say.

"I was being polite. It's a job for an Abomination."

There it is. A dirty job for a dirty guy. She had a good time saying it, too. "What if I don't do it? What if I tell you all to fuck off, and find a way back to Pandemonium myself?"

"Jim," says Alice. "Please."

Vehuel says, "That's an option, of course. And you're right, but remember this. Without the sword, the war will go on. And God—Mr. Muninn, as you like to call him—will lose. The loss of Heaven, and the final and irrevocable damnation of all mortal souls, fallen, and loyal angels will lie squarely on your shoulders."

I look around at everyone. Daja is confused and scared. The Magistrate is practically licking his lips he's so excited. Traven looks overwhelmed seeing an obscure story in his obscure books coming true. Hell isn't Hell. The Devil isn't the Devil. Next you'll tell me that Mickey Mouse is just a guy in a costume.

The looks on the angels' faces range from bemused to angry and, in the case of Alice, worried.

"I told you this was a real-estate scam. You're a hard-sell bastard."

"It was necessary."

"You enjoyed it."

"A bit."

"I was right. All you angels are assholes."

"By your definition, yes," she says.

I look around, trying to figure an angle, but I can't find it any more than I can find a way home. It hits me hard that I'm probably really stuck here, that maybe my whole life has been manipulated to put me here at this moment.

"Fuck. Okay. I hate you celestials, you know."

Vehuel cocks an eyebrow.

"Even Alice?"

I look away for a minute. Rub a knot at the back of my neck.

"Talk to me like that again and I'll let Heaven and all the rest of it fall just to watch you burn."

"Jim, please," says Alice.

When I turn back Vehuel tries to stare me down. It doesn't work. She needs me.

"Very well," she says reluctantly. "Please accept my apology."

"Fuck that. Where do I go?"

"To Gan Eden."

"The Garden of Eden? I definitely remember burning *that* to the ground."

"Not that Eden. The evil, mocking one Maleephas built here. It lies just behind the ruins of his palace. You'll find the Lux Occisor hanging from a tree in the center."

"Just like an angel," I say, shaking my head. "Now I know why you don't want to touch it. You don't want to handle one of the big man's great fuck-ups."

Johel takes a step in my direction, but Vehuel holds up a hand to stop him.

"Will you retrieve the sword and fulfill your destiny?"

I give them all a big toothy smile.

"It must twist you up inside knowing trash like me can do something you can't."

"Then you'll go?"

"Yeah. I'll go. Just so I can tell you to kiss my ass when I bring it back."

"You've made a wise choice," says Vehuel.

"Careful. You're going to talk me out of it."

"You don't have to go alone," says Alice. "I'll come with you."

I look at the other angels, then back at her. "No. You'll be tainted meat like me if you do. And you have to live with these pricks. I don't."

"Be careful."

"I always am."

"No, you never are."

"Just this once, then."

The Magistrate hasn't said a word this whole time. He just stands there like a mantis, all insect patience and killer instincts. I wonder how much of this story he knew? Maybe all of it. Certainly enough to go along with dragging the gun all this way.

I nod to Traven and look around for Cherry, but she's gone. Probably off rattling cookie jars looking for pennies in empty houses.

I walk into the ruins.

FOR A PALACE, the place isn't that impressive. I've seen bigger mansions in Beverly Hills. Still, considering it was probably the first thing the first fallen angels built after their nine-day tumble from Heaven, it's all right. I step over fallen beams and a few blackened sticks of furniture. Half a door on my right. Melted glass from the windows. It glazes a pile of blackened bones like a thick coating of ice. I kick through the debris to get a better look and uncover a whole skeleton. Is this what's left of Maleephas? Why is there anything left at all? He should have blipped out of existence here and slid down to Tartarus. Unless it's not him, but the remains of whatever hapless fallen angels first built the palace, long before

Tartarus even existed. If that's true, this place is even older than I thought. Maybe old enough that, like Vehuel said, even angels could forget about it.

Most of the grounds around the palace are as fried as the house. There are more bones out back. Maybe I was right. It could be a graveyard back here, an honored burial place at the first palace for the workers who built it. What a way to end up. From sitting at Mr. Muninn's right hand to a pile of bones in a barbecued condo in the heart of Nowhereville. At least the beetles got a good meal out of the whole sad wreck of a rebellion.

Okay—no more maudlin shit until I find the Light Killer. I wonder if it would be all right to kill the Magistrate when I hand the sword over to the angels. I might have to. He isn't going to let it go easily. At least there's that to look forward to. Now I just have to find the damn thing.

Finally, at the top of a blackened hill, I come to a fence. The fire from the palace came most of the way up here, but it didn't get past the big iron gate sealing the place shut. The lock is so old and rusty that it shatters with one good kick. I go inside, and sure enough, I'm back in Eden. Of course, the plants here aren't as Hello Kitty bright as the other Eden. The stunted trees are gnarled and bent. The few flowers left look like living razor blades and little meat grinders where the scattered remains of beetles fertilize the fetid soil. Pale vines follow me as I walk, cooing and sighing, hoping I have oatmeal for brains and will get close enough that they can drag me off and eat me at their leisure. And at the center of all this treacherous merriment is a skeleton tree. It's sturdier than the others we've seen. Taller and thicker. Its branches are as big around as my leg.

And hanging from one of them is a golden sword.

It's a little hard to believe at first and, honestly, a little disappointing. I mean, after all we've been through, all the attacks and traps, I was expecting a Sphinx to ask me some riddles or at least a few shambling zombies. But there's nothing here but me and a dumb tree.

Fuck it. Let's get the pigsticker and get out of here. I've got people to kill.

The tree is in a little bed of purple and puke-yellow flowers. I stroll through them and reach up to grab the Light Killer when a stabbing pain shoots up both legs. I jump back and check myself. There's no blood, but the bottoms of my leather pants are shredded. I squint at the flower bed, looking for the razors and meat grinders from earlier, but what I find is even better.

It's a whole plot of flowers ranging from a few inches to a foot high. They have petals like roses, but in the center of each blossom is a bright white set of teeth. They snap and snarl at me when I get close enough to give them a once-over.

The front teeth are sharp with big canine fangs at the edges. The big ones are like Rottweiler flowers, while the little ones bark and nip like Pomeranians with an attitude. There's a good six feet of them between me and the tree. I look around for something to smash them with, but everything in here is as mean as these mutt posies.

Think, goddammit.

I have to go all the way back to the palace and carry an armload of unburned chair legs and arms. I toss them carefully among the fleabag flowers, and they land in a rough rectangle about eighteen inches wide and long enough to reach from where I am to the base of the tree. When I'm satisfied with the shape, I get out my plastic bottle and splash Aqua Regia all over the wood. The little dog mouths lap the stuff up. Enjoy the drink, puppies. It's going to be your last.

I crouch by the edge of the flower bed and spark the phoenix lighter. The Aqua Regia explodes into flame, burning me a nice path through the hungry mouths. I actually feel kind of bad for the little curs. It's not their fault they're a cannibal florist shop. Unlike most of the havoc, they were bred to be the way they are.

I drink the rest of the Aqua Regia and wait for the flames to die down. When they're low enough that I'm reasonably sure I'm not going to go up like a Roman candle, I walk carefully through the little walkway I've created. The flowers on either side of the path growl and stretch their stupid stems to get a piece of me, but they can't quite reach.

When I get to the tree I don't touch the sword right away. I take out Doris's butcher knife and probe around the branch. After all, the tree in the other Eden had a snake in it. Who knows what kind of nefarious wrigglers might be hiding in this one?

But the blade comes back clean and with no bite marks. I sniff it and don't smell any obvious poison. And I didn't trigger any booby traps. Still, I don't exactly want to reach up there and just grab the sword. I should have kept the golden blade instead of being all magnanimous and giving it back. Lesson learned: once you get a weapon, never, ever give it up. Unless it's the amber blade. That one I promised to give back, but that's a special case. Now that I think about it, I wonder if it might be useful here. If there is something hiding in the branches, maybe it will kill it before it gets a piece of me.

I put away the butcher knife and take out the amber blade. Probe around the branch the way I had a couple of minutes earlier, but this time it's different. The moment I touch the tree, there's a crack. The trunk sags a few inches and slips to the side. Branches fall off all around me. Shit. I killed the thing. It's funny watching something die that's older than anything you know. I don't exactly feel bad about it, but it's another reminder of how everything snuffs it somewhere, sometime. Maybe I should get over being dead and figure out the best way to spend eternity. For damn sure it isn't going to be in this weed patch.

Finally, the branch right above my head snaps off. I have to duck out of the way, then twist around to catch the falling sword. The moment I have it in my arms, I, very carefully, slip the amber blade back inside my coat.

The flames have died down enough on my walkway that the nearest dog blossoms can reach me. I have to jump out of the flower bed to keep from getting gnawed to death.

And that's it. I have Mr. Muninn's sword in my defiled Abomination hands and neither of us exploded or turned into a pillar of salt. The gold is beautiful, but I'm surprised. I mean, it's just a sword. I was expecting something that vibrated with power the way the amber blade does. This is just a sword. And it's light for gold. I swing it through the air a few times. The weight is perfect. I'd really like to keep it for a while and play with it, but there's a bunch of grumpy killers and angels and a soon-to-be-dead messiah waiting for me.

I remind myself that I can't get too anxious about doing in the Magistrate. Not with Daja around. She doesn't realize I'd be helping her, and I won't have the time to explain to her the facts of life. So, just like every other goddamn thing on this fun-house ride, I'm going to have to wait and pick the right moment. And Daja isn't the only one I'm worried about. I have to make sure Traven is clear of the havoc before I do anything. But I've waited this long. A little longer won't make any difference.

THEY WAIT FOR me at the edge of the ruins. It doesn't look like anyone wants to get closer to the spooky junkyard, so I put on a little show. Swinging the sword. Spinning it. Flipping it end over end into the air and catching it just before it hits the ground. Alice laughs, but Vehuel and the other angels look like they're about to have kittens, so I let them off the hook. Stepping out of the ruined palace, I toss Vehuel the sword. She plucks it out of the air more gracefully than I ever could. Angel show-off.

"You're welcome," I shout before taking a deep and obnoxious bow.

The angels crowd around Vehuel, laying hands on the sword like sixties teenyboppers trying to touch the holy hem of Jagger's tailored suit.

"It's beautiful," says Vehuel.

I pat my pockets, looking for a cigarette. Find a pack of Maledictions with one last soldier inside.

"It's pretty," I say, "but until you've had a Singapore sling at Bamboo House of Dolls don't talk to me about beautiful. Carlos is Picasso with little umbrellas."

No one is paying attention. Here I am telling these halo jockeys about the best place in L.A. for a celebration drink, but none of them hears a word. They're all too busy wanting to get back to Heaven for milk and cookies. An angel wouldn't know fun if it showed up in a blimp with dancing girls and a full bar.

Traven and the Magistrate go over to cop a feel from Excalibur, leaving Daja alone. I walk to her and offer her the Malediction. She takes it, has a couple of puffs, and hands it back.

"Thanks."

"Anytime."

"That's it, then? That's God's sword?"

"That's it."

"I thought it would be bigger."

"Me too. It's light for gold. But I guess Mr. Muninn can do what he wants with the molecules or atoms or whatever."

I hand her back the cigarette. She puffs and hands it back.

"I don't understand anymore. We take it back to the weapon, make it work, and then what? Do we have to drag it back into Hell?"

"I'm not dragging that thing one more foot."

"A lot of people feel that way. Maybe they'll take us to Heaven with them to fight."

"I doubt that. Odds are they'll take the gun and piss off back home, leaving us here with a pat on the ass and a promise to call the next day. But they never call."

She gives me a look.

"What are you talking about?"

"It's a metaphor . . . or maybe a simile. I'm not sure. What

I mean is Vehuel and the rest are done with us. They have what they want and they don't care about us any more than the Magistrate cares about those morons he's been dragging through the desert."

"That's not true," she says. "He cares. You just misunderstood."

"Sure. It's all a misunderstanding."

I give her the last of the Malediction. She finishes it and absently drops it on the ground. It's hard when your parents disappoint you and doubly hard in Hell when you thought you were having Sunday dinner with the messiah. Whatever Daja was when she got Downtown, she's more screwed up than when she got here, and that's not fair. Of course, fair doesn't mean anything in this universe. The winners are the schemers and the ruthless who take what they want, not the suckers standing around hoping for an even break. Still, it's one more reason I'll enjoy killing the Magistrate.

But I might not get the chance. I think some other people have the same idea.

The angels with their supersonic ears hear them first. By the time Daja and I notice them, the mob is practically on top of us. Or rather, from the way they're spaced out, two different mobs come at us side by side. This is definitely a pitchforks-and-torches situation.

Johnny is at the head of one mob. Wanuri leads the other. Two mild-mannered personalities. Nothing bad can come of this.

Wanuri shouts, "Daja! Magistrate—be careful!"

"Is that the sword?" says Johnny. He's holding Doris's *panabas*. There's no way she gave it to him voluntarily. I scan

Wanuri's bunch and see her with them, a deep gash across her forehead.

"Hand it over," Johnny says.

See, this is what I meant by fair. The problem here is that while Wanuri and her group are clearly looking out for people they consider friends, Johnny's horde is twice as big. The only thing keeping his bunch from ripping hers apart is that Wanuri was smart enough to keep control of the guns. Almost everyone in her group is armed. So, why aren't they shooting? I have a bad feeling I know the answer.

Johnny is flanked by Billy and Frederickson. Barbora is nearby with a small contingent of Hellions. She nervously taps a length of pipe against her leg. The mob behind them looks tired, hungry, and desperate. I'm sure they're going to listen to reason.

Vehuel holds the sword across her chest.

"The Lux Occisor belongs to the Almighty, not damned mortals and fallen angels. You will not have it."

"Look," says Johnny in a more reasonable tone. "We're going to take it. Yes, you're bloody angels and all the rest of it, but even with those sparklers you call swords, there are only six of you. There are a lot more of us and you can't take all of us down."

Vehuel takes a step toward the crowd. A few of them back up.

"Do not test my patience, mortal."

Johnny points at her.

"We know you can die."

He points to me.

"That shit stain there killed one of you by himself. I figure all the rest of us together must equal six of him."

"You don't," I shout. "Go home before they chop you into kitty litter."

"You're next, mate. We take the sword and then we settle with you."

I turn to Vehuel.

"In that case, feel free to kill them all, starting with Chopper Read up there in the front."

"Why do you even want the sword?" says Daja. "What good is it going to do you out here?"

"He does not want it out here, do you, Johnny?" says the Magistrate. "You and your serfs will drag the weapon all the way to Pandemonium. That is your plan, is it not? You will set up your own private fiefdom in Hell's ashes and crown yourself its king. The master of ruins. That is quite a title, Johnny. Your mother would be so proud."

"Leave her out of this."

"Of course. I did not mean to offend. But I am curious: How do Frederickson and Billy feel about being your lackeys once you have secured your kingship? Or do you plan on killing them, too?"

"Enough!" he shouts. "We'll have the sword or your head, or maybe we'll have both. How does that sound to everybody?"

That idea gets a nice rise out of Johnny's glee club.

The Magistrate says, "Wanuri. Would you mind killing Johnny and his confederates if they move toward the angels?"

"With pleasure," she says.

Johnny shakes his head.

"They're bluffing. I helped to move supplies from the trucks to the ship. There was barely any ammo left. Miss *boong* and her tribe have a lot of guns, but I know for a fact that half of them are empty."

Yeah. That's what I was afraid of.

I look hard at Wanuri. Her eyes glance nervously left and right. Johnny is right. She's bluffing. There's no way to stop what's going to happen. Maybe six angels really can hold off this many psychos, but a lot of people I kind of like are going to get hurt. I wonder how many people I can take with the amber knife before they take me down. I also have the na'at, the Colt, and the butcher knife. Dying again isn't what I hoped for today, but I should be able to take a fair number of Johnny's idiots with me to Tartarus.

Alice comes and stands beside me.

"Don't worry. I'll protect you," she says.

"That's my line."

"Yeah? How's that Gladius of yours coming?"

"Sure. Kick me when I'm down."

I look around. Traven has gone to stand with Wanuri's group. Cherry, however, is still missing.

Alice shouts, "Vehuel!"

I turn and see something I've never seen before. An all-out brawl among angels. Johel and a dark-haired female are on top of Vehuel, trying to wrestle the sword away from her. The sixth angel is already dead.

Oh, fuck. They're rebels.

Me and Alice run over. While Johel and Vehuel continue to fight, the dark-haired woman gets up and manifests her Gladius. Alice never stops running. She manifests hers and the two of them slam into each other in a thunderclap of noise and light. I head over to help, but they both extend their wings and flap into the air. Not much good I can do there. So I do the only thing I can think of: I jump on Johel's back and get an arm around his throat. He lets go of Vehuel and does a quick flip, throwing himself on top of me. With all that armor on, he knocks the wind out of me just long enough to jump to his feet and manifest his Gladius. He's fast, but so am I. He brings it down hard and the ground sizzles around it when he misses. No way this is going to be a fair fight without my Gladius. So I do the only logical thing.

I cheat.

With one hand I pull out the na'at, and with the other hand, I reach into my coat. Extending the na'at to its full length, I flick it at Johel like a whip. The Gladius slices through it like a blowtorch through Rocky Road. Too bad. I'm sorry to see the na'at go, but using it did give me enough time to get out the amber knife. He sees a blade in my hand, but just laughs at the skinny thing. Then he charges me.

I throw the knife.

At first I can't be sure anything happened. But then Johel starts pulling at his chest, trying to get his armor off. His Gladius goes out and he falls on his back, breathing hard. I guess Samael was right. The knife does go through angel armor. Good to know. I run to get the knife back, but it's not there. I roll him over and there's blood on his back. The knife went all the way through him and embedded itself in a nearby tree, which is also extremely dead. I run and grab the knife, scanning the sky overhead for Alice.

She and the dark-haired angel are still fighting. Vehuel

struggles to her feet, leaking pearly angel blood. When I get to her, she shoves the Light Killer into my arms saying, "Guard it." Then she leaps into the air and disappears.

This leaves me in a slightly awkward position. While Johnny and his clown show weren't about to jump into an angel rumble, they're not nearly as reluctant to come after me.

"Little help here," I shout.

"Don't do it, Johnny," says Wanuri, leveling her rifle at him.

He says, "Do you even have any bullets, you slit?"

"One way to find out fast."

He makes a quick, unconvincing feint in her direction and she backs up a step.

Fuck.

"That's what I thought," he says, laughing, then calls back to his people. "Get him."

This is where things get weird. Again. Remember how I was kind of disappointed about how there weren't any traps or tricks by Maleephas's tree? Funny thing. It turns out there was something, only it was very old and probably a bit rusty and it took a while to get cranking.

Because all around us, the skeleton trees begin to come apart. Branches unwrapping from around each other. Trunks splitting apart and moving on their own. The pieces start to connect for me. Whatever happened to all the hapless fallen angels when the town came apart? Funny thing. They never left. They *are* the trees.

All around us, trees come undone and naked bodies— dry skin stretched over brittle bones like hundred-year-old roadkill—lumber down the hills in our direction.

Up and down the line, Johnny's troops begin to scream. You see, Wanuri's bunch ran up the side of the road close the buildings, while Johnny's kept to the side of the road that ran along the base of the hills. Like the beetle attack earlier, the shambling tree zombies overwhelm Johnny's line with sheer numbers. To give them credit, Johnny's troops go down fighting. Barbora takes down three with her pipe before she's dog-piled and disappears. Billy almost makes it out of the fight with two zombies on his back and one on his front. Frederickson . . . well, they go for his scalped head like it's a bargain buffet on a Sunday after church. He vanishes, one arm flailing like he's trying to hail a cab.

I grab Daja and we take off running for Wanuri's group.

She and everybody else with a loaded weapon fires into the hobbling piles of gristle. They take down a lot, but Henoch must have been a pretty big town. There are plenty more behind them. I run down to her with the sword in my arms.

"Come on!" I shout.

"Where?"

"To the gun. We can make it work now."

I don't have to tell any of them twice. We sprint back to the crossroads like the freaked-out bunnies we are. I want to say that we all make it, but things don't work out like that. A lot of people get taken down along the way. Most of the dog pack I know is in front of me. So is Traven. I look up, hoping to catch a glimpse of Alice, but all I can see are flashes of light when Gladiuses smash into each other. I turn away. I don't want to know what happens until it's over. I know if the wrong angel comes down I can kill it. That's all I need to know.

"Where's the Magistrate?" yells Daja. The idiot stops for a second and I have to grab her and drag her behind me. I want to tell her that wherever he is, he's fine. He's a goddamn angel. And no sooner do I think it than the prick appears from the crowd, running alongside Daja like they're out for a jog in the park.

When we get to the gun, me and the Magistrate leap up onto the flatbeds and run to the rear. Daja, Wanuri, and some of the others climb up behind us, but are too slow to keep up.

When we get to the rear of the gun, I pull open the breech and look at the Magistrate.

"How do we use it?"

"I do not know," he says. "The stories never specified how the weapon worked."

Of course not. Vehuel would know, but she's occupied at the moment.

"Look around," I say. "It has to fit somewhere."

By now, Traven and the rest of the dog pack have caught up.

"Look around for where the sword might go in," I tell them.

A moment later, Traven says, "Here. This might be it."

He points to an indentation in the breech. There's a slot where it looks like something could slide in.

"Try it," says the Magistrate.

I bend down, and when I hold the sword out straight, it fits perfectly into place.

Big smiles all around, but they don't last long. The tree fuckers are shuffling down the hills and the crossroads.

I slam the breech shut and lock it into place. There's a lever on the Magistrate's side.

I nod to it.

"Do it."

Grinning like a school kid on a snow day, he grabs the lever and pulls.

Exactly nothing happens. No boom. No shudder. An absolute zero.

"Try it again," I shout.

He pulls again and it's the same big nothing.

He says, "You must have put it in wrong."

"Let's see."

I open the breech and pull out the sword. Halfway out, it snaps and falls to the flatbed in pieces. I pick up one of the shards.

"It's wood. It's wood painted gold."

"That cannot be," says the Magistrate.

He reaches for some of the splinters, but I push him away. The dead are just about on us. I climb on top of the gun.

"If you're alive, duck, motherfuckers!"

I start screaming Hellion hoodoo as loud and fast as I can in every direction.

The first couple of hexes knock the forward wave of skeletons down, but the ones behind climb over like a swarm of rats. I keep shouting, going easy on the hexes until the last of Wanuri's people are clear. When they are, the skeletons are right on us. Now I shout the rough stuff. The kind of hoodoo I used out on the river. I turn the air around the dead into fire until the road and hillsides are a solid carpet of flames. Some of the dead keep coming, but they're slower than before. With each step they fall apart piece by piece and are easy for the havoc to take down.

I climb down off the gun and stand with the others, breathing hard. While they scan the road for any dead bastards out for a stroll, I look up at the sky. No flashes up there anymore. Whatever was happening is over. I get out the amber knife and wait to see who comes back.

A moment later Alice and Vehuel slam to the ground a few feet behind us. I jump down and run to them, grabbing Alice in a big hug when I get her. She hugs me back, but more of her attention is on Vehuel. I look over, and see why. There's a hole you could put a fist in over her heart.

"What the hell happened over there?" I say.

"Johel and Phanuel were traitors," says Alice. "Some of the officers have been going over to them for some time. I guess even a few generals."

Traven stands nearby and looks over my shoulder.

He says, "Is there anything we can do for her?"

Alice holds her boss's bloody hand.

"I don't know."

Vehuel opens her eyes.

"Did you try to fire the weapon?" she says.

"Yeah. It didn't work."

"Yes, it did. It worked perfectly."

I look at the Magistrate, Raziel fucking archangel in disguise. I say, "It was a test."

Vehuel touches my arm, and between Alice and me, we're able to pull her upright.

"Yes. A test. For us, the generals, and for the damned and fallen who might want such a weapon for themselves."

The Magistrate holds a piece of the golden wood in his hand.

"I do not understand. Why would you come all this way just to test us? If you had not appeared, we might never have found the Lux Occisor, which would render our crusade pointless. But you brought us here. Why?"

"To test you, too, Raziel," says Vehuel. "And you failed."

Hearing his real name does not put the Magistrate in a good mood. He grips the wood harder.

"Careful," says Vehuel. "The wood is made from Neshi-yyah Bane, the Hellion Tree of Life. Deadly to angels. Touch any part of the Lux Occisor other than the gold and you will see for yourself."

He stares at the wood, holding it carefully in his long fingers, and stands up. He looks down at Vehuel.

"Test me you might," he says. "But I am still here while you will soon be gone."

Daja doesn't seem to even register the threat. Instead, she says, "Who's Raziel? Why is she calling you that?"

"It's father of the year's real name," I tell her. "He's an angel. An archangel, in fact. Only he snuck out the back door. Now he's looking to kill both God and Lucifer." I go to her. "And he was using saps like you and the havoc to get the only thing he wanted. The Light Killer."

The Magistrate comes around Vehuel and stands by me and Alice.

"Tell me I am wrong, Mr. Sandman Slim," he says. "I admit I did not recognize you at first. A dirty wretch lost in the desert with a mad story about Death. But when I did, I knew we were kindred spirits. You spent years in Hell killing Lucifer's generals. Even when you were Lucifer, you kept Hell at bay. You convinced the Almighty to open Heaven's gates, but he was too weak. I am not. You are not. God and Lucifer are one entity now. If we destroy one, we destroy the other. Imagine it. A universe without rulers. Where each soul and celestial is free to chart their own destiny. Admit it. Does that not sound like an idea you could have had?"

I shake my head.

"And I thought Samael had daddy issues, but they could do a whole college course about yours."

"It's true, then, Magistrate," says Daja. "You've lied to me and everyone else this whole time."

"Quiet, child. There are things you do not understand. I am doing this for your benefit as much as mine."

"A few minutes ago you said the havoc didn't matter! That they could all die and it would mean nothing to you. Were you serious?"

"Of course he was," I say. "And he meant you, too, by the way. I'm sure you're a nice pet to have around, but sooner or later he's going to get bored with your questions or your neediness. Then off to Tartarus you'll go. Right, Raziel?"

Angels are fast, but archangels are fucking *fast*. The next thing I know he's pulled Alice to her feet and is holding the wood from the Light Killer to her throat.

"Empty your pockets," he says. "I know that you did not spend a week in the wilderness just to come back with a false promise and a cigarette lighter. Death gave you something else. Give it to me. The great weapon may be a lie, but my crusade continues. I will destroy the despot who rules the universe."

"Don't listen, Jim. Please," she says.

I look at her. She's not afraid at all. She really is a warrior and is ready to die for her cause. The problem is, I'm not ready to sacrifice her for it.

"I know what you want. Death's knife. Let her go and you can have it."

"Are you mad?" says Vehuel. "He will kill us all and then storm Heaven. With Death's weapon he will be unstoppable."

I shrug.

"You people should have thought of that before you made the knife. And before you let assholes like this walk free. You *tested* him? You should have killed him the moment you laid eyes on him."

"That's not the Almighty's way."

"Well, it's mine, and if I ever see this prick again I'm going to rip his head off."

"The knife please," says Raziel. "My patience is not infinite."

I reach into my coat pocket and slowly take out the amber blade.

"Lovely," says the Magistrate. "Now set it on the ground between us."

I drop it in the dirt.

Vehuel lies back down, rubs her eyes with the heels of her hands.

"You fool. You have doomed Creation."

"Fuck Creation. Your kind broke it a long time ago and now you're blaming me for taking care of one of the few people I ever cared about?"

"Don't do it, Jim. Take it back," says Alice.

"I can't let you be murdered twice."

"Enough," says Raziel. "Move back and take Vehuel with you. Once I have the amber knife, you may have your little angel back. Of course, you might find that her opinion of you has changed."

"I don't think so. We are who we are. Isn't that right, Alice?"

"That's right," she says, and closes her eyes.

Raziel says, "For one last time. Move back."

"No."

I raise my boot and slam the heel down on the knife, shattering it into a million pieces.

"What have you done?" he yells. But that's the last thing he manages to bleat out of his smug face.

Raziel lets go of Alice and collapses to his knees. The piece of wood falls from his hand. As he goes down, I see Cherry behind him. She's trembling. I get it now. She stabbed the bastard in the back with a piece of the killer wood before I even had a chance to move. I wonder how long she'd been planning on killing him? It took her long enough.

Alice is on the ground next to her boss.

"Are you mad?" Vehuel says. "Out of sentimentality you destroyed Death's weapon? Do you know what this means?"

"That if I destroy nine more I get a free sandwich?"

"Without death, mortal life has no meaning. I know that seems cruel, but endless, pointless life is a true Hell. And you have brought it on all of your own people."

"No I didn't."

I pick up the amber knife. It's in one piece.

"But I saw you crush it."

"I'm half angel, remember? If I can't do hoodoo that will trick another angel, then what am I good for?"

Alice swats my leg.

"You idiot. What if it hadn't worked?"

"I knew it would. Come on, now. You knew what I was doing."

"You're insane. I had no idea at all."

"See? I fooled her, too, and she's known me a lot longer than you halo polishers."

Slowly, Raziel's body fades and soon it's gone.

"Is he dead?" says Daja.

"Yeah. Sorry."

Wanuri puts an arm around her and Daja starts to cry.

Cherry stands with her arms wrapped around herself. She looks like she just saw a ghost, a unicorn, and Hello Kitty having a three-way in a clown car and they didn't invite her.

I walk over.

"Nice trick," I say.

"You're welcome," she says a little absently. "Is killing someone always like this?"

"Just the first couple of times. After that it's like folding socks. But that's just me."

She takes a couple of breaths and blinks, getting herself together.

"Okay. Wow. That wasn't what I expected it to be."

"Maybe you ought to sit down."

"I'd like that. Can we go somewhere and talk for a minute?"

"Sure."

I take her around the side of the flatbeds where no one can see us.

"If you want to throw up or something, it's okay. Everyone's first kill is rough."

"No. I'm okay," she says. "That's not what I wanted to talk about."

"Say what you have to say, but no stupid 'let's fuck' lines. I'm sick of that."

She looks around, making sure we're alone.

"I helped you, right?"

"I just said so."

"That means you owe me."

Great. Where is this going?

"Maybe. What do you want?"

"I don't want anything. I want to help you some more. I can save you. Don't you want to go home?"

I get a really bad feeling in my gut and it's not from being hungry.

"Just say what you want to say, Cherry."

"All I've wanted to do is help you, ever since you got here. I mean, I was surprised as anyone when I saw you, but then I told them and they said it was okay."

"*Who* did you tell?"

She hesitates. Balls and unballs her fists.

"I don't want to say it. But you know."

"Then I'll say it for you. Wormwood."

"Yes."

Oh, Cherry. How many bad decisions can you make in one life- or death-time? I want to snap her neck. I want to find more of those tree shamblers and feed her to them. But she did save us, fucked-up motives aside, so I just talk.

"That angel attack. The town full of Legionnaires. Those ships on the river. You were telling Wormwood where we were and where we were going."

"Of course. That's the first thing they wanted to know."

"All those breakdowns along the road. Were those you, too?"

"Some," she says like I caught her stealing from the collection plate. "They wanted us to go slower so they could keep an eye on things."

"You know, a lot of people died along the way because of your bullshit. All those pathetic souls in those little towns."

"But *you* didn't. I always made sure you were safe."

"Because Wormwood told you to."

"Yes. But for me, too. I don't want to be alone again."

"Of course."

Her face gets hard.

"Fuck you, Jimmy. Don't talk to me like that, like I'm one of those bar girls you used to con into buying you drinks. You let me die, but I saved your ass a dozen times down here. Don't forget that."

"And you murdered a hundred people and made Wormwood a fortune. So don't try to guilt me into anything." Something nags at me. "Why do they even care about me anymore?"

"That's the thing. They care a lot. Hell needs to change, just like you say. But not too much. Just enough."

"Just enough so they can keep making money off the war. Day-trading on damnation futures. What else?"

"I don't know. But when they heard you were here, they knew you could mess up their plan. Now, though, now that you can't leave, they can make things easier for you."

I turn and go. It's the only way to keep from wringing her neck. Cherry grabs me from behind.

"Don't walk away from me. I don't want to be alone down here and neither do you. You think Alice is going to stay in this pigsty with you? She's got her wings, and the moment Heaven calls, she's going home. I like you, Jimmy. We need to stick together. Wormwood can set us up nice."

I turn and look at her hard. She stands her ground.

"You helped with Raziel, so I'm not going to kill you. But that's the best I can do for you. Good-bye, Cherry."

I head back to where Alice and the others are waiting. I only get a few steps when I hear the distinctive sound of the hammer being pulled back on a revolver. I turn around. Cherry is pointing a very shiny Colt Python at me.

"I swear to God I will, Jimmy. Wormwood will cut me off if you walk away. I can't be alone down here anymore. You don't know what it's like."

"Yeah. I do. I know exactly what it's like."

I head back to the others.

"I'll do it. Take one more step."

I look at her again. Crane my neck a little to get a better angle.

"Cherry. There are no bullets in that gun."

Her hands start to shake like the Python suddenly gained fifty pounds.

She says, "I'm doomed, you know. They're going to kill me. What am I supposed to do?"

"First off, when you're bluffing somebody with an empty gun, don't use a revolver. As for the other stuff, good luck and fuck off."

I leave her there and go back to the others.

"What was that about?" says Traven.

"Nothing. Just saying good-bye to an old acquaintance."

Alice is holding Vehuel up.

"How is she?" I ask.

"Bad. She wants to talk to you."

Normally, an angel should already be healing by now. The fact Vehuel isn't is a bad sign. I kneel down beside her.

"Shouldn't you be getting up? Mr. Muninn is probably holding dinner for you."

She smiles a little. Shakes her head.

"Alice will make my apologies for me."

Alice's hands and armor are stained with Vehuel's blood.

"What can I do to help you?"

"Since when does Sandman Slim help angels?" Vehuel says.

"I'm not helping an angel. I'm helping Alice's friend, so shut up with the halo stuff."

Alice says, "Listen to her, Jim."

"I am."

"No. The 'shut up and listen' kind of listening."

"Right."

"I was here to test you, too," says Vehuel.

"Yeah? How'd I do?"

"Even with all your anger, you didn't want the Lux Occisor for yourself."

"I didn't need it. The na'at is a sword."

"Hush," says Alice.

"Right."

"But your na'at is gone," says Vehuel. "And you didn't sacrifice Death's blade even for someone you loved."

"If the trick didn't work, I would have."

"So you say now. The important thing is that God has a message for you. Are you ready to hear it?"

Nothing good has ever come from anything that begins with "God has a message for you."

"Sure."

"He invites you to join him in Heaven, as a warrior or simply a resident. He also says that you know he could compel you to come, but he won't do that. You may come to the golden city with us right now, but it must be your choice."

"Free will. It always comes down to free will, doesn't it?"

"Always."

This isn't what I was expecting to hear. I was ready for more of a "Thanks for not killing too many of the wrong people, now keep the hell out of the way, the grown-ups have work to do."

I look over at Traven and the remains of the dog pack.

"Tell Mr. Muninn thanks, but I'll stay Downtown."

"Jim. No," says Alice. "What are you trying to prove anymore? And don't start in on the Abomination bullshit. If God doesn't care, no one else will either."

"First off, yes they will. If I know anything about angels, it's that they're a snooty bunch. Present company excepted."

"Thank you," says Vehuel.

I look at Alice.

"Second, I know that you're all right. They like you up there and you can kick angel ass. That's about as good as it gets. But third, there's people down here who deserve better."

Traven says, "Stark, don't be a fool."

"Until they can go, I can't go."

Alice says, "You are such an asshole."

"I can't argue with that."

"What about me?" she says. "I'm just supposed to say 'It's been nice. See you around' and just leave you here? If you don't go, I don't go."

"Now who's being an asshole?"

"Tough. I'm staying."

"You're a warrior now. You can't do that from here."

"Which is why you should come with me."

"I can't."

"Please be quiet, both of you," says Vehuel. "I don't know how Heaven could ever stand the two of you at the same time. But I know it must."

I get up.

"My mind is made up."

"So is mine," says Alice.

Vehuel says, "Might I point out something to you both."

"Go for it."

"The Lux Occisor must be returned to Heaven."

"Why? It's a fake," I say.

"But few know the truth and that's how it must remain. Angels on both sides of the conflict will rethink their positions when they learn that God has recaptured his thunderbolt sword."

"Fucking hell. I can't even begin to count up the lies I've heard since Samael dumped me back down here. I'll tell you one thing, even when he was Lucifer, he didn't lie the way other angels and Mr. Muninn do."

"Cry, gnash your teeth, and rend your garments all you want, little Abomination. The sword must be returned. If you don't do it, then Alice must, and one wrong touch could kill her. Are you really so stubborn that you'd risk her life?"

I look at Traven.

"You're smart. Isn't there something in your books about this? Some kind of magic Saran Wrap or doggie bag we can put it in?"

"I'm afraid I'm out of magic doggie bags."

Alice is giving me that look she used to give me back in L.A. The one that says, *You know you have to go to the dentist. You know you're going to the dentist. Why are you screwing around about it and making it a hundred times worse?* And she was always right. Not wanting to do something isn't the same as knowing you're not going to do it. Fair isn't an option in this universe.

On the other hand, blackmail is.

"I'll go under one condition."

"What's that?" says Vehuel.

"Traven and what's left of the dog pack get to come, too."

"What's the dog pack?" says Wanuri.

"It's what I called all of you behind your backs."

"Charming."

"Don't ruin your chance for Heaven by making ridiculous demands," says Traven. "We'll find our way back to Pandemonium and join the other refugees."

"I accept your offer," says Vehuel.

"Really?" Traven says. "Well. Thank God for ridiculous demands."

"Wait—did you just extort our way into Heaven?" says Wanuri.

"Yeah," I say. "You, Traven, Daja, Doris, and Gisco. But it has to be your choice. You can stay if you want."

"Fuck that. I'm not going to crawl around in shit forever when I can have wings and armor like her," she says, turning to Alice. "I want a flaming sword to hurt some bastards."

"The right bastards," says Alice.

"Of course."

"Just making sure."

I look at the others.

"What about the rest of you?"

They nod and grunt affirmatives.

"Can I bring my knives?" says Doris.

"You should probably leave those," Alice says.

"I was afraid so." She takes them off one by one and tosses them into the road.

Gisco grunts something.

"Yes. They can fix your leg," says Alice. "That's one of the archangel Raphael's specialties."

That gets an enthusiastic nod.

"What about the rest of the havoc?" says Daja.

I look over at the remains of the messiah's terror squad. They don't look so scary now with no vehicles or food or water. And there's a lot fewer of them than when I joined the show.

"Which way is Pandemonium?" I ask Vehuel.

"Due east."

I point east and shout, "Go that way. There's food and water in Pandemonium. Then head south. You'll find other souls there. Sooner or later, Heaven's gates will open. You don't want to miss it."

Just a few leave at first. Then small groups, and finally the rest, start the long walk east. Cherry stands there like maybe I'll tell her our conversation was a joke. She's a wreck and always has been. I can forgive her a lot, but not Wormwood. Finally, she gets the idea and follows the others.

"That's taken care of. Now I guess we grab the Light Killer."

"Every scrap and splinter. Leave nothing behind," says Vehuel.

"Getting barked at by angels. Heaven is going to be fun."

We spend the next half hour scraping up pieces of the sword from the flatbed and the road. We wrap everything in a moldy curtain Daja grabs from one of the abandoned houses. All except one little pinkie-size piece that we almost missed. I stick that in my pocket. After one last look around, I take the heap to Vehuel.

"That's it. Let's get going before you make us sweep up the whole Tenebrae."

"I don't think she's going anywhere," says Alice.

She's right. Vehuel is already starting to fade. But she's strong. It's a long time before she disappears completely. I help Alice up. Her eyes are red, but she doesn't shed a tear. She's a fighter and there are still things to do. There will be plenty of time to cry when she gets Upstairs. I won't let her do it alone.

"I'm very sorry," says Traven.

Alice just nods.

"What do we do now?" says Wanuri. "She was our ticket out of here."

"No," says Alice. "I can take you."

I shift the bundle under my arm.

"Then let's go. Henoch smells and I'm sick of the lies and a thousand other kinds of bullshit down here."

She says, "Jim, you touch my shoulder. Father, you touch his. The rest of you, touch the person in front of you."

For a second, I hope that she has to fly us there. I haven't been on a roller coaster in years and wouldn't mind a Disneyland moment on our way out of Hell. Instead, Alice looks at the clouds overhead and says a few angelic words. It's not Space Mountain, but it's still pretty good.

It's like she punches a hole in the sky with fire. A blazing circle appears in a particularly dark cloud bank, and spreads wide, its edges burning bright with crimson flames. When she decides the hole is wide enough, and without any kind of fucking warning at all, she blows out her wings and leaps into the air, dragging me and everyone else with her. There's a lot of wind and some turbulence on the way up, but it's not exactly the roller coaster I was hoping for. It's more like a freight elevator a million miles high.

As we climb through the clouds, lightning crackles around us. A storm blows up, smashing rain and hail down on us. A few remaining shards of the divine light glass tear at us. It's like the clouds knew we were coming and Downtown saved one last fuck-you for us on the way out.

Okay—now we're in the roller coaster. The crosswinds get worse. There's glass in my face and hands. I squeeze the bundle with the Light Killer close against me. It would suck very hard to drop it now. Each flash of lightning illuminates things hiding in the clouds. Miles high, with claws like skyscrapers and wings wide enough to smother all of L.A. They are truly pissed about our little excursion Upstairs. They roar and howl, and their voices are the thunder and lightning that come close to knocking us off Alice's back. But I tighten my grip on her armor and close my eyes against the glass. After all I've been through Downtown, I don't want to end up in Heaven with just one eye.

Static electricity and volcanic heat burns us as lightning flashes in every direction, missing us by just a few inches. The roar of Hell's guardians and hurricane winds hurt every bit as much as anything I fought in the arena. Just about the time I'm going to tell Alice that I changed my mind and that she should drop me off at the nearest Denny's, it all stops. The noise. The wind. The rain and lightning. It's gone. I look down and watch the burning hole above Hell fizzle out and the giant guardians pulling the clouds closed around them.

So long, you dinosaur-looking motherfuckers. You did your worst and we made it out on the wings of one lone, not-too-tall angel. Think about that for the next billion years, King Ghidorah.

As bad as the ride up from Downtown was, where we are now is flat-out unsettling. We're nowhere. Empty space. Astronaut territory. Stars wink and pulse around us. Comets and the occasional meteor flash by, but none of them try to kill us. That's a nice change. It takes me a few minutes, but I finally figure out where we are.

This is the fall. The limbo the first two Lucifers and their playmates fell through after Mr. Muninn kicked those kids off his lawn. It took them nine days to hit bottom. After our run through tornado asshole alley just now, I'm not sure any of us can hold on for that long. But it can't be nine days for angels, right? I mean, they fly. Hellions just plummet like eggs dropped from a frat-house roof. The utter fucked-up emptiness of this place makes me feel kind of sorry for Samael and his bunch. I've never felt such a sense of being *nowhere* before. So far from everything—good and bad—and so empty inside. And Samael had to go through this for nine days. That would make anyone, even an angel with an ego the size of Texas, a little crazy.

Soon I see that I was right. A bright pinprick of light flares in the distance. It's either Heaven or we're about to get hit by the 3:10 to Yuma.

Lucky for us, there are no actual trains in limbo, just paranoids like me. It isn't long before we see actual goddamn gates up ahead. They're gold and even bigger than Hell's flying guardians, which, if you ask me, is a bit much. I mean, angels are about as tall as regular-size people. Why do they need gates the size of Everest? It's like Mr. Muninn was getting ready to sell the place and went a little crazy with the upgrades.

When we're close enough to see details of the gates, they're even worse than I thought. They look like solid gold—of course—shaped like fucking huge arches. There are towers and spires and rose windows set into the walls on either side of the gates. It's all one big, epic Gothic orgasm. I don't know what I was expecting, but it wasn't the fancy-ass fence at a gated Ren Faire community. This is Brentwood with cherubs.

Worse, the bars on the gates are animated. They bend and twist around each other, forming shapes. There's an explosion of light, then the birth of angels. Some angels start to hang stars in the sky while others build worlds. Fuck me. It's the birth of the universe. Who is Mr. Muninn trying to impress? I think not going to Hell is pretty much what the souls who end up here care about. They don't need a slide show while they're getting their passports stamped.

But I really have nothing better to look at, so I keep watching. By now the angels have moved on to creating air and water. Then microscopic organisms. That's good news at least. God believes in evolution. Then animals show up, and finally, the crown of Creation, us ridiculous human assholes. But he left out traffic jams on the 405, reality TV, and selfie sticks. Talk about propaganda.

Outside the gates, Alice lands us on a courtyard made of marble slabs as big as a Safeway parking lot.

Everybody oohs and aahs.

Alice folds her wings and stands next to me.

"Well?"

"Please tell me it's not all like this."

"Of course not. Heaven is just a regular place with trees and houses and libraries and parks."

"And bars?"

"Yes, bars."

"And movie theaters. You promised me movie theaters."

"Yes, movie theaters. It's just that seeing as how it was everyone's first time here, I thought I'd take you through the formal entrance."

I look up at the gates. The floor show is starting over. Lights. Angels. Stars. The whole bit.

"Isn't there a nice alley with a Dumpster out in back of a taco place? Can't we go in there?"

Alice gives me a look.

"I'm driving, so we're going in the nice way." She points past me. "Look at Father Traven. He's enjoying himself."

"Indeed I am."

His eyes are as wide as Escalade wheel rims.

"See? That's a positive attitude. Give it a try."

I shift the bundle around in my arms.

"I did it once. I got a rash."

Alice watches the others enjoying themselves.

"Fine—if you can't be nice, then be quiet. Just until you see how things work around here. I swear you're going to like it."

"Introduce me to Sam Fuller. That would be a good start."

"Excuse me," says Doris. "Are there animals here?"

"You mean animal Heaven? It's right over the big red bridge. I'll show you later," says Alice.

Doris beams. "Then it was worth the storm. I've missed Tootsie, my cat, so much."

Daja says, "I miss Oscar. He was my ferret."

Wanuri makes a face. "You had a ferret? They're just weasels who learned a few tricks."

"Have you ever actually met one? They're sweet. Lots of people have ferrets."

"Lots of crazy people," says Gisco.

Everybody stares at him. Of course. We're in Heaven. Everybody can talk to everybody.

It's nice to understand you, Gisco, but fucking hell. It's already so fucking sweet here. Like being in Disneyland forever. And I already got off the only good ride.

Wanuri says, "Matilda, my ex, had a whole fish tank of scorpions. Those don't count as pets, do they? Are there scorpions in Heaven?"

Alice thinks for a moment.

"Believe it or not, that's the first time the subject has come up. But I can ask."

"I hope not. And I hope they ate her."

"What did I just say about a positive attitude?"

"Sorry."

Daja walks away from the group. I follow her.

"Are you going to be okay with Raziel gone?"

"I guess. It's just that between him and this, it's a lot to take in all at once."

"They probably have therapists in Heaven."

"They better. Who's that?"

I look at where she's pointing. Someone in a suit sharp enough to cut a diamond is headed our way. I walk over to him.

"I see you made it," says Samael. "And you brought some little friends. You always were sentimental."

"Careful. It's that attitude that got you the Lucifer gig. Do you want to go back to that?"

"Not for all the tea in China."

I hand him the moldy drapes wrapped around the Light Killer.

"Hold this. I have to get something."

"Why is it every time I see you my cleaning bill goes up?"

I take out the amber knife.

"I told you I'd get this back to you soon."

"No thank you."

"But I'm done with it."

"Are you sure? You might want to turn around."

I look over my shoulder just as an armored angel swoops down at me, his Gladius raised to take off my head.

I roll onto the marble floor and back onto my feet. The winged bastard misses Samael by a few inches, but Samael doesn't move. Always the show-off.

By now the others have dropped their kitten and bunny chatter and noticed me fighting for my fucking life.

"Sarosh!" shouts Alice.

Sarosh. Now at least I know the name of the guy who's going to relieve me of the misery of eating organic muffins forever.

The angel makes a sharp turn and shoots back at me. I shout some Hellion hoodoo and it has about as much effect as reading cupcake recipes to a lobster.

You're in Heaven, dumb-ass. Hell magic isn't going to work here.

While I'm trying to improvise some Sub Rosa hoodoo, on the off chance that Heaven allows us magical types any leeway at all, Sarosh lands. And runs at me like Toshiro Mifune in full samurai mode. At least if I had a na'at I might be able to put a little distance between us. But I have nothing other than the amber knife, and I'm really trying to not start out in Heaven by killing an angel. Of course, there is another angel in the vicinity and she's not the shy type.

Alice hits Sarosh boots first at about a hundred miles an hour. The blow smashes him into the marble floor hard enough to bury him a good six inches. But the prick gets up. He's bloody and his nose is a little off center, but the hit hasn't slowed him down much. That doesn't faze Alice. She lands and smashes her Gladius into his, knocking him back a few feet. That just pisses him off. He shouts and charges her. Sarosh swings his blade, but when she goes to block him, he slips under and tags her in the belly. It doesn't stop her, but I can tell that it hurt like hell. Then Sarosh is on her, raining one chopping blow after another onto her Gladius. Wounded, Alice can't take the crazy ferocity of the hits and goes down on one knee.

I look at Samael and he shakes his head. He's still Death and Death can't take sides. But I'm sort of Death now, too, so I rush Sarosh from behind.

When he raises his Gladius high for a killing blow, I grab his armor and shove the amber blade straight through the back of his holier-than-thou skull.

So much for a quiet entrance Upstairs.

His Gladius goes out and now he's the one who drops to his knees. Alice gets up and shoves her Gladius into his chest, bringing it up sharply and splitting him neatly in half. He blips out a second later.

I run to Alice and grab her.

"Are you all right?"

"Yeah," she says. "But part of the blow slipped between two armor plates and tagged me. I'll be fine, but I need to sit down for a few minutes."

The others come over. I let her down slowly and kneel next to her.

"That was a hell of a shot at the end, splitting him like that." She does a grimacing smile.

"I thought you'd like that. It's the kind of thing I've seen you do."

"You've seen me fight with a Gladius?"

"What? You think I haven't been looking in on you when I could?"

"Very sneaky."

"It's no fun watching movies all the time without you."

"So, I'll just hold this forever, shall I?"

It's Samael. He's holding the drapes out as far from his body as possible.

"How about two more seconds? We're having a moment here."

He looks away.

"Now that you're up here, I'm going to start sending you my cleaning bills."

"Feel free."

"They're expensive."

"I'll get a job."

"As what? There aren't a lot of openings for wandering assassins in Heaven. The best you could hope for is bouncer at one of the beach bars."

"Like college dudes and party bros doing tequila shots?"

"Exactly."

I look at Alice.

"You didn't tell me about any of this."

She says, "Thank you, Samael. Thank you for making it a hundred times harder to get him to stay."

He just raises an eyebrow.

He says, "They play reggae, too. All day and all night."

I wonder if I can walk to Pandemonium from here?

"Damn. Not *this* fool," Samael says. "I hoped never to see his ridiculous face again."

"Who?"

"Oh no. It's Michael," says Alice. "He went to the other side. Now he's a rebel general."

The archangel Michael sets down gracefully on the marble. It's easy to see why Samael hates him. He's handsome. Like right up there with Samael's cover-model looks. Only Michael is meaner around the eyes. If he was mortal, he'd be the kind of good-looking guy who spends too much time in bars complaining about foreigners, chemtrails, and Area 51.

Alice grabs my coat.

"Help me up."

"Wait a minute."

As far as I'm concerned, Mr. Universe isn't the real problem. The real problem is the twenty other rebel angels hovering over him. Mr. Muninn invited me here, you'd think he'd be a good enough host to help me get past the damn gates. But like so many other times when I could have used a little Heavenly help, he's a no-show.

I look at Samael.

"I suppose you can't take sides here either."

"Oh no. Actually, I can kill all the rebels I want."

I hold out the amber blade to him, but once more he declines.

"I think you should hold on to that for a while longer."

"What are you going to use, though? Can you manifest your Gladius? I saw you use two of them once."

He sighs. "There's another downside to being Death. I have a pretty amber blade that will kill anything, but I lost my Gladius."

"Fuck."

"I agree completely."

Alice grabs me.

"Help me up. If I'm going to die, I won't do it on my back."

I pull her to her feet. She does her best to stand straight up, but she can't quite do it.

Michael heads for us.

"If it isn't Sandman Slim, the monster who kills monsters. Isn't that what they call you?"

"I prefer Abomination. It fits better on a T-shirt. I'd comp you one, but we don't have any big enough for your ego."

"Why would you say that? You don't know anything about me."

"You're an archangel who hates his dad, has a neurotic thirst for power, and when the war is all over, you have a plan to set yourself up as a tinhorn messiah with those goons up there as your brownshirts. Am I in the ballpark with all that? I think I am."

"You have a big mouth and make a lot of assumptions about your betters."

"I just helped kill an archangel exactly like you Downtown, so I'm acquainted with your type."

He thinks about that for a minute.

"Who did you kill?"

"Raziel."

He laughs and so does his peanut gallery.

"That imbecile? He couldn't even pick a side, so he ran off to the hinterlands with his tail between his legs."

"He had nice things to say about you, too."

"Did he? What did he say?"

"That you're a coward, and even though you might not

have liked him, you were always jealous of Samael because he's smarter than you and has bigger balls."

"Feel free to leave me out of this conversation," Samael says.

Michael rubs the back of his neck.

"You're aware that I'm an angel, correct? I can tell when mortals are lying. And you're lying."

"But I'm not a hundred percent mortal. Can you be a hundred percent sure when it comes to anything about me?"

That stops him for a minute. He turns to Samael.

"What's that you're holding? You're friends with this thing. Are you doing his laundry now, too?"

"If only it were clean laundry," Samael says. "Care for a sniff?"

Michael looks from Samael to me to Alice.

"You don't look too well, my dear," he says.

"Attack me and see how bright my Gladius is."

"All in due time. Who are your friends?"

He points to Traven and the dog pack.

"Don't worry about them," I say. "They're just some strays Alice picked up on the way."

"Good," says Michael. He turns to his goons. "Kill them."

"Okay. Wait. They're with me."

"See? You were lying and I knew it."

"You don't have to kill them because you're pissed at me. I take back all that other stuff I said about you. You seem like a swell, reasonable guy. Let's talk this over, bastard to bastard."

That really makes him smile.

"In that case, you're all free to go. Enjoy Heaven."

The others look at me.

I tell them, "Don't move." To Michael I say, "What's the catch?"

"You know exactly what the catch is," he says.

"Before I decide, tell me something. Did you see what happened or did someone tell you we had it?"

"Guess."

"Wormwood. They told you."

He looks at the bastards hovering above us.

"What a clever monster he is. I'll keep his head on my mantel and take it out every now and then to scare children."

His people chuckle.

"You're very ugly, you know," he says.

"So I've heard."

It looks like I have one thing in my favor. He knows we have the Light Killer, but he doesn't know it's broken and a fake. Maybe I can do something with that.

"Listen, we both know I'm not just going to hand you the sword."

"Fine. Kill his friends."

"See, I was right. You're a small-time little shit with a big ego."

He holds up his hand for the attack squad to stop.

"You really should stop talking or I'll kill your friends slowly in front of you."

"I'm saying if you are who you say you are, send the glee club home and the two of us fight for the sword and my friends."

"Stop it," says Alice. "You're being an asshole again."

"Just because I'm an asshole doesn't mean I'm wrong. This

kind of thing is pretty much all I've done for the last twelve years."

"What would Candy say? Your ego is as big as his. You think she'd be proud of you being this stupid?"

That almost knocks me back, but I suck it up and say, "I've spent a lot of energy trying not to think about Candy. This is not a good time to bring her up."

I take a couple of steps toward Michael.

"What do you say? The two of us for the sword, Alice, and my friends."

"Done," says Michael. "But my troops won't be leaving. You're a well-known trickster and I won't have it. This is a fight to the death between the two of us. No hoaxes or illusions. And no technicalities. If I think you're cheating, all of your friends die."

"Cool. Let me just say a couple of good-byes in case I break a nail."

Alice says, "Please don't do this. Let's fight them together."

"As long as I have Death's knife, Mr. Universe isn't hurting anyone."

I squeeze her hand and go to Samael.

"Sorry to drag you into this."

"Don't apologize. This is more fun than I've had in a long time."

"Just tell me one thing. If I fuck this up, can you get the amber knife and kill these pricks?"

"With great pleasure."

I shake his hand and go to Alice.

"You brought up a lot of old feelings in me."

"You did that to me, too."

"Heaven with you is very tempting."

"But L.A. with Candy is more," she says.

"Yeah."

"But you can't go back."

"If I stayed here, she's all I'd think about. I'd be useless to you and everyone else. That's not Heaven for anyone."

"You choose now to stop being an asshole? You have terrible timing."

"Whatever happens with these guys, it was worth it to see you again. I hope you know that."

"I do."

I kiss her on the cheek and get up wondering if I'm the dumbest guy to ever reach the pearly gates. But when I close my eyes, it's Candy's face I see.

"I'm sorry I let you down," I whisper. "I told you I'd never leave you alone or go back to Hell without you and I blew it. Whatever you're doing, I hope you're happy and keeping Kasabian in line. I'd come back to you if I could, but I can't and that's okay. I'm not pushing your memory away again. If you're the last thing I see before I go to Tartarus or whatever happens to the dead up here, I'll go out happy thinking about you playing your guitar worse than anybody in California. It was fun being monsters together. I just wish it could have lasted longer."

Michael says, "As I drove the serpent from Eden, so shall I kill you today, Abomination."

I rub my hands on my coat to make sure they're dry.

"Was that you with Adam and Eve? That was a dick move shoving a couple of naked morons into the wilderness. I bet you come to Earth just to trip blind people."

He manifests his Gladius. I take out the amber knife.

He frowns.

"Are you going to fight me with a stick?"

"It's very pointy. It'll really leave a mark."

"No tricks," he says.

"No tricks. Just me and my stick."

He doesn't say anything because a second later he's in the air, coming down like a falling star.

I need to time this just right. No more fuck-ups or half-assing it. I'm going to get one, maybe two shots at this, tops.

I really don't want to lose to this guy. I'd rather work the reggae bar with ganja-head white-boy nitwits than let Mr. Universe get his smug way.

Michael closes in fast.

I bend my knees, dropping my weight back.

See you around, Candy. Stay sweet.

When he's just a few feet away, I let my legs go and roll, so I drop down on my back.

Damn, but archangels are fast.

I get the amber knife up exactly where I want it, but he rakes his Gladius across my chest. My vision goes black for a moment from the pain. When I can see again, I'm very pissed off.

Even though I got Michael square in the chest with the amber knife, he's standing nearby fresh as a fucking daisy. There isn't even a mark on his armor.

When he sees me staring, he checks himself. Nope. Not even a skinned knee. He points at my hand.

"What exactly is that?"

He looks over at Samael.

"Did you give this buffoon your blade?"

Samael shrugs.

"Father isn't going to be very happy with you."

"He seldom is. But at least I'm not boring."

"And I am?"

"No. Of course not. You're terribly interesting. Read any good books lately?"

"I'll deal with you later."

He turns back to me.

"Didn't we just agree to no tricks?"

"It's not a trick. It's a knife."

"And no technicalities either."

"What technicalities? You have a fucking sword. And you can *fly*. I have a knife. What's your problem?"

"My problem is that that isn't an ordinary knife. You're part of a conspiracy with Death. That's my problem, trickster."

"I'm supposed to fight you with a sharpened Popsicle stick? You have the best sword you can, I have the best knife I can. Calm down and let's fight."

"Have it your way. But when you're dead, I'm killing all your friends myself."

"Thank you."

"For what?"

"For this whole thing we're doing right now. Between Hesediel, Alice, and Vehuel, I'd forgotten for a minute how much I hate angels. You're a billboard for everything wrong with your kind."

"Aren't you wondering why I'm not dead?" Michael says.

"Yeah. I am actually."

He slaps his fist against his chest.

"This isn't angelic armor. If you had any brains at all, you would have recognized it. It's Father's armor from the first war. And it's immune to Death's touch."

Samael says, "To be fair, I didn't recognize it either. It isn't filled out. You simply don't have the physique for it."

"Now I'm going to kill you, too."

"I said you were boring."

While the two brothers bicker I rummage around in my foggy brain trying to come up with any way I can get the knife close enough to Michael to slip around his armor. The problem is that he's right. Aside from being deathproof, the armor covers every square inch of his body except his face. What are the chances of him letting me get close enough to poke my chopstick up his nose?

That's it, then. I have nothing. All I can do is play for time and try to give everybody a few more minutes of life. Even if I can return the knife to Samael, he can't get through the armor any more than I can. Sorry, everybody. I blew it again.

Sorry, Candy. At least this is the last time I'll ever disappoint you.

I lower my center of gravity and move into a fighting stance. I look ridiculous with my useless knife sticking out like the antenna on a thirty-year-old cell phone.

Michael manifests his Gladius and runs at me. I stand my ground hoping to get in a shot at his face. When he's a few feet away, he lets the Gladius go out. I thrust the knife at his eye, but miss by a mile. Instead of finishing me, Michael pulls back a big armored fist and punches me over my chest wound.

I think I must have blacked out for a second from the force

of the blow because when I look around, I realize I'm floating in limbo.

This is going to be a humiliating way to die. There's no gravity and nothing to grab on to. I pump my arms and legs trying to get some traction, but nothing happens. I know that everybody by Heaven's gates can see me. That's going to be their last memory of Sandman Slim: him flailing away like a bloated tick trying to roll himself off his back.

I don't know what the hell Michael does next, but a moment later I'm rocketing back to the golden gates. The Colt slips out of my waistband and tumbles into empty space. Big deal. A lot that would have helped against an archangel. I feel around my boots and coat. The na'at is long gone and now the gun. All I have is Doris's butcher knife and the amber blade. The only other thing I find is the pinkie-size piece of the Light Killer in my pocket. I don't think he's going to let me shove that through his face either, so I do the only thing I can think of. I eat it.

A second later I'm back at the gates and Michael is holding me off the ground by the front of my shirt.

"We can't keep meeting like this," I say. "People will talk."

Michael looks back at his troops.

"Am I done here? Should I just kill him and finally rid creation of the Abomination?"

Lots of cheers and hoots from the cheap seats. I blow them a kiss.

Michael manifests his Gladius.

"Wait. I should do this so Alice can see."

He turns and I wave to her.

"Hi. Can you see me all right?"

She nods.

"Good."

I purse my lips and spit in Michael's face.

He wipes it off.

"You filth," he says. "You spawn of corruption. You living defilement of all that is holy."

I spit again. It's a nice solid quantity, too, and it hits him right in the eye.

This time he drops me. He screams. His hands go to his face, tearing at his eye. It's turning red and starting to bleed.

"What have you done to me?"

"I gave you the sword, just like you wanted. Well, a bunch of little pieces of it. It tasted bad. Looks like it feels bad, too."

He's down on his hands and knees now. I lean over so I can see his face. He's pale and sweating. I kick him upright. Then jam the amber knife into his bleeding eye and pull it out again.

It's messy and bloody, but honestly, I'm feeling pretty good about myself. I think about how I'm going to buy myself a drink and maybe not work in the reggae bar after all.

But this is an archangel and I'm a moron.

Even as Michael starts to fade and die, he manifests his Gladius. And shoves it right through my heart.

The fire is so intense that I don't even feel it. I just get very cold because for the second time in not all that long, I am no-shit dying. I have just enough time and strength to throw the amber knife to Samael. He drops the bundle and he and Alice run straight at Michael's troops. I wish I could stick around and see how it comes out, but Michael is going and so am I and that's how the song ends.

So long, dog pack. See you around, Traven.

I'm sorry I disappointed you again, Alice. Some days it seems like the thing I'm best at.

Thanks for the laughs, Samael. Now do what you do best with angels. If they move, kill 'em.

I don't say good-bye to Candy this time. I already did that. I just hold her face in my mind as I fade away. And it's okay.

I'M IN THE dark for a million years. Or maybe just a second. I don't wear a watch, so I'm just guessing.

Then there's light. It's so bright it's like a knife through my brain. Then my chest spasms and I cough. It's not pretty. Garbage comes up from my lungs. The more I cough, the more my eyes water. The more my eyes water, the more my nose runs. I'm blind and in pain and probably a disgusting mess—nothing new there. But I can't stop. Wherever I am, whatever is happening, it goes on for a long time.

When I can finally catch my breath and my eyes stop watering, someone hands me a towel.

I must look like a wino who just won the Most Bodily Fluids Leaked in One Sitting prize.

I wipe myself down and then someone takes the towel away.

A man says, "Open your eyes. What do you see?"

I can't quite make out the voice. "Light. Just bright light."

A shadow moves across me.

"Can you see that?"

"A little."

"Good."

"Alice?"

"What did he say?"

It's a woman.

"Alice?"

"That name I know," the woman says. "It's his lover."

"The old one?" says the man.

"Yes. The new one's name is Candy. Or Chihiro, depending on who you ask."

I reach out for them.

"What the fuck is going on?"

I try to stand, but my legs are string cheese and I fall on my face. It's not so bad, really. There's less light down here. I can see furniture. It's nice stuff. Maybe antiques. They probably have good yard sales in Heaven. I can also see feet. Around a dozen of them.

Hands grab me and help me up.

I'm wearing some kind of gown. Great. Mr. Muninn put me in a fucking choir. I'm definitely not in the mood for that. I don't even do karaoke.

"Is this Heaven?"

Whatever bunch owns the twelve feet laughs. Someone helps me sit down. It's goddamn hard and uncomfortable.

"We like to think so," says the woman. "You keep closing your eyes. You have to open them so they get used to the light."

I do what she says and this time I can make out faces. They're not distinct, but I can see enough to know that there are four men and two women.

"How are you feeling? You already look better. You're getting some color back," says one of the women.

"Can I have some water?"

"Of course."

A few seconds later someone presses a paper cup into my hand. I down the whole thing. My throat spasms a little. It's very dry.

"Feel better?"

"Yeah. That helped. Where am I?"

"You said it yourself. Heaven."

"Then why do I feel like such shit?"

"You've been dead a long time."

"How long?

"Eleven months, two days, and three hours," says one of the men.

"That's not so long in Heaven."

"It depends on how you define Heaven," says the woman. "We've always felt that Los Angeles is as close to Heaven as you can find in this funny old world."

I open my eyes and look around the room a lot harder. Faces come into focus. One in particular.

"You're Eva Sandoval."

"Very good. I see death didn't scramble your brains completely."

I look around the room. There's the nice furniture. Old, pricy-looking paintings on the walls. White lilies in a crystal vase on a side table. I'm lying on a pool table covered in plastic sheets.

I look at Eva.

"You're fucking Wormwood."

"That's a complicated notion these days, but you're not entirely wrong."

I swing out an arm to grab her, but my body doesn't want

to cooperate. She steps back and I almost fall off the table. Again.

"Where am I? What's happening?"

"I already told you. You're in Los Angeles."

"I'm alive?"

"More or less."

"What does that mean?"

"I'll explain later. See if you can walk."

A couple of the men help me up and I take a few feeble steps to a chair. It's as far as I can go, so I give up and flop down.

I look around for Eva again.

"Nice chair."

"I'm glad you're enjoying yourself."

"Never felt better. A second ago I was in Heaven with my friends and now I'm here with you creeps. What, did you bring me back so you can kill me again? Hurry up. I have places to go."

"In Hell?"

"Don't sell me short, Eva. I made it all the way Upstairs. Right to the pearly gates. Only they're not pearly. They're gold and really ugly."

"Heaven," she says. She speaks to the others. "That makes sense. We completely lost track of him in Hell. He must have found his way to Heaven somehow."

"I just said that."

"Ask him how," says the man, ignoring me.

"My sparkling personality, you Wormwood prick. All of you can fuck off. If this is the world, prove it."

"Of course," says Eva. She goes away and comes back with the little box in her hand.

"What's your greatest fear?" she says.

"Flan."

She presses a TV remote into my hand. There's a flat panel the size of Raziel's motor home on the wall. I hit the power button. A crisp hi-def picture of some women appears. They're all wearing too much makeup and lots of ugly jewelry and most have had mediocre plastic surgery. They're arguing, all shrill and fake and over-the-top. I have to watch for a couple of minutes for it to make sense. Then it does and I feel as cold as when Michael's Gladius was burning me up.

"This is one of those angry-housewife shows."

"Good boy. And what's this?"

She puts her hand around mine and changes the channel.

A skinny guy with freckles is singing the blues. He thinks he's B. B. King, but he's more like a coyote with a sore throat.

"It's a talent show."

"Right again."

"Oh God."

"Welcome home, Mr. Stark."

"No. It's a trick. I'm in Hell. No one brings you back from the dead just to make you watch reality TV."

"Do you believe you're back from the dead?" say Eva.

"I'm not sure. Why would Wormwood bring me back?"

"As I said, the whole concept of Wormwood, at least on the mortal plane, is a bit of a mess. Factions. Splinter groups. Bankruptcies. A few murders."

"A lot of murders," says the man.

"Quite a lot," says Eva.

"Good. Rip yourselves to shreds. If you brought me back to see it all happen, thanks. This ought to be fun."

Eva pulls over a chair and sits next to me.

"We didn't bring you back to watch us come apart. We brought you back to help us put things back together again."

I'm starting to feel almost like I believe her and that I am alive. That last thing she said got my heart beating fast.

Eva says, "For one thing, you'll save a lot of lives and a lot of ordinary people's livelihoods. You know we control a lot of investments. Well, many of them are falling apart and losing value. Innocent, ordinary people are losing everything."

I hate the way she keeps saying "ordinary people." Still, I say, "Tough. They shouldn't have worked for you in the first place."

"Most don't know that they are, but let's forget money for now. Some of our more radical offshoots haven't been satisfied with merely playing the markets on things such as famines and communicable diseases. They're beginning to manipulate them. Pneumonic plague outbreaks. Ebola. It's all very ugly."

"They're even manipulating the damnation market," says the man. "Insider trading on human souls. Imagine it. Doomed to Hell for eternity so that a broker could get a bigger bonus this quarter."

"You're lying."

"You said it yourself," says Eva. "We're Wormwood. What wouldn't we do?"

She's right. It sounds exactly like something Wormwood would do.

"What does this have to do with me?"

"I told you. We need to rein things in. Bring in the outliers. Restore some order to the system."

"And you want me to help you do that?"

"Yes."

"Forget it. Kill me. You think Hell scares me? It's you people that scare me."

"That's not all we're offering," says the man.

"Eva, who the fuck is this guy?"

"I'm sorry," he says. "I'm Barron Sinclair."

He says it like it's supposed to mean something to me. When he holds out his hand to shake, I hold up the remote and turn off the TV instead.

"As Sinclair said, the chance to save lives and livelihoods isn't all we're offering," says Eva.

"What else do you people have that I'd want?"

"How about your old life?" says Sinclair. "All of it."

Eva says, "When you finish your contract with us, you can go back to your friends. Candy, Kasabian, the others. Even your silly video store is still there."

"Why should I trust you?"

"Because as an act of good faith, we can give you something I know you want perhaps more than anything else."

"What?"

"The Room of Thirteen Doors."

"Now I know you're lying. The Room is gone. *Occupado.* Full of old gods or a new universe. Anyway, it's off-limits."

"Not to us. The Room is empty and waiting for you."

I look around at all the ugly, earnest Wormwood faces. They look more scared than I am angry. And it's not me they're scared of. It's something else. Maybe they're afraid of each other.

"How can you have possibly gotten control of the Room?"

Eva says, "We don't have control. Only you can control it. We just swept it out for you."

"How?"

"Do you really want to discuss transsubstantive metaphysical plane displacement? Or do you want to see the Room?"

"I can go right now? Just walk right out of here?"

"Yes."

"How do you know I won't bolt?"

Sinclair leans in.

"Remember when you asked Eva if you were alive and she said 'more or less'?"

"It's actually a lot less than it is more," says Eva. "Without our intervention, there's a time limit to how long your body will hold together. If we pull the plug, so to speak, you will begin to decay just like any other corpse."

I touch my face, my left arm. No flesh there. Just a black Kissi prosthetic.

Fuck. I really am alive.

"How did you get my body in the first place?"

"Don't be stupid. We paid off someone in the coroner's office."

"And you've kept me on ice ever since. For how long?"

"We told you: eleven months, two days, and three hours."

"It's getting closer to four hours now," says Sinclair.

Almost a year. I was in the Tenebrae with Raziel and his sick crusade for almost a year. It's not as bad as eleven years the last time I was Downtown, but it's bad. It's long enough that people begin to forget about you and move on with their lives.

Bad enough that coming back could be another kind of Hell. But, if there's a chance . . .

"I want to see the Room."

Eva says, "Of course. You'll notice that we've arranged the lights so that there is a nice shadow in the corner near the lilies."

When I get up this time, I can stand on my own. Eva gets behind me and unties my filthy hospital gown. I'm naked as a baby bird. Sinclair hands me black pants and a shirt. They're silk. It takes me a while to get them on. My motor skills aren't quite there yet. When I look down, there's a pair of black loafers by my feet. If I have to wear loafers forever, then I really am back in Hell.

I put on the shoes and head for the shadow.

"Don't forget to come back, Mr. Stark. Without our help, your body won't last more than an hour."

I don't look back. I just step into the shadow.

And there I am. The Room. It's real. It's cool and clean and I can feel the old sensations of being here. That I'm in the still, silent center of the universe where nothing, not even Mr. Muninn, can get me.

I walk around, trailing my hand over the walls and each door. The thirteenth door is still nailed shut. The others don't look like they've changed at all. I take a few deep breaths, just getting used to the feeling of real air, not Tenebrae or Hellion stink, in my lungs. My heart is racing a hundred miles an hour. I'm actually afraid these Wormwood geniuses brought me back just so I can have a heart attack and die all over again. I lean against the cool stone. Breathe in through my nose and out through my mouth. After a few minutes, my heart begins to slow and I can relax. I want to try all of the doors at once, but the one that interests me the most, I'm afraid to open.

I walk to it and grip the ring sealing it shut. One turn of my wrist and it opens. I step through.

It's night and I'm in Hollywood. On Las Palmas Avenue, just north of Hollywood Boulevard. Across the street is Maximum Overdrive, the video store where I live with Candy and Kasabian. There's a music practice area in the storage room. Kasabian has a little apartment on the first floor. Candy and I live upstairs.

I want to go across the street and bang on the door, but my feet won't move. I could go in through a shadow and surprise them, but then I remember something.

Eleven months, two days, and four hours. Dead almost a year, maybe strolling in while they're having burritos isn't the best strategy. And Eva said I only have an hour. An hour won't be enough inside, whether they're happy to see me or not, but I hope to hell they'd be happy.

Instead of rushing over, I just take it all in. I'm home and it's real and I don't have to rush. I can think about it and figure out my best move.

But is that the right thing to do? It's been almost a year. For the first time in a long time, I'm genuinely, to-the-bone scared. It's too much. I can't take it all in.

My heart starts racing again. I rub my chest. It hurts in more ways than one.

What am I fucking doing here? Wormwood is blackmailing me with the one thing they know I want. If I ever said yes to them about anything, I'd never be able to get out. I'd be just like them and deserve Hell more than I ever have before.

That's it, then. I can stand here and rot or I can go back and tell them no to their faces.

I'm about to step into a shadow by a scraggly palm tree when the front door to Max Overdrive opens and Candy walks out. She's with Allegra and Brigitte. They talk for a minute. Laugh. It's simple and normal. A dumb little snapshot of friends going out, probably heading to Bamboo House of Dolls for a drink. I'm jealous and afraid and I want to run over to her and let her know I'm alive. But only for one more hour.

A cloud that was blocking the moon moves and the street lights up. Candy turns in my direction and for a second I think she sees me, but she's just watching a moth dive-bombing a streetlamp.

I can see her face, but there's not a goddamn thing I can do about it.

I walk into the palm tree's shadow and out again into Eva Sandoval's house. All six of Wormwood's finest gasp when they see me.

Eva says, "That's quite a startling trick, Mr. Stark."

She's holding a drink in her hand. I take it and gulp it down. It's bourbon. Very good stuff. It burns just right.

"My name isn't *Mister* Stark. It's just Stark.

"And you've got yourself a deal."